D0722290

KANSAS BLEEDS

COLTON BROTHERS SAGA

Kansas Bleeds

Melody Groves

FIVE STAR
A part of Gale, Cengage Learning

GALE
CENGAGE Learning·

Farmington Hills, Mich • San Francisco • New York • Waterville, Maine
Meriden, Conn • Mason, Ohio • Chicago

GALE
CENGAGE Learning®

LIBRARY OF CONGRESS CATALOGING-IN-PUBLICATION DATA

Groves, Melody, 1952–
    Kansas bleeds : Colton Brothers Saga / Melody Groves.
      pages cm. — (Colton Brothers Saga)
    ISBN-13: 978-1-4328-2807-3 (hardcover)
    ISBN-10: 1-4328-2807-X (hardcover)
    1. Brothers—Arizona—Fiction. 2. Arizona—History—Civil War,
1861-1865—Fiction. I. Title.
PS3607.R6783K36 2014
813'.6—dc23   2013041351

First Edition. First Printing: April 2014
Find us on Facebook– https://www.facebook.com/FiveStarCengage
Visit our website– http://www.gale.cengage.com/fivestar/
Contact Five Star™ Publishing at FiveStar@cengage.com

Printed in the United States of America
1 2 3 4 5 6 7 18 17 16 15 14

To Myke and Mykie,
Two "Peas in a Pod"
And
To all the good men and women who gave their lives
fighting for what they truly believed in.

ACKNOWLEDGMENTS

Thanks to my husband, Myke, who braved Kansas winds to help with my research for this novel. His help was, and still is, invaluable.

And thanks to editor Clark Whitehorn, who allowed me to fulfill every writer's dream . . .

CHAPTER ONE

August 12, 1862

Luke Colton squatted, his hand above his shoulder clamped over his horse's muzzle, hoping, praying she'd stay silent. One sound and they'd be discovered. As close as he was to the Kansas River, maybe the rushing water would drown out his breathing. And maybe the tall weeds and bushes would conceal him. Maybe.

He hadn't meant to get this close to Quantrill and his boys. In fact, when he'd heard they'd raided a town on the Missouri side of the river, he'd relaxed. Let his guard down, which wasn't the smartest thing he'd ever done. No, he'd taken his time riding back from Kansas City west toward Lawrence and his home, knowing danger lay behind him. But instead, it was at his elbow.

William Clarke Quantrill waved toward a stand of willows, mere feet away from Luke. "Jesse. Clarke. One of you get the map. Meet me by that tree."

Luke recognized Quantrill from the pictures plastered all over the newspapers and on the wanted posters around town. In the pictures, the renegade's beady brown eyes, separated by his famous Roman nose, stared off into air, like they were contemplating who to kill next. Under the nose, Quantrill's mustache drooped over his thin lips. And right here in flesh and blood, he stood what looked to be a good five inches shorter than Luke. Quantrill's woolen shirt, high heeled boots, and a drab slouch hat hiding most of his sandy brown hair, gave him an unassuming appearance. However, he was mean, through and through. And here the man stood, less than ten yards away.

At one point a while back, Luke had considered joining up with Quantrill. In some ways, they seemed to think alike. Neither liked what the Union was doing, and while Quantrill rode the country supporting his beliefs, Luke argued with Pa and anyone who would listen—not too many anymore. Quantrill's methods were more brutal than his, although the Raider leader got things done. But, remembering stories Luke had heard, he was sure teaming up with this man wasn't the best idea. Quantrill was violent, killing people indiscriminately. Luke hadn't killed, and had no intentions to.

Late-afternoon heat sent sweat down Luke's back and dripping down the sides of his face. A fly chose that moment to land, then walk across his cheek. He snuffed at it, but the fly appeared oblivious to the slight puff of air. Luke's legs ached from crouching in the brush, one arm gripping his horse's reins, the other around her muzzle. His arms tingled, but he didn't dare move.

Footsteps, grass crunching underfoot, a twig snapping. His heart pounding.

Quantrill's clipped New England accent grew into a staccato rhythm. "This is where we were, Jesse," he said. "Independence, Missouri. Home of the so-called Santa Fe Trail."

More footsteps, rustle of tall grass parting, then the thud of a body lowering itself to the ground. Both men chuckled.

"Hell, Bill. Independence ain't so independent no more."

Quantrill's baritone voice sailed across the weeds. "Sure as hell ain't. That was some fun, eh?"

"Sure was." Jesse's words softened. "You reckon the Confederates gonna give you a promotion? I mean, you were truly righteous back there. Leading everybody . . . your guns blasting. Pure poetry."

"Whatever they wanna do is fine by me. Just as long as I can lead these raids, I'm content."

Silence pounded against Luke's ears. He eased his head around a clump of wild cherry bushes. An arm and part of a shoulder. Could be Quantrill, could be the other man, Jesse something.

"Now, I hear the rest of them sonufabitch Yanks ain't turning tail and running like they should." Quantrill clicked his tongue. "Guess they ain't heard of us yet."

"They will, though, Bill. After yesterday, they will."

A cork popped. Someone swallowed a long pull. The cork squeaked back into the canteen.

"Where we planning on hitting next?"

Cigar smoke roiled under Luke's nose, gray puffs infecting his eyes. He released the reins and pinched his nose. Holding his breath, his eyes watered.

"Hell, Jesse, any place's as good as the next. I'm thinking Shawnee, but all them damn Jayhawkers need to be killed."

More smoke.

"You mean, just the soldiers?"

Quantrill spit. "I mean anybody who ain't a Confederate. Hell, kids grow up, don't they? Hell, look at you, kid. What're you now? Fifteen?"

"Next month," Jesse said. "Fifteen next month."

"That's what I mean. Already grown up." Quantrill's voice took on a hard edge. "We gotta stop 'em."

More footsteps. Running footsteps parting the brushes. Luke cringed, waiting for a gun to press into his back.

"Hey, Bill, Jesse." The words were a bit out of breath. "Me and Amos spotted tracks back yonder."

"So? Lots of people use this road."

"But they're fresh, real fresh. And appears to be stopped right around here somewheres."

Luke chanced a peek at the speaker. A young boy, wide-brimmed hat flopping around his ears, no more than thirteen, pointed in his direction.

"You sure?" Jesse stretched to his feet, eyes darting left and right. "I don't see nobody."

William Quantrill also stood, map in hand. "Jesse, you go scout around. See if you see anything. I'm gonna study this map a mite longer."

Luke held his breath, aware at any moment he'd have to leap onto his mount's back and spur her for all she was worth. Which wasn't much. She was a solid horse, but a bit slow. Luke glanced down at his numb legs, still bent. A brown spider, its eight legs spreading out to a gold-dollar size, was busy making its way up his thigh. He flicked it off and as he did so, his horse blew out air.

"Hey!" The kid snapped around toward Luke.

Luke swung up, spurring his horse as his rear settled into the saddle. An Osage plum thicket slowed him, the branches whipping his face as he ducked, trying to keep from being knocked out of the saddle. His face stung like a Bowie knife had sliced him, but he couldn't stop or even worry about it now. Currant plants, ripe with red berries, grabbed at his legs.

Shouting, hollering, thundering hoofs slashed at the air. Luke leaned forward, draping himself over his horse's neck. If he could get out of this tangle of bushes, he figured he'd make it to a footpath he'd spotted back a ways. He sure as hell wasn't going to lead Quantrill toward his home. That would be crazy.

He rode.

A bullet splintered the tree next to him.

He ducked and rode harder.

As much as he wanted to give his horse her head, let her

choose the best way out, Luke reined right, then left, around trees, past boulders and then out into the hills.

He rode.

One mile. Five. Eight. Winded, his horse slowed. Waning sunlight dimmed the hillside, turning bushes into men, low hills into mountains. Luke trotted down the narrow footpath, until he spotted a cabin below, set off under a canopy of willow tree branches. A long look behind him—no one. Did he dare hope?

He pulled his horse to a walk and listened. No furious pounding hoofs, no shouts, no gunshots. His horse wheezing, his own heart pounding, he reined up long enough for his boots to hit the ground. He led his horse toward the cabin, hoping it was empty or whoever lived inside was friendly. He'd hate to have to explain himself in the dark.

Mosquitoes buzzed, lighting on his neck, his face, his hands. Like a madman, Luke swatted and whacked, but his gyrations seemed to bring more. He reached for his hat but instead felt hair, his hat lost somewhere behind him. He'd just have to continue swatting and hope they'd get their fill and quit biting.

Another quarter mile and there was the cabin, its wood front in desperate need of paint.

Whitewash peeled off the door like strips of the white ash tree surrounding it. Luke stood back, wispy smoke curled out of the stovepipe, the single window glowed gold, a welcome beacon. A smile raised one side of his mustache and a sigh escaped his chest.

He'd be all right. At nineteen, he had no intention of dying.

"Hello the house!" Luke yelled louder than he'd anticipated, his voice echoing against the hill behind the cabin. To his right stood a barn, a single-stall affair with a loose board jutting out near the corner. On his left sat an old wagon and plow.

Before he could shout again, the door creaked open, a

shotgun stuck through. "Come closer there, fella. Slow now. Move fast and I'll shoot."

Luke's hands eased up as he walked forward. "I'm lost," he said. "Hoping for a barn to bed down in. I'll be gone at first light."

"Damn right you'll be gone first light." The man held the shotgun chest high. "Stop right there. Hand over your piece, butt first."

Luke did. His holster felt light once his Colt left its leather home.

Light poured from the open door, backlighting a man, wide-shouldered, taller than Luke, sturdy-looking. He stepped off the porch and halted a couple feet from Luke. Without a word, he grabbed Luke's gun. The man's dark eyes roved up and down Luke's body.

"Hmmm." The man's shoulders relaxed. He eased the shotgun down. "Guess I should offer you some grub. It ain't much, but it's fillin'. The wife's a good cook with what we got."

He jerked his head toward the house, stepped forward, then stopped. "Wait."

Luke froze.

"Wash up at the trough out back. I'll walk with you." The man half turned and shouted toward the house. "Ginny. Set another plate. We got company."

Luke's stomach growled. Before now he hadn't noticed smells of cooking sausage mingled with something he didn't recognize. But whatever it was, it had to be delicious.

Hands and face washed, horse tethered to a hitching post, Luke sat at the table eyeing the mound of sausage and greens piled in a bowl. He bowed his head during grace, then waited while the man—Tom Whitman he'd said his name was—took most of the food. The woman, her light-brown hair tied back in a ribbon, helped herself to a spoonful. Luke knew he could've eaten the entire bowl all by himself, but scraped what was left onto his plate.

"Thank you, ma'am, for sharing your food. I do surely appreciate your kindness." After enjoying the aroma sailing under his nose, Luke attacked the meal.

As he ate, Luke studied the couple. Tom was probably in his early thirties, but she appeared to be five, maybe ten years younger, about Luke's age. Virginia, as she'd been introduced, would be a mother by year's end, Luke figured. Not that he was a judge of expectant women, but when Sally's stomach pooched out like that, she had delivered Adam about four months later.

Luke cut his eyes sideways at Virginia. Pretty. Well, more like radiant. Her smooth cheeks pinked with the cabin's warmth, and her brown eyes danced when Luke commented on her fine cooking. Luke chided himself for lustful thoughts, but, damn, she was a fine specimen of womanhood.

Judging by the calluses on Tom's hands and the dirt under the nails, he farmed. Admirable enough job. Pa farmed a bit, too. Luke knew he should stay a day and help out as payment for their hospitality, but he had to get back to Lawrence, talk to the town's council, or at least his pa, and let them know about Quantrill. Or would he?

While Virginia cleared the table, Tom extracted two cigars from the tin humidor, offered one to Luke, then walked outside. Luke followed on his heels.

Puffing, enjoying the cool of the night's breeze, thoughts of his wife and son walked across Luke's mind. What were they doing now? He hoped Sally wasn't worried he hadn't come home tonight. She knew he'd been to Missouri and more than likely it would take two days. If he didn't get home tomorrow, she'd really be worried. But, if luck held out, he'd be home in time for supper.

15

Tom puffed a white "o," then turned to Luke. "What part you say you're from?"

"Lawrence. Got a house in town. My folks' farm's just on the outskirts."

Tom's gaze roamed over Luke's body. This scrutiny wasn't nearly as friendly as Virginia's had been. "Why'd you say you were over here for?"

He hadn't, but Luke had nothing to hide. "I drive freight wagons for Gibson's Mercantile in Lawrence."

"Don't see no wagon." Tom pointed his cigar into the dark. "Besides that, your horse come in all lathered up, blowin' hard." He bent closer to Luke. "Still don't see no wagon."

"I delivered it *and* supplies to a general mercantile, Watkins Mercantile, in Kansas City. Brought my own horse along and left the team there." Luke shrugged and chose to explain further. "Ran into a gang of border ruffians on the banks of the Kansas River. I hightailed it back here and lost 'em, I reckon."

"I reckon."

Dozens of crickets chirruped night songs. A bird, possibly an owl, sliced through the darkness overhead. A dog, hair matted and stickers clinging to its tail climbed onto the porch and lay at Tom's feet. Tom regarded his cigar and then faced Luke. "You with him?"

"Him who?" Luke feared he knew the answer.

"Quantrill. You ridin' with Quantrill?" Tom backed away pointing his cigar at Luke's face. "Got scratches there. You sure as hell don't look like no delivery fella, either. And there's no wagon."

Luke shook his head. "Sir, I ain't with Quantrill. Got these scratches from a bramble bush when I was running away." He glanced behind him at the open door. Virginia stood in the middle, golden glow outlining her shapely figure. Luke shrugged. "I'll be leaving first light, just like I said."

Tom turned to his wife. "Ginny."

Before Luke could think, Virginia held the shotgun against her shoulder, aiming at Luke's chest.

"She don't miss, Mister Colton," Tom said. "My Ginny's the best pig hunter they is around here. One wrong move, and you'll be a dead pig."

"W-what?" Luke knew he stammered.

"Put your hands behind your back, nice and slow, Mister Colton." Tom spun his fingers like a ballerina's pirouette. "That's right."

Tom tied him tight. Scratchy rope cut into Luke's wrists. No matter how much he strained, the binding held.

"Sorry to have to do this, Mister Colton," Tom said. "But half of me's thinkin' you're lyin'. And the other half ain't yet decided. So, I'm gonna let you sleep in the barn tonight, then at first light you'll ride out, just like you said." Tom pushed Luke toward the barn. "But instead of you ridin' out, it'll be me and you. We're goin' to Independence, see the sheriff there. I'll let him decide your story."

"But—"

"Can't have you Bushwhackers traipsin' all over creation, ransackin' my farm, destroyin' my crops, and . . ." Tom glanced over his shoulder at Ginny. "Takin' advantage of our women. No, siree. You no-good scoundrels gotta pay."

"But . . ."

Shoved, Luke tripped over his own feet. His pistol left behind in the cabin wasn't doing him any good right now. A plan. He needed a plan.

17

CHAPTER TWO

The ropes tightened with every pull as Luke struggled to free himself. Hands tied behind him and a post jammed against his back, he sat on the dirt floor surrounded by clumps of manure and hay. His backside burned with numbness.

One dark hour dragged into the next. Had something happened to the sun? Maybe it was daylight right now and somehow Virginia's cooking had affected him. Or was he asleep? No, not possible.

A plan. He had to come up with a plan.

Another dark hour. Footsteps of something tiny, a mouse perhaps, tapped across the barn. Then soft footsteps, most likely a cat.

Dawn crept like an old woman to her milk cows until slivers of daylight squeezed under and around the barn door. It flew open. Luke recoiled, reeling from the blazing light. Tom's face loomed.

"Time to get goin'." Tom untied Luke's ropes.

"No need to do this, Mister Whitman." As he lurched to his feet, Luke rubbed his tender wrists, the skin red and raw. "I'm not with Quantrill."

Legs rubbery, he staggered outside to his horse and managed to saddle her with hands and arms of lead.

A shotgun pointed at his chest spurred him along. He swung up into the saddle and nodded to Virginia behind the gun. "I'm not the enemy, ma'am."

"Best get movin'," she said.

"Thanks for the grub." Luke automatically reached up to touch where his hat brim should be, looked at the pointed shotgun and reconsidered. He nodded.

Both men rode in silence until the tree-lined trail intersected the main road, the road used by the Oregon Trail immigrants. Wide, dirt packed hard by hundreds of overweight wagons, the route led straight past Luke's home.

Luke eyed the walnut-handle Colt tucked in Tom's waistband. Was that his? The man seemed in another world of thought. Now or never.

Luke gigged his horse, reined hard right heading west, and rode low as he attempted to outrun a bullet. His heels spurred into her sides frenetically, until dust and dirt clods hid his captor from view.

He listened for pursuit, then glanced behind. Sure enough, Tom broke through the fog of dust, trailing several yards behind. Tom took aim. Luke hunkered down lower, then reined hard right.

Bang!

Fire burned his right arm. It hurt like hell, but a quick look confirmed it had only seared his flesh. Luke gritted teeth. Reining left, then right at full gallop, he tensed, waiting for the next shot.

His horse's labored breathing beat staccato in rhythm with her pounding hooves.

Another mile, then he looked back.

No Tom.

CHAPTER THREE

Luke Jeremiah Colton winced more from the noxious smell of liquid Sally swabbed up and down his arm than from the pain. Besides making his eyes water, it stung like a swarm of bees. And his mother hovering over him brought nothing but heat to his cheeks and anger to his chest.

After galloping home, Luke had ridden to the barn and taken care of his horse. Little Adam ran from the house and wrapped his arms around Luke's legs, almost tripping both of them.

"Watch what you're doing!" Luke bit off further harsh words, but his blood-encrusted arm throbbed and fatigue leadened his footsteps. Sleeping—rather *sitting*—on the hard ground in a dark barn all night had taken its toll.

"Up?" Adam raised his outstretched arms.

"Not now." Luke gripped the two-year-old's hand and together they marched outside.

He hadn't even closed the barn door before being swarmed by Ma, Pa and Sally. All talking at once, fussing, fuming, and fretting. The cacophony of concern followed him into his house.

As Sally continued to fawn over him, Ma worked in the kitchen fixing them supper. The banging and clattering of pans a testament of love for her family, the aroma of chicken frying wafted out of the kitchen and pulled at his nose. His stomach rumbled while he fought down anger. Pa's pacing back and forth in the living room made him squirm. A lecture was undoubtedly forming in Pa's head.

The wooden chair grew hard under his rear, and for the first time in the last few minutes, he felt naked with his cotton undershirt down around his waist and his bare chest open to the warm house air. He squirmed again.

Pa's brown-eyed gaze. Sally's questions. *Where've you been? Did you get lost? Are you all right? Why'd anyone want to shoot you? Do you have to go back?*

He shrugged for the hundredth time that hour. "Not my fault. I was riding over in Missouri. A day there and a day back," he said. "Supposed to be an easy trip. Didn't know I'd end up on the receiving end of a gun."

No way in hell he'd tell them how he'd run into Quantrill and a couple of his Raiders. Besides, how was he supposed to know they'd attacked the town of Independence the day before? And how was he supposed to know a nice farmer would turn into a lunatic with a gun? Sure as hell wasn't his fault. Maybe, just maybe, if he asked nicely, his whole family would let him be. Let him sit and mull things over for a while.

Pa glared at him.

"About got your fool head blown off, Luke." Pa paced halfway across the living room, the rag rug softening his footfalls. He nodded toward Sally. "Almost left her a widow."

"But, I didn't," Luke said. "On either count."

Luke's glib response ignited an already short fuse. Pa went up like cheap Chinese fireworks.

"It's just that type of attitude getting people killed today. Needless killing. Senseless killing." Pa stepped in close until his shaking finger almost touched Luke's nose. "If those damn Bushwhackers would leave well enough alone, we'd all get along fine." He pulled in air, running a hand across his mustache. "I apologize for the language, Sally. It's just . . . well, sometimes, this *husband* of yours makes me see red."

Pa pronounced "husband" like it was somehow evil. Luke's

anger simmered.

"You'd see it different if you weren't a Union-sympathizing Jayhawker." Luke's upper arm burned like a fiery horseshoe was stuck to it. A glance at his arm proved him wrong. "You know, if they'd leave Kansas a slave state, *like it was voted,* the South wouldn't have to fight anybody."

"The only reason it voted slave was because those no-good Bushwhackers come over from Missouri and voted." Pa pointed east. "Then they rode back on across the river. You tell me how a state that's got only two thousand voters can cast eight thousand votes. Tell me. That some kind of miracle?"

"From what I read, it was legal," Luke said. "And if the stinking politicians like Jimmy Lane worked *for* the people instead of against 'em, we'd have a decent place to live. We all would. Hell, Pa—"

"Watch your language!" Pa's eyes narrowed and a vein throbbed on the side of his neck.

"All I'm saying is they wanted to be sure almighty Washington don't take sides. Each state should have equal say in matters."

"They already do," Sally said as she wound a strip of cotton material around Luke's arm. "And the Jayhawkers are right, although their methods are wrong. Stealing horses like Doc Jennison does is wrong. But, your pa's right. The Bushwhackers need to be stopped. We prayed for it in church this morning."

That was it. Luke didn't need his father-in-law, the almighty Reverend Burroughs, leading his congregation into praying for death and destruction of the *wrong side.* And he sure as hell didn't need a lecture from his pa or his wife. Luke would think whatever the hell he wanted, believe whatever he wanted, *do* whatever he wanted. Maybe, with some thought, he'd find out which side he was truly on.

He bolted to his feet, pulling Sally's fingers from the ends of binding she tied. Luke waved her hands away and glared at his pa. "I'm going outside." A couple of long strides took him to the door. "And smoke."

Ten giant paces from the barn, his haven for smoking and thinking, a vice-like grip on Luke's upper arm stopped him. He wheeled around to face Pa.

"Look, son," Pa said. "I didn't bring you and your ma and your brothers all the way out here just to get you killed. We've spent over five years working this place, making a home, a living. Hell, if I hadn't believed we could have a better life than what Pennsylvania offered, we'd have stayed there."

Luke didn't want to talk. He wanted a smoke.

Pa frowned. "Hell. This whole place is a powder keg. You weren't old enough to remember, but before we moved here, border ruffians sacked this town. Burned and looted. It was a sight." He shook his head. "We helped rebuild. Hell, you even helped rebuild Gustav's barn. Remember?"

Luke didn't care. What was done, was done. "What's that got to do with now?"

"Ain't your fight. Anybody going up against the likes of James Lane, whether riding with Quantrill or not, they'll get killed," Pa said.

He chewed on Pa's words. As he shrugged into his undershirt and then the shirt hanging from his waist, he wanted, no, *needed* the cigars kept in the barn. Sally wouldn't let him bring them in the house, which was fine with Luke. Gave him an excuse to take refuge in the barn, away from all the racket.

Luke faced his pa. "So, you a Jayhawker? Why do you hold with their Union thinking? Hell, they've stolen everything that ain't nailed down. Acting like that ain't good for America. They've killed, looted, robbed . . ." Luke looked toward the house. "Hell, maybe even raped anybody what got in their way. And you're on their side?"

"Dammit, Luke!" Pa's wide shoulders shook. "Don't you get

it?" His voice boomed. "This is the United States of America. *United—*"

"Not no more, Pa."

"States." Pa continued. "We need to stand together, not fight and bicker. Apart . . . well, each country'll have to start over and then try to live in peace as neighbors."

"Won't be peace for a long time." Luke edged toward his sanctuary.

Pa shook his head. "The Union will win this war. The slaves will be set free. As they should."

Luke exploded. "There you go again! You know this war ain't about slaves. The North's playing that card because they're losing. Slavery's an issue they think they can win on." He marched back and forth. "Hell, Pa. George Washington, the father of this country, *your* country, owned slaves. So did lots of others. They still do. Seems like the politicians're talking out of whichever side of their mouth gets votes." Luke lowered his voice. "What kind of leader is that?"

Silence wedged between the men until Pa walked away, slowed, then returned to Luke. Pa's eyes swept the ground. A good man, but hardheaded. There was no way, no *words*, to change Pa's mind. Luke sighed. "I'm sorry it's come down to this, Pa. I don't agree with what you're saying."

"I'm sorry, too," Pa said. "I was hoping you'd join me."

Luke shrugged. "Sorry. Can't. The Jayhawkers are wrong. The North is wrong."

Pa leveled his gaze on Luke's face. The men stood eye to eye. "You telling me you're a Bushwhacker, boy?" Pa cocked his head. "A Bushwhacker just like those Missouri gunners, Quantrill and that James fella? Frank James?"

"No—"

"Why don't you go ahead and ride with Quantrill? Kill innocent people? Turn against your country?" Pa pointed a finger at Luke's chest. "That'd make your ma real damn proud."

Luke narrowed his eyes, fisted his trembling hands. "I ain't riding with Quantrill at this particular moment, but I sure as hell could be." As angry as Luke was, he wasn't about to give in. "Maybe I should."

Pa's shoulders slumped. "Don't do it, son."

Luke folded his arms across his chest. "Each state has a right to make its own decisions."

Luke had read in the newspaper that the Confederates were holding their own. All they wanted was fair and equal treatment by Washington. Those almighty politicians who held the life and death of Americans in their greedy, corrupt hands were yellow dogs.

Pa interrupted Luke's thoughts. "You're as stubborn as your brothers." He gripped Luke's shoulder and shook him. "This damn war's divided too many families. Sure as hell don't want it dividing ours."

CHAPTER FOUR

Joseph Frederick Colton sat at the kitchen table and thought, paper in front of him, pen in hand. He regarded the pen as if it would write the letter itself. He knew what he wanted to say, to ask, but the exact words wouldn't come. He again dipped the stylus into the ink bottle, and penned the date.

August 15, 1862.

Dear

He gripped the pen. Which of his three other sons should he address it to? Pursing his lips, a habit which put him in touch with his deepest thoughts, he thought of each of his boys. Now good, strong men. Even the youngest, Andy. Eighteen this November, still, he too, was a man.

"Your ink's drying out."

Brigid's soft words startled him. She flashed a smile and sat next to him. "Who're you writing to?"

Joseph ran a hand over his mouth and returned the stylus to the ink. "Not sure. One of our boys needs to come home and pound some sense into Luke. He won't listen to us."

She patted his hand. "Call them all home."

Joseph nodded. "Would be nice, indeed. But Trace is sheriff of all Mesilla, he can't get away." He stared at the table. "Heard it's a big town now. Three thousand."

"Still, I'd love to meet Teresa and get to know our grand-daughter." Brigid's words were softened by a tinge of melancholy. "Holding a picture isn't the same as holding a child."

Joseph leaned back. "Andy would be better. He's got a solid head on his shoulders, plus, he's single. He can give up his job at the livery stable in Mesilla. Don't like him doing so much blacksmithing, anyway. After a while, it gets tough on a body."

"He'll be deputy by year's end, he says." Brigid McConnell Colton's gaze swept over Joseph's face. "Blacksmithing. Just like you when we first met. I remember a big, handsome man with lots of muscles." She smiled, squeezing his upper arm. "I imagine Andy looks a lot like you at that age." Longing etched her face. "He was just beginning to get his shoulders when he took off."

"Two years can make a difference," Joseph said, unwilling to go down the path which would surely bring tears to his wife. It was hard having three of her boys so far away. New Mexico Territory might as well be the moon.

She tapped the paper. "Maybe James should come. He's working with Andy, but he's only driving wagons. Possibly they could spare him. Of course, he'd bring Morningstar, and I'm not sure she'd want to make the trip all the way out here."

Birds chirped outside the window as Joseph considered. There was so much he wanted to ask second son James. It would take a thousand letters to cover it all. "James would be the best choice. Give us a chance to talk. Maybe he'll tell us about his stint in the Union army." And last year's run-in and capture by Cochise, Joseph thought. Had his two oldest sons been tortured? Unsure whether to tell Brigid what he suspected, he decided to let James do the explaining.

"If Morningstar comes," Brigid said, "she and Sally might become friends. Two of my daughters-in-law in the same town. Woddn't tha' be gran'?"

At times like this, when she got excited, her Irish accent escaped. Something else Joseph loved about this woman.

27

Joseph dipped the stylus in the ink. "It's settled. James. He and Luke are close. Gotta be James."

Brigid nodded, patted Joseph's arm and stood. "Maybe address it to all three." She kissed the top of his head. "And tell them we love them and miss them."

CHAPTER FIVE

Mesilla, New Mexico Territory
August 1862

James Francis Michael Colton sat on his veranda watching the rising sun. If he leaned far to his left, he could see part of the Corn Exchange Hotel, its white plastered walls glinting vibrant rose-gold. Even farther left to the east, the Organ Mountains rose in jutted peaks of deep purple, standing sentinel over the Mesilla Valley.

Mesilla, perched on the banks of the Rio Grande which overran every year, was the largest town in the territory. It was also hub to freighting and stage lines. Wide fields of cotton, lettuce, alfalfa and grapes brought added wealth to the area.

To his right, James spotted a woman, her lace mantilla draped over her head, walking with her husband toward the San Felipe de Neri church. He thought about the church, its steeple standing tall and proud on the north end of the plaza. The church where he and Lila were supposed to get married last year. But Cochise interfered and Lila married somebody else. Uncontrolled tightness filled his chest. He glared into memories. *If Cochise hadn't captured me and Trace. If . . .*

Cochise had taken everything from him. He and his brother had recovered physically, but both sported vicious scars. James fought to push aside those memories, but at times like this, they were relentless. Chanting, drumbeats, screams—his and Trace's—and the ever-vigilant nerves kept him from sleeping.

Like terrified wild horses, they raced through his head. Although today was a beautiful morning, he couldn't shake the terror.

A walk will help. Trace should be up by now. A quick note to the sleeping Morningstar and he left.

Down three streets, across the *acequia madre,* the main irrigation ditch, the lifeblood of Mesilla, and then up another street took him to his brother's house. Smells of bacon frying and coffee boiling rumbled his stomach. A quick tap on the door, then he pushed into the house.

"You're just in time." Teresa's voice sailed from the kitchen over a baby's giggles and gurgles.

James followed his nose into the kitchen. "Time for coffee, I hope." He poured himself a cup. "Yours is always better than mine." Baby Faith sat in her high chair, waving her arms at a familiar face. He ruffled her brown hair, which curled in the back.

"Gettin' bigger every day." James couldn't help but smile at the wide eyes and innocence on her beautiful face. A face resembling Trace's, yet Teresa's green-brown eyes and steady gaze were evident, too.

James sipped his coffee then peered out through the kitchen into the parlor. "Where's that brother of mine? You know, the really handsome one? Looks exactly like me? Lives here."

"Guess you haven't heard. There was a fight early this morning over at Sam Bean's. Trace said he had to arrest four men, and none of them wanted to go to jail."

James pulled out a chair at the kitchen table and eased into it. "Bet that was exciting."

"By the time it was over, Trace'd been punched—"

"He all right?"

Teresa nodded. "Gonna have a good black eye, but Sammy got his leg broken." She tsked. "Trace said one of those drunks fell on Sammy and pinned him."

"He gonna be all right?" James liked his brother's deputy. Even though Sammy Estrada was wide-shouldered and bull strong, his bones would break like anybody else's.

Teresa pointed the fork over her shoulder. "He's over at Doc's right now and Maria's with him. She thinks he'll be up and around in no time." She turned back to the bacon. "Trace should be here any minute."

A slow sip while James considered. "So that means Trace is out a deputy until Sammy heals up." He wouldn't mind stepping in to help, be his big brother's deputy, but even if Trace agreed, the town council more than likely would vote him out *pronto*. The town still saw him as a crazed Indian captive turned Indian lover, not the hero the army had given a medal.

He was getting better. He hadn't beaten up anyone, nor had he drunk himself into a stupor since marrying half-Apache Morningstar a couple months ago.

A sharp knock at the door, then it opened before James could get to his feet.

"Ummm . . . bacon and coffee, my favorite." Andy marched into the kitchen and shook hands with James. "You're out and about early."

Teresa handed Andy a filled cup and gave him a quick hug. "You are, too. Trace tells me you were there when the fight started."

James' brother, tall enough to have to duck going through six-foot doorways, bent over and kissed baby Faith on the top of her head. Andy's entire demeanor softened whenever he was around her. James fought a grin—the disarming grin all four brothers inherited from Pa. They also inherited his height and broad shoulders. Family. So close, so comfortable. This is what his ma and pa had preached since James could remember. Family first.

Andy scooted out a chair and sat, his long legs stretching

under the table. He slurped then spoke over his coffee. "Yep, quite a fight. More like a brawl. Never seen so many chairs and fists flying at one time."

"I'm glad you weren't hurt," Teresa said.

"Me, too." James nodded as Teresa poured more coffee. "But my question is, what were you doing down at a saloon at that hour? Should be home in bed. Asleep."

"Couldn't sleep."

James leaned back. "Why? You're doing hard physical labor all day. Till way past sundown." He pointed his cup at Andy. "And with Bergstrom working you more and more on the black-smithing jobs, you oughta be exhausted."

"And what about you, older brother?" Andy raised one eyebrow as he emphasized *older*. "You work, too."

"I got the easy jobs now, but soon I'll be pounding horseshoes, too." He rubbed his right palm, the puffy knife scar running side to side.

Teresa slid filled plates in front of James and Andy. "You remember being his age, James. Hasn't been *that* long ago."

More like a lifetime. Memories of home in Kansas raced through his mind. He'd been jealous of older brother Trace riding the Santa Fe Trail into New Mexico Territory in search of a new life. James couldn't wait to be old enough to go, too. And now, here he was. At the ripe age of twenty-one. Twenty-two next month.

James couldn't dismiss his brother's late night. James wore the mantle of protective older brother willingly. "So, Andy. Go out a lot, do you? How come I didn't know?"

Fidgeting with his fork. A long sip of coffee. A deep breath. Andy set the cup down and met James' stare. "Sometimes . . . well, sometimes Trace lets me tag along on his sheriffing rounds. You know, just kinda keep him company."

His brother didn't need company. Before his capture by Cochise, Trace had been a stagecoach driver and those men were in charge of everything—the coach, the passengers, the mail. They were hired based on strength and character, their leadership ability. Trace had more than his share of all that. No, Trace didn't need company to walk the streets of Mesilla at night. More than likely, he was preparing Andy as a second deputy. Trace had mentioned that with the town growing like it was, another lawman would be welcomed. And Andy would turn eighteen in November. Old enough to take the oath.

Was James jealous? Sure. He wanted the job. But why had his brothers gone behind his back? Wasn't like them.

Then again, maybe they had to. There were times James would pick a fight just to feel a fist on his face. Just to feel the adrenaline push through his body. Just to feel . . . something.

James eyed Andy staring at him. Teresa, too, a pan of eggs in hand, frozen midair.

"I'll ask again, James." Teresa frowned. "You want more eggs?"

"You all right?" Andy pointed his fork at James' plate. "You about dug a hole clean through to China." Breakfast, mushed into tiny pieces, was pushed to the plate's rim.

James wiped his mouth and then stood. "I better go. Star's expecting me." He nodded to Teresa. "Thanks for the coffee . . . and . . . food."

Before he reached the door, Trace opened it.

James stepped back while his brother entered. A raised welt glowed under Trace's left eye. Trace cocked his head toward the kitchen. "Had breakfast?"

"I was just going." James brushed past Trace and stepped outside.

"Wait." Andy followed, dug into his vest pocket and held up an envelope. "We got a letter from Pa I picked up at the post office. Something's wrong."

"What?" James reached for the letter. "Somebody die?"

"Nah." Andy shook his head. "It's Luke. Pa said it's real important one of us come home." He handed it to Trace. "Here. You read it."

The look on Trace's face as he scanned the letter knotted James' stomach.

CHAPTER SIX

Lawrence, Kansas
1862

On this warm late-summer morning, Luke rode south and east to meet Quantrill. Wanting to be rested before meeting this legend, nevertheless, Luke had spent a long night tossing and turning, mumbling. Sally had offered a glass of warm milk sometime in the dark, but he had declined, his stomach tied in too many knots.

Damn Pa and his Jayhawker sympathizing. He was wrong. And the farther Luke rode, the more his determination cemented itself, to prove to Pa that the Confederacy was right.

Maybe joining up with bloodthirsty Quantrill wasn't such a good idea. On the other hand, maybe he could help Quantrill and his Raiders end this damned war. Decision made. What he was doing was right. Damn Pa and his sense of righteousness. Damn those Jayhawkers and their rampages. Damn the entire Union army.

Setting up a meeting with Quantrill had been easy. Too easy? While buying a gun to replace the one Tom Whitman had taken and a hat replacing the one blown off during the chase, a casual conversation with Pete Brunson at Otis Mercantile turned his thoughts. Pete rode with Quantrill and didn't mind telling certain people about his adventures. A couple good words from this man and Luke's meeting was set. Luke mulled over Pete's last words.

"Just be careful. This is Quantrill you're dealing with, not some mild-mannered Bible-thumping preacher." Pete shook hands with Luke. "His lieutenants ain't no thumpers either."

Reflecting on Pete's words, Luke rode southeast most of the morning while the sun did its best to warm the world. After crossing the Pottawatomie River, Luke spotted a stand of wild cherry bushes in a swale up ahead, four horses munching on the leafless branches. Quantrill and his gang already here? Luke pushed down anxiety, straightened his shoulders and reined up.

Sitting on his horse was Quantrill. Luke recognized him from his earlier encounter. The Bushwhacker's Roman nose and dark-blond hair a dead giveaway. Luke swung out of his saddle, his boots hitting Kansas dirt. He nodded to Quantrill.

The leader stared at him. "Luke Colton?" Quantrill pronounced the name quickly.

"That's me," Luke said. A cursory survey of the four riders. Two he recognized from pictures in the newspapers. Frank James and Cole Younger. Luke probed his memory for the last face, then he had it. Jesse from the first time Luke had seen Quantrill. Could he be Frank James' younger brother?

Quantrill, who hadn't bothered to dismount, looked down. "And you think joining up with my Raiders will do what, exactly?"

Luke detected a glint of humor in Quantrill's eyes, or was that insanity? Maybe both. Luke's mumbled question on his ride over repeated itself. *What the hell am I doing?*

He shoved doubt aside. "Well, sir," Luke said. "Me and my friends feel like we ain't making one diddly damn difference with this war. We're tired of seein' our friends die . . . and for what?"

"You got a plan?" Quantrill cocked his head, reins lying limp in his hands.

"Not much of one," Luke said. "We got men in town willing

to supply us guns, but unless we can stop them Jayhawkers from coming in and helping themselves to our supplies, to our whiskey, our . . . women—"

"Nobody messes with our women." Cole Younger pointed a finger at Luke. "Not nobody."

"If we don't do something right now," Luke continued, enjoying his rant. "Well . . . then we might as well just pull the dirt up over our graves ourselves."

What was right was right, and Luke knew, no matter his own family's leanings, riding with Quantrill was right. There needed to be an end to this war, the atrocities committed by both sides, and other than joining the Confederate army, which he had no intentions of doing *ever*, Luke figured this was the best way to set about doing it.

Silence hung in the air like a warm breeze. "What is it you do, Mister Colton?" Quantrill asked. "To make a living, that is?"

One hand gripping reins, Luke used the other to point northwest. "Up in Lawrence, I haul freight for Gibson's store. Been doing it couple years now."

"Freight, huh?" Quantrill regarded Luke. "That'd make a damn good cover. You can haul just about anything and get away with it. Can't ya?" He chuckled and reached down, extending a hand.

Luke shook with Quantrill.

"We can use you. Welcome aboard, Mister Colton," Quantrill said. "Got any ideas right now?"

Luke did. He wanted to start gunrunning, a plan he'd been hatching for weeks. Luke's friends, the Iverson brothers, had talked about heisting a wagonload of British-made Enfield 1853 rifled muskets.

"You bring me those rifles, Colton, and you can ride up front with us."

CHAPTER SEVEN

Luke drummed his fingers against the splintery post in Pa's barn, the movement bringing throbbing to his mostly healed arm. Damn, it was hot in here. Sweat pasted his shirt to his back. Stifling Kansas heat enveloped him like a wool blanket. How many times in the last couple of minutes had he glanced at the barn door waiting for it to open? How many more minutes would he wait? He half expected Pa to come home early and discover everyone. If that happened, there would be hell to pay.

And what the hell was keeping the Iverson brothers, anyway? Everyone else was here. His gaze trailed around the six-stall barn revealing men sitting on nail kegs and hay bales, their conversations quiet. Luke counted thirteen. Lucky number.

Luke itched for something to do, something to calm his fidgeting. A smoke, he thought. He patted his vest pocket, then gave up the search. Lighting a match in this tinderbox would be a disaster. He'd have to wait.

"Anybody know about the Iverson boys?" Luke asked.

A man in the back shrugged. "Should've been here by now."

"Maybe got waylaid by Quantrill," another man mumbled, then spit into the sawdust.

"Bet they met up with Billy Anderson," a third offered. "He's a real nice fella, I hear." Chuckles and guffaws bounced around the barn.

Anderson. Quantrill. Ruthless, murdering men. Why again

had he joined up with Quantrill? Pa. It was Pa's fault.

What would Pa do when he got back from town to find his barn filled with men? Luke hadn't asked permission to use the barn, taking advantage of his folks being away for the day. If he'd used his own barn, Sally would surely find out. Yeah, Pa would be angry all right.

A shred of guilt tugged. Had it already come down to that? *Family comes first,* Ma preached. It's not the first, nor the last thing. It's the *only* thing.

Luke squirmed at more uncomfortable thoughts and pushed them aside. He turned his attention to these men, good men, who represented a growing resentment of the way Kansas and the United States dealt with states' rights. The Confederacy had the right idea. Leave Kansas and the rest of the states the hell alone. Those who wanted to be a part of the industrial world like New York and such, fine. Let the states create their own laws. Now, Luke and "the boys" would take matters into their own hands, their way.

The big question sat on his chest like a sack of grain. Would he tell them he'd joined up with Quantrill? That this meeting and impending mission was to prove himself to the feared Raiders' leader? Some of these boys didn't trust the man and would leave. Then Luke would have to waste valuable time rounding up new recruits. No, he'd keep quiet, ride with Quantrill when asked, run guns with this group.

Luke dug into his vest pocket and pulled out his watch. The hands were closer to the hour of three than of two. Manure smells colliding with leather smells wafted around Luke's head. Heat brought out odor, not to mention flies. He swatted, then cursed.

"How much longer we gonna wait, Colton?" Albert Perkins, part-time accountant and part-time bartender, paced the length of the barn from the wall to the doors. "Don't have time to spend hangin' around here." He peeled off his felt bowler and pushed on the wide doors, their groan echoing as they opened. Al peered out. An oath mumbled under his breath, he slapped his hat back on his head and turned to Luke. "Hell, I got chores need doin'. I'm leavin'."

"Wait a minute." All right. This was it. Now or never. Pa would be getting home within the hour. "Close the door. Please."

"It's hot in here," Al grumbled. "Why the hell you insist on keepin' it closed?"

Two men stood and ambled toward the doors. "Damn hot," one said.

Luke held up a hand. "Nobody needs to know we're meeting here. Don't want somebody riding by and see us in here like this."

"Sit down, you three," Smitty Jenkins said. His shaggy blond hair hung at his lean shoulders. He moved toward Luke. "He's right. We gotta be careful."

"Easy for you to say, *deserter*." Albert Perkins' hands fisted. "What d'you know? Hell, you turned tail and ran from the last battle of Northern aggression."

Most of the men jumped up, intent on the argument at hand. Harvey Tillman, a dirt farmer who, despite his skinny build, had fists that were legendary in a fight, kicked up sawdust as he made his way to join Smitty.

Luke had to take control before everyone took to swinging. He'd never get his group together if they did.

"Time to create platoons," Luke said. "We'll divide into three groups." He gazed at the flushed faces of men he was about to ask to risk their lives.

One man, plaid shirt half tucked into his dirty wool britches, spoke over the mumbles. "First. We need us a name. If we're gonna be an army, shouldn't we call ourselves something?"

Absolutely, Luke thought. What better way to keep the spirit alive than a moniker?

"Ideas?" he said, relieved the men had calmed.

Suggestions sailed around the barn.

"How's about *Colton's Cutthroats*?" someone shouted.

Instantaneous agreement exploded.

"Now that's settled," Luke said. Even to him, his words sounded filled with pride and anxiety. He knew he'd burst if he didn't get this group moving in the right direction. The Iverson boys could catch up if and when they got there.

"Let's get out of this oven, Colton." Albert Perkins started for the doors, three others behind him.

"Wait! Let's assign platoons first."

" 'Bout damn time," Al said. "Me and Janovich here—"

"I'll do the assigning," Luke said. "We'll need three platoon leaders. They can choose their team." He searched faces he'd known for a while, a couple he'd known just recently.

"Well," Al said, "I ain't servin' under no army deserter." He glared at Smitty Jenkins.

"He ain't no deserter," Harvey Tillman countered. "He was just smart. Left afore he got himself shot dead. Any man in their right mind'll do that."

Smitty Jenkins straightened his shoulders. "I ain't gonna explain myself to nobody. You either want me riding with you or you don't. Your choice."

Luke stepped in front of Al and held up both hands like the orchestra conductor he'd seen one time he'd gone to Kansas City when Ma had insisted her boys be exposed to good music. But now, instead of conducting musicians, Luke was conducting men. Men who just might kill each other rather than a Jayhawker.

"Settle down, men." Luke met the gaze of each, then began the speech he'd rehearsed. "Today is a red-letter day. We've come together, no, *banded* together to set Kansas on its ear. No, to set the United States on its ear. No, to set the *world* on its ear." He waited for rumblings of support to race through the group. "Instead of joining the Confederate army, we're creating our own."

Two men raised fists in the air. "Army. Army." They chanted while a few others joined in. Luke stood, admiring their exuberance, waiting for them to quiet.

When some had regained their places on the hay bales, Luke continued. "That's right. We're an army now. Our goal is similar to Quantrill's, but we don't need his help." Luke hated that lying to his men was necessary for now.

"We can do this ourselves." Luke took advantage of the stunned silence. "Smitty, I want you to be in charge of platoon number one."

Jenkins, easily six inches taller than Luke and three years older, stared at each man. "I'll do a good job, right ya are. Got me some battlefield experience."

"Your help will be needed." Luke turned to a boy about his younger brother's age who leaned against a post. If wide eyes and open mouth were any indication, he'd been soaking in every word. Luke nodded at him. "Hopper. William Hopper."

The teenager glued his eyes on Luke. "Sir?"

Sir? Luke liked that kind of respect and the admiration that went with it. Why not? Luke was a natural born leader and now he was proving it. He pointed at the freckle-faced Hopper.

"You. I'd like you to be platoon leader number two. All right?"

Hopper saluted. "Yes, sir. You can count on me." A lopsided grin slid up his face, his brown eyes dancing with excitement.

"Good." Luke was on a roll now and excitement butterflied in his stomach. Now, for the last one. He pointed at Harvey Tillman. Maybe Albert Perkins would be a good leader, maybe not. But Luke wasn't sure the accountant-bartender could keep his temper when a cool head was needed. Albert was fine in a

42

bar fight, but that was about it. Harvey Tillman would be better as a leader. At least he wasn't hotheaded.

"Harvey, let's make you one of the unit's commanders. You'll be platoon number three," Luke said.

Harvey's shoulders pushed back, his chest expanded. "I ain't never been a leader before."

A wide smile revealed several gaps in his teeth. His blue eyes swept across the circle of men. "Ain't that righteous?"

Nods from a few.

"You've plenty of work ahead of you, Harvey. We all do," Luke said.

"You're making Harvey a platoon leader?" Albert Perkins flapped his arms against his side. "What about me?" He shook a pointed finger in Luke's face. "You're makin' a huge mistake. He can't write or even cipher numbers, much less lead. What're you thinking?"

Luke met Albert's glare. "I'm thinking he'll do fine. Keep his head. Lead with his knowledge of people. Don't have to have book learning to be smart."

"Leave 'em alone, Al!" A voice from the back sailed over the men.

"He hits as hard as you do," a second man said.

"Who says? I'm the best fighter anywhere." Al brought his hands up to his face, then slowly fisted both. "I'll punch any man who says different."

"What kinda weapons do we got?" William Hopper's question turned heads.

Luke took advantage of the distraction. "If the Iversons ever get here, we'll know what we can get our hands on." *Just hope it's the Enfields like I told Quantrill.* Luke cringed at the thought of not delivering as promised.

Albert Perkins snorted and headed for the barn doors. "Ain't got time for this. How do we know Luke ain't one of them Jayhawkers? Huh?"

"Simmer down," Smitty said. He stood eye to eye with Al. "Luke wouldn't do that to us. Besides, we don't need to be fightin' between ourselves. Hell, fightin' the Union's enough."

"What d'you know?" Al shoved Smitty, who rocked back two steps.

Luke stepped in between, holding Al's right arm. "No need—"

The barn doors squeaked open. Luke, Al and Smitty snapped around, Luke's eyes adjusting to the strong light boiling in. Two men, silhouetted against the sun, stepped in and closed the door. Luke squinted. The Iverson boys. Finally.

The taller of the two tilted his hat back on his head. "Sorry we're late. Horse threw a shoe." He sauntered up to Luke eyeing the grip he had on Al. "We . . . miss anything?"

Luke released Albert's muscled arm and nodded to Smitty who took a step back.

Gunnar Iverson looked from man to man. "What's goin' on here?"

Silence filled the barn.

Albert Perkins let his shoulders drop. "Nothin'." He eyed Gunnar and then Luke. "Sorry, Colton. Didn't mean anything. You know, it's hot—"

"It's all right, Al," Luke said. "We're about done here."

Smitty stared at Gunnar. "You get those guns?"

Gunnar Iverson's blond eyebrows arched over his blue eyes. "Ya betcha we did. Big ones."

Tobias stood at his brother's shoulder. "And . . . with enough ammunition to blow up the whole state of Kansas."

CHAPTER EIGHT

Luke squinted at the map laid out on his dining table. Under the oil lantern's golden glow, it was hard to make out which farm was which, which stream ran where. But he couldn't sleep until he had a better plan. He'd already tossed and turned earlier tonight until he figured he had bruises from rolling. And he knew Sally had awakened, if her mumbles were any indication.

His finger traced the winding Missouri River's path from north of Saint Joe down toward Independence. Luke froze, finger on that town. Nope, he didn't want to go back there. Leastways, not any time soon. From what he'd read in the paper and heard around town, Independence had been ransacked pretty good by Quantrill and his boys. And, he'd heard in whispered rumors, Quantrill was aiming to expand. With Luke's help, certain town leaders in Lawrence could be singled out. Hopefully, that would keep this town from meeting the same fate as Independence.

Luke turned the map sideways. Maybe it would make more sense this way. The Iverson brothers had told Luke to meet them at a wagon crossing where the river makes a sweeping westward curve, about fifty miles north of town. Two, maybe three days—one long day up there and two back. He didn't like being gone from home any more than necessary. Time was, not many weeks ago, he'd take off for days at a time, prowling like a cat in places he wasn't really welcomed. Usually he had a good time—what he remembered of it.

But now, he worried about Sally and the boy . . . and his folks. If the raids spread out and got closer to home, his folks could stay with Sally here in town.

Focus back on the map, Luke cocked his head and recounted directions. "Skirt past that fort at Leavenworth, take the trees—"

A soft hand on his shoulder. Luke jumped.

Sally.

He clutched his chest with one hand and released the crumpled map with the other. "You near scared me to death." Luke frowned up at his wife. Her blue eyes widened.

"Shhh. Adam's asleep." Sally's mouth curled up at both ends, a trait Luke couldn't resist. It reminded him of pictures of elves, those little Irish creatures he'd seen in picture books.

He grasped her hand and pulled her to his lap. Her hair in his face smelled like lilacs. The familiar fragrance always stirred passion in Luke. Tonight was no exception. He pulled her close, his hands gliding over her slightly pooched stomach. Maybe by year's end, he'd have a second son.

She peered down at the map. "What're you looking at?"

She wasn't to know anything about this. Luke kept his dealings with Quantrill, the Iversons and the rest of "Colton's Cutthroats" a secret, and he had no intentions of telling her. She'd be safer not ever knowing.

"Gotta drive another load of freight to Independence tomorrow. Just looking to see where I'm going," Luke said.

Silence grew in the cozy dining room. Sally breathed heavier than usual, Luke swallowed twice, the clock in the corner thrummed with each beat of Luke's heart.

A minute stretched into two. Sally broke out of his embrace and stood pointing. "Independence is east, not north."

"I know." Luke chose the offensive. "Just wanna take a different route this time. Do you mind?"

She placed Luke's hand on her belly. "Your children need a pa." With a frown, she started for the darkened bedroom, then stopped and turned around. "I don't know what you're up to, Luke Jeremiah Colton, but you've been to Independence dozens of times. You know all the roads."

She disappeared into the bedroom and closed the door.

CHAPTER NINE

Leaving early the next morning wasn't easy. In fact, leaving at all was tough. Sally was no fool, and she was right. But he couldn't stop what he was doing. He wouldn't turn tail and run because he had a family. He wasn't special. Everybody had brothers, sisters, children, wives. And he firmly believed the Confederates were right, and he'd pledged his life to run gun blockades. He would do everything in his power to help the South win.

As Luke drove the freight wagon north out of town, he mentally checked the map. By mid-morning he should reach the banks of the Missouri, where he'd meet up with Harvey Tillman. Leaving town separately lessened the chance of anyone seeing them together. The first real act of Colton's Cutthroats was about to get underway.

Late-August heat settled around Luke. Oppressively hot. Despite the little breeze from his ride, flies perched on his shoulder. One even dared land on his nose. He swatted. Maybe a run would soothe some of his nerves. Reins clutched in both hands, he let out a *"Yee haw!"* The horses bolted.

A low hill provided enough height to afford a view of the meandering river shimmering in the sun. Luke pulled to a stop, his horses blowing hard. He'd run them almost too much. Fortunately, his load was light this time. Just two nail barrels, a box of carpenter's tools, and three boxes of food, all destined for a farm north of the fort. He grinned. Trading loads with the other driver had been easy. Maybe too easy, but that just-off-the-boat Italian immigrant didn't speak enough English to tell their boss about the last-minute switch. If he tried, Mister Gibson didn't understand most of what Luigi said. A signed receipt was a signed receipt. It didn't say who the driver was.

Luke had plenty of room for the guns the Iverson boys were supposed to have. Luke brought extra canvas paulins to hide the weapons. The thick sheets would keep prying eyes away and the rain off if it were to happen.

Not a cloud in the sky, Luke pried off his hat, ran his sleeve across his forehead and fanned his face with the wide-brimmed hat. A sip from the canteen, his hat back in place and he was ready to find Harvey.

Harvey Tillman was waiting for him underneath one of the few trees growing along the river. As skinny as Harvey was, Luke had almost mistaken him for a sapling.

After a quick dinner of ham and biscuits, and cornbread that Harvey had brought, Harvey tied his horse to the back of the wagon, jumped in, and the two men drove along the river.

They passed the time discussing the war, the new Springfield rifles, the trusty British Enfields, Quantrill, crops, weather and women. The last topic made Harvey squirm and Luke warm. They changed subjects.

Late afternoon brought a standstill to all conversation. Luke and Harvey rode in silence, the treeless rolling hills of eastern Kansas in Luke's sight. He kept an eye on the river while following the well-worn road paralleling it.

Luke calculated they were closing in on Fort Leavenworth. They'd made good time, and if his map was anywhere close to accurate, it wouldn't be too far now. Considered a Union stronghold, Leavenworth served as a supply station and provided escorts for Santa Fe and Oregon Trail travelers. However, the Cherokees and Kiowas were still a problem, and they continued harassing settlers moving west.

"Looky over yonder, Luke." Harvey pointed northwest.

Blue-suited soldiers rode in two columns, heading straight toward Luke's wagon. A red, white and blue guidon waved over the heads of the 4th Cavalry Regiment. Luke chewed his lower lip. What the hell did they want? He had planned to avoid them, and now here they were. As much as he wanted to veer away, he knew he couldn't. No, he'd have to endure.

The soldier in front held up his hand, and after the patrol had stopped, saluted Luke. "Sergeant Williams, sir."

"Luke Colton and this here's Harvey Tillman." Luke chided himself for giving their real names. What the hell was he thinking? Not a very good start to a career as a Rebel gunrunner.

The sergeant rode closer. "Mind if I ask your business out here?" His blue eyes traveled up and down Luke, then across Harvey. "Got some renegade Kiowas making life miserable in these parts."

Luke cocked his head toward his wagon. "Ain't got Kiowas back there, Sergeant. I'm delivering freight, not Indians. We're out of Lawrence."

The sergeant brought his shoulders back, his buttons straining at his chest. His gaze roved again over Luke then back to the wagon. "Mind if I have a look for myself? Some independent businessmen are selling whiskey to the Indians." He rode up to the wagon, tilted and shook the nail kegs until he heard metal rattle, pawed through the box of food, and then tossed the paulins back. He scanned the rest of the wagon bed, then replaced the canvas. "Providing whiskey to Indians is against the law, you know."

Luke bit his lip again, swallowed twice, then realized he'd been holding his breath. Anything to keep from yelling at this Blue Belly. "I *know*, Sergeant." Damn, it was hot, and not a breath of air.

Sergeant Williams pointed behind his troops. "The fort's just over the rise there." Another scan of Luke. "You're welcome to rest there tonight. Get a fresh start in the morning."

Like that would ever happen. Luke nodded and squinted up at the sun. Still a couple of useable daylight hours. "Thanks all the same, Sergeant. Maybe another day." With that, he snapped the reins over his team's back, and they left the troops behind.

Well out of the soldiers' earshot, Harvey raked his hand through his hair. "Damn, that was close. Suppose we'll ever see them again?" He fanned his sun-blotched face with his hat.

"More'n likely," Luke said. "Sure don't like being scrutinized like that."

"Being what?" Harvey fitted his hat and raised one skinny eyebrow at Luke.

"Scrutinized," Luke said. "Examined. Taken apart piece by piece. Makes me uncomfortable."

"Yeah, me, too."

Another hour slid by in silence. Green rolling hills gave way to sunburned brown flat. At times, far off in the distance, Luke spotted a farm or small settlement. And off to his right in the distance, a sea of black, shaggy bodies grazed in the late-afternoon sun. But all along the way, they'd met only one other wagon on this road. That was all right. The fewer people who saw Harvey and him, the better.

And then there they were. The Iverson brothers. Gunnar and Tobias, their wide shoulders matching their wide smiles. They waved from their wagon parked under the only cottonwood within view. Despite the waters from the river, only reeds and wild cherry bushes lined both sides of the steep banks.

Harvey waved as soon as he spotted his fellow Cutthroats. Luke snapped the reins and the horses picked up speed, trotting toward the tree.

"Thought you'd never get here, Luke." Gunnar held out a

hand and leaned across Tobias.

"Damn Blue Bellies decided they wanted a powwow," Luke said.

"Hell, yeah." Harvey jumped down from the wagon and shook hands with Tobias. "They even invited us to supper." A quick grin flitted across his face, raising his thin lips into a crescent. "But we politely said 'no, thanks' and rode off. Didn't we, Luke?"

"Shoulda give 'em a piece of your mind, Harvey," Tobias said. "I'd of told 'em right quick they was on the losin' side. I'd of told 'em—"

"No, thanks is what you would've told 'em, Tobe." Gunnar shoved his brother across the wagon bench until he sailed off the end. "Harvey's right. Don't be drawing attention to us." He jumped down and lowered the wagon's gate.

Tobias and Gunnar peeled back the buffalo hides and duck paulins. Two dozen .58 Enfield rifles lay glinting in the fading sun. Luke whistled long.

"Beauts, ain't they?" Harvey ran his hand down one barrel. "Takes one of them Minie bullets, don't it?"

Luke picked one up and sighted it. "From what I've heard, you can fire three times a minute if you've got a full charge of black powder."

"And," Gunnar said as he aimed one. "It's deadly at three hundred yards. Hell, Luke, you could run like Lucifer's on your tail, and I'd still drill you. Right through your head." He chuckled. "But that wouldn't do any damage, since it's empty. No, I'd aim for your butt."

A couple more playful threats then the men sobered, the weight of this undertaking on their chests. Luke replaced the rifle and then cut his eyes sideways to Gunnar. At twenty-three, this man had already fought too many battles of his own, and they showed. Etched in his forehead was a drunken, abusive father, a mother dead before her time, another younger brother lost to war. No wonder Gunnar kept close watch on Tobias. He was the only family left in the Iverson clan, and no doubt, Gunnar would keep Tobias safe.

But was running guns across Union blockades the way to keep your brother safe? Hardly.

While Luke and Harvey carted the furry skins and paulins to their wagon, Luke realized that his own younger brother, Andy, had done something of the same for James. One and a half years ago, at the age of sixteen, Andy joined the Union army to fight alongside their brother. *To keep James safe.* And Andy ended up shot, nearly killed by a Rebel bullet. But in the end, James saved his entire Union regiment from an Apache attack. He'd even received a medal, along with a sliced up hand and chest.

Yep, Gunnar was a lot like Andy.

"We'll get more where these came from, Luke." Gunnar nudged him with his shoulder. "You listening or just trying to think?" He wagged his head. "See? I knew your head was empty."

Gunnar set his armful of rifles down on the paulins and then arranged them next to each other, stock to barrel. Luke rolled the bayonets in another canvas sheet, and nestled them up near the front of the wagon.

By the time Tobias and Harvey finished packing the weapons, the sun had turned orange-gold casting gray-blue shadows over the hills of thistle, clover and verbena. More canvas, then the skins covered the rifles. Luke moved the nail barrels and food box onto the fur to help hold down the skins in case of wind. With nothing to run interference, the wind blew most of the time in eastern Kansas. But high winds only came in the form of tornados. And Luke prayed there wasn't one in his future.

The four men settled in for the night under the cottonwood. The campfire, along with a bottle of whiskey Tobias provided, warmed their spirits. The evening passed with food and stories.

Lots of stories. Most, Luke figured, held a bit of truth.

Luke lay with his head on a sack of beans, a thin blanket covering his body. Firelight flickered in its last spasms of life. "Gunnar? You think Quantrill's right?"

Silence.

Gunnar turned onto his side. "Maybe. But I don't like the way he goes about the business. Gotta be a better way."

Tobias poked the fire, which sparked to life then just as quickly faded. "He's a scary sumabitch, that's for sure. I wouldn't ride with him."

CHAPTER TEN

Morning light danced on Luke's face, warming his exposed cheek. He flipped onto his other side, determined to remain asleep. However, aromas of coffee intermingling with frying bacon brought him to his feet. Tobias and Gunnar raised their coffee cups at him as he stumbled toward the fire. Harvey slept rolled up in a blanket.

By the time Luke finished his second cup of coffee, Harvey started his first. Within half an hour, breakfast was eaten, pans and dishes cleaned, fire doused, horses fed and watered, pistols inspected, harnesses checked and rifles double-checked.

Gunnar pointed. "Me and Tobias gotta head up north where we can get our hands on more guns. We'll be gone a couple weeks, and we'll contact you as soon as we get back."

Luke and Harvey gave a final handshake to the Iverson boys, then turned the team around. A brief stop to drop off the freight and they would be headed home. Once they reached Luke's barn, they'd hide the rifles there until it was time to hand half of them off to Quantrill. As he bounced along in the wagon, the Iversons' promise of more British Enfield rifles echoed in Luke's head. Three dozen next time. The Enfields were proving to be just as valuable as the Springfields. Harvey's voice interrupted Luke's thoughts.

"Where you suppose them boys are gettin' those rifles at?" Harvey squinted behind him. "And where're they gonna get those Springfields at? Those're mighty hard to come by . . . unless you steal 'em."

How had Harvey survived these many years on his own? Luke pushed both eyebrows skyward. "I don't remember them *buying* them, do you?" Immediately, he regretted the sarcasm.

"No, don't reckon so." Harvey sighed loud and long. "Too bad they gotta steal 'em. Too bad we gotta shoot 'em. And shoot each other."

Now for Harvey, that was deep thinking. Luke liked Harvey Tillman, ever since they were in their early teens and in school together. They hadn't been close, but certainly friends. Luke promised himself to be more patient with him.

The morning passed in idle chatter. Following a quick mid-day meal of ham and biscuits, the men started off again, hoping to get to the barn by nightfall. If Luke had planned right, they could stash the weapons and no one would be any the wiser. By dark, Sally was always inside the house fixing supper. No need for her to go out there.

Harvey sat swaying with eyes closed, while Luke counted the rabbits in the fields. Again. He'd lost track at seventeen. The flat, open, treeless prairie stretched out on all sides of their wagon and the monotony brought no new thoughts for Luke. Nothing but thinking about getting these weapons safely to the barn.

Once he got to the barn, he'd hide half the rifles way in the back. The other half Albert Perkins was supposed to come get, arranging for the rifle disbursement. The moment Al took what he thought was all the rifles, Luke would take the rest to Quantrill.

A whoop and holler brought Harvey to his feet and Luke spinning on the seat. Behind them, bearing down at full gallop, rode a dozen or more Kiowas. Luke slapped the reins and yelled at his team, even though he knew they could never outrun these

Indians, these men whose horsemanship was legendary. But he'd try.

Harvey pulled his gun from his waistband, swiveled around on the seat and fired. The Indians kept coming.

One hand on the reins, Luke tossed his Colt to Harvey. "Try with this."

Harvey shot. The Indians bore down harder.

They covered nearly a mile before two Indians grabbed the harnesses and pulled back.

Two more Indians, feathers sticking out of their black hair, jumped into the wagon bed. One held a knife close to Luke's throat.

Luke tried to swallow and yank on the reins at the same time. Breathing proved impossible.

Before Luke could bring the wagon to a stop, Harvey sailed from the wagon seat onto the ground, somersaulting down a low hill. Two Kiowas pounced on him, the sun reflecting off their knives.

A hand pushed hard, and Luke tumbled off the wagon seat. He hit the ground, rolled, then scrambled to his feet. What looked to be a hundred Indians attacked at once.

Luke yanked his Colt from its holster, aimed at the closest Kiowa and fired. The man flew back, screaming as he hit the ground. Before Luke could get another shot off, a body—muscular, powerful, sweaty—plowed into his back and wrapped its arms around him. Struggling like a captured wild boar, Luke dropped to his knees, the Indian's hold lost.

Crawling, then leaping to his feet, Luke clutched his gun and swung at the closest Kiowa. *Thwack!* The Indian crumpled to the ground. Before Luke could cock his gun and shoot or swing at another, four Indians pounced on him, forcing him down, pushing his body to the ground. Fists punched his face, his stomach. Feet rammed into his back, his legs, his head.

A face or two blurred then cleared. Scowls—wide scowling faces glared at him.

Hands—tough, leathery hands grabbed at his clothes.

Feet—moccasined, powerful feet kicked, again and again.

Luke squeezed his eyes tight, praying for this to end. And he prayed he and Harvey would survive. But he hadn't heard even a whimper from that direction.

The ground hard under Luke's body, he rolled to his right in time to spot a leather legging and attached moccasin barrel toward his face.

A moan. Luke brought his hand up and gripped his head. Something crusty covered his face gluing his eyes shut. Throbbing, pounding, his head was ready to explode. In only a matter of seconds, his brains would splatter everywhere.

Another moan. Was that his? Luke dug the caked blood from his eyes, then willed them open. One obliged, but the other remained shut. He patted his left eye and discovered it was swollen, too swollen to open. He'd have to navigate with one. But, was he blind? Even with one open, he couldn't see a thing. Luke rolled onto his back, the agony of movement reminding him he was alive.

He blinked then rubbed his good eye. Stars. Stars in the night sky. As he lay there, the river gurgled, frogs *charrumped,* and something small skittered into a nearby bush. But then there was something else. Another noise. Breathing. A moan. Luke frowned. It wasn't him. Harvey! Had to be Harvey.

Luke froze. But maybe it wasn't Harvey. Maybe it was an Indian he'd taken down.

Maybe the Indian was crawling over to kill him. Stab him. Shoot him with his own gun. Luke rolled away from the breathing and then pushed up to his knees. Every muscle, every joint, every hair on his head hurt, all screaming at him. If he could get to the wagon, pull himself up, use it for cover . . .

Eye adjusting to the scant moonlight, he spotted no wagon, no horses, no nothing. Just stars. Using all the strength he could muster, he stood, his muscles and body complaining. He ran his tongue over his lips and tasted blood.

The prairie stretched in all directions, more night noises coming alive.

Harvey. He had to find Harvey. And if he came across an Indian, he'd have to fight. Somehow. After turning in a circle, Luke lurched forward, hoping he'd stumble across his friend . . . his still-alive friend.

As Luke searched, his head thundered. A couple times he stopped, gripping both sides of his head, waiting for the pain to lessen. Something across his forehead, a cut maybe, stung and burned. He tried to ignore it. With the morning sun, he'd take better inventory of his injuries.

And then there he was. Harvey. Lying face down in the grass at the bottom of a low hill.

"Harvey?"

Luke shook the thin shoulders then rolled him over. A moan. This time Luke knew it had come from his friend. How had they both managed to survive?

"Harvey," Luke said. "Wake up. You're all right."

Luke sat by Harvey until the prairie glowed with predawn sun. A better inspection of his friend revealed a deep slice across Harvey's forehead. Luke felt his own and realized he had one similar. "Hell and damnation, Harvey. We've been almost scalped." He peered across the rolling hills, waiting for an Indian to attack. "Sumbitch."

Soft glowing light brought new life to the prairie. Those Indians more than likely had found the rifles and left him and Harvey for dead. Rifles, Luke decided, must be more valuable than scalps.

But what about Quantrill? He had given specific orders he wanted those weapons. What would that leader do to him? Speculation brought a lump to his throat.

Leaving Harvey where he lay, Luke limped to the river. On his bruised knees, he splashed water on his face, wetting his neckerchief to swipe at dried blood. He felt better. With one eye still swollen shut, the other was at least able to focus. The cool water helped.

"See you ran into some indigenous heathens, Mister Colton."

Luke jumped, spun around, fumbling for his Colt lost to the Kiowas.

Sergeant Williams cocked his head, part of a smile pushing up his mustached mouth. "Looks like they took your wagon, too."

"Sergeant," Luke said. "You about scared me to death."

A detachment of four soldiers sat atop their horses.

And why hadn't Luke heard their approach? He frowned.

The sergeant turned to one of his men. "See to his wounds, Corporal." Williams dismounted and handed the reins to another soldier. "I'm guessing it was Kiowas did this to you. Part of Satanta's renegades. I warned you they were out here."

Gripping his wet bandanna, Luke envisioned wrapping it around the sergeant's neck. Instead he held it against his swollen cheek, the coolness soothing the throbbing. Luke gritted his teeth. Tightness filled his chest. He pulled in air, started to speak, and then stopped. Another breath.

"Could you help my friend over there?" Luke asked. "Maybe take him back to the fort?"

CHAPTER ELEVEN

A solid handshake. Using his other hand, Luke gripped Harvey's shoulder, rocking his slender frame, the cotton-stuffed mattress bouncing with the movement. "You rest up here, get better." The stench of rubbing alcohol, combined with the overall odor of sick people, turned Luke's stomach. The sooner he made his escape out of this army hospital room, the better. He'd already spent too much time there. A day and a half and he was itching to leave.

Although he wasn't itching to run into Quantrill.

Luke fitted his hat down tight over the bandage wrapped around his head. With the wind whipping the grass already this morning, the ride home would prove fearsome. The wind rattling the windows and his frayed nerves already on edge, he jumped at every sound. The soldiers had assured him the Kiowas weren't anywhere around. Today.

Harvey Tillman's swollen mouth pushed upward, fat lips resembling a grin. "See you when . . . *business* picks up."

"You just rest, heal up, then I'll buy you a beer." Luke tossed another smile at Harvey, turned and stepped into wind and daylight. The door slammed behind him.

The hat brim shielded his eyes from direct sun, but damn, it was bright outside. No clouds, just sun. Wind tugged at his hat. He squinted at the soldier holding the reins of a dun, at least sixteen hands high. She looked fast, too. *Just in case.* Luke chided himself for his nerves. But he had good reason. A real fine reason.

While being tended the day before, Luke had talked to the doctor who had pointed out that both Luke and Harvey had, indeed, been scalped, but the hair hadn't been lifted. Whoever had started the process, he said, got sidetracked which proved fortuitous. The cut required only a few stitches.

Sergeant Williams remained perplexed as to why the Kiowas hadn't finished the job. Luke knew. Harvey knew. But they weren't telling.

Luke swung up and adjusted his weight in the saddle. Sergeant Williams headed toward Luke, his stride intent on interception. Maybe if he spurred hard, Luke could get past the gate sentries and out into the prairie before that Blue Belly could prattle at him. Nope, the sergeant's long legs covered ground too quickly.

"Mister Colton." Sergeant Williams raised a hand. "A moment."

A moment was way more than Luke wanted to give this man, but he swallowed impatience and waited.

"Just wanted to tell you, we'll probably run into you again." The sergeant pointed south. "Got reports a couple of Bushwhacker groups are trying to raid this part of Kansas. We'll be heading out first thing tomorrow."

And? is what Luke wanted to say. But he instead chose to say, "Bushwhackers, Sergeant? Like who?"

"A fella named William Quantrill. Got a sidekick, supposedly a cousin or something, named Clarke Blackhorn. Evil sumabitch." Williams brought his shoulders back then moved in closer to Luke and squinted against the rising sun. "You heard of either of 'em?"

Breakfast smells, bacon, coffee and something Luke couldn't identify, emanated from the sergeant like waves of rotten fruit.

Luke fought down his own rising breakfast. "Everybody has, Sergeant."

"Maybe so," Williams said. "I was hoping, since you seem to be out often on business, if you'd keep your eyes peeled for Captain Quantrill, we'd appreciate it."

"Wait a second here, Sergeant." Luke's good eye twitched while his swollen eye closed. He gripped the reins tighter. "He's a captain?"

"Sure enough. Been commissioned captain as a Missouri Partisan Ranger." Williams shook his head. "Don't that beat all? But the Union army's declared him an outlaw. We will find him and bring him to justice."

"And if he's killed in the process, that's just too bad?" Luke asked.

While Luke didn't hold to killing, he certainly didn't hold to the way the Union interfered with everybody's lives. Confederates still had the right idea.

"If he's killed, Mister Colton," said Williams, "it's his own damn fault. You live by violence, you die by violence." He frowned up at Luke. "You sure you ain't a Bushwhacker . . . or a Confederate?" He spit.

"Did I say I was?"

Williams paused. "No."

Luke turned the conversation back to the original topic. "So you want me to spy? For the Union army?"

Sergeant Williams chuckled. "Not exactly. Be more like our eyes and ears out in the field. We can't be everywhere at once." He glanced behind him toward the closed door to the hospital. "And since we patched you and your friend up . . ."

"Hell, Sergeant, if you want payment—"

"No." Williams held up both hands. "Not money. Just information. Be our eyes and ears. Let us know what you find. Especially about Quantrill. I hear he's around these parts."

Luke gave a feeble salute. "Thanks again for the doctoring. I'll leave this horse in the livery stable in town and be sure he's fed and watered."

Sergeant Williams touched the brim of his hat. "Glad to know you're on our side, Mister Colton."

Luke set spurs into the sides of his horse, and trotted out of the fort gates and into freedom.

CHAPTER TWELVE

The first day back home passed without incident. Sally doted on him, catering to his every twitch, every groan. Luke promised himself not to moan louder than he really felt, but he admitted he enjoyed the attention. Even toddler Adam spent time on his lap, playing with the white gauze bandage wrapped around Luke's head.

He'd told Sally about the Kiowas, but reported them near Independence, not Leavenworth. She seemed to have believed the story. However, when his folks came over the afternoon of the second day, Pa was harder to convince.

Joseph Colton sat on Luke's couch and leaned elbows on knees, eyes glued on Luke's face. The brown eyes traveled over the bandaged forehead, down to the half-swollen eye ringed with black and blue streaks, and stopped on the split lips. Luke fidgeted under the scrutiny. He rocked back and forth in Sally's favorite chair.

Pa's questioning stare always upset Luke, ever since he was around twelve. Admittedly, that was about the time he'd started acting on his own ideas and not always obeying Pa, but here he was a grown man, still nervous about talking to him.

"Kiowas, you say?" Pa asked. "I'm surprised they're over around Independence."

"That's where they were. Over there. Renegades from Satanta's tribe." Luke played with a corner of his mustache. "Came outta nowhere."

Pa frowned. "Sure pack a wallop, don't they?"

Luke nodded, touched his tender cheek, and winced. "Probably a war party. Twenty, thirty at least."

Laughter and a high-pitched squeal sailed from the kitchen. Sally and Ma undoubtedly were playing with Adam. He loved his grandma and clung to her leg every time she was near. Sally had announced they would make a special supper in honor of Luke's survival. No doubt, Adam was "helping."

Luke's thoughts returned to his pa now sprawled back against the couch, looking as if a nap was next on his agenda. His six-foot frame, the muscles and wide shoulders, ideal for a man his age who worked as hard as he did, took up half of the couch. As much as Luke wanted to sit on the other half, enjoy its softness, its security, he chose to stay in the hard, wooden rocking chair. Safe from Pa's reach.

Not that Pa ever hit him. At least not in years. He wasn't an overly strict parent, but expected his sons to obey. He never asked twice. Luke thought back to a time when he and James decided to go to a favorite fishing hole instead of school. They hadn't been there an hour when Pa showed up. Mad, sure he was mad. But it wasn't until they'd each caught two catfish that Pa decided he'd "found his boys" and marched them on to school.

What he told Ma was never revealed, but they ate fish that night.

"Why don't you lie down for a while, Luke?"

Ma's gentle voice startled Luke awake.

"You know I don't hold to drinking during the day," she said, "but with your bruises and that nasty cut, I think another shot of whiskey wouldn't hurt." She gripped his arm. "Here, I'll help you up and then get your . . . medicine." Ma smiled. One more thing he loved about her.

Pa snored while Luke groaned up to his feet and made his way to the bedroom.

Chapter Thirteen

Bored. Four days and Luke was bored. All the well-wishers had come and gone, meals brought and eaten, even swollen bruises had shrunk and faded. The only excitement was his itching stitches. It seemed as if young Adam delighted in running in and out of the room shrieking at top volume, or wrapping his little arms around Luke's leg as he walked, sending both to the floor. Sally's patience had grown thin, and she expected Luke to feed himself and Adam, bring in firewood and resume his usual "before the attack" duties.

He did what he could, reminding himself Sally was a fine woman, although a bit moody in her delicate condition, and she probably didn't realize how grouchy she sounded. After the baby came, in another three months, she'd be back to normal. He could wait. Although, admittedly, patience was not one of his stronger suits.

While he sat on the couch, enjoying its softness, its security, bootsteps thumping onto the porch startled him. They weren't expecting visitors today, and it was Adam's nap time. Two hours of blissful afternoon quiet about to be disturbed.

Before Luke could ease his sore body off the couch, pounding echoed throughout the house. How could knuckles rap like that? Luke cringed. Quantrill?

Fighting down the knot in his throat, Luke turned the knob.

Albert Perkins' hand was raised, ready to knock again, when Luke yanked open the door.

"You alone?" Albert's little round pig eyes swept the living room.

"Sally and the baby are napping." Relieved, Luke stepped back and waved him in. Luke took the rocking chair while his visitor stood, fidgeting. Luke pointed. "Sit down, Al."

"Can't stay." Albert eyed the empty couch then perched on the edge. He leaned forward and lowered his voice. "The rifles. They're wanting our rifles."

"Who?"

"*Them.*" Albert mopped his forehead with a blue-checkered handkerchief. "Them who paid for the rifles. And if we can't do it today, they said they can't wait."

Not Quantrill, Luke decided. The other people who wanted the Enfields. He pulled in air and expanded his chest. His shirt buttons strained. "You tell 'em we had 'em but they got stolen?"

Albert nodded.

"By the Indians?"

Another nod. "And I can't get any of the other Cutthroats to help me. Said they're keepin' their heads down."

Luke ran his tongue over his healing lower lip. He still tasted blood, still heard Indian whoops when he closed his eyes. Sometimes he shook.

Albert shrugged. "Luke? What'd we do? I mean, hell . . . we promised those Enfields, and now . . ." His listless eyes sparked for a moment, then returned to their dull brown. "I hear that Quantrill's gonna supply some."

The ones we were supposed to deliver. Luke ran a trembling hand over the back of his neck, feeling a shrinking lump at the base of his skull. "I guess keep doing what we need to do. Gotta get guns, good guns, to our men. I know those damn Blue Bellies think they're winning. I mean, hell, they won at Pea Ridge—"

"Our Southern soldiers outnumbered the Yankees, and we

still lost." Albert shook his head.

"Yeah. We even lost at Mill Springs. Hell, even Forts Henry and Donelson," Luke said. His stomach hurt.

"You're right there," Albert said. "But what about Vicksburg? Our Kentuckians run off those damn Yankees. All it took was a couple of cannonballs aimed at their boats." He smirked, dug around in his vest pocket, then held up a cigar. "Ran away like scared little girls. Bet they won't be trying anything that foolish again around Vicksburg. No siree."

"Hope you're right, Al."

" 'Course I'm right."

A shake of Luke's head brought a quick wave of nausea. He blinked and fought down the urge to throw up. "When I was back at Fort Leavenworth, the sergeant told me they'd be sending out troops, stationing them all along the Kansas–Missouri border."

"And I'm sure they're hell-bent on taking our guns, too." A scowl brought a hint of life into Al's face, along with a tinge of pink into his cheeks. "Can't let 'em do that."

Luke paused, and then regarded the accountant-bartender. Somewhere under this man's boring exterior lurked a man of passion. A man of conviction. A man not afraid to get dirty.

Luke gave him another look. Albert Perkins hid it well.

"So when d'you think we'll get more rifles, Luke?"

Pursing his tender lips, Luke played with the end of his mustache, the only part of his face pain free. He peered toward the closed bedroom door, then swung his attention back to Perkins, and lowered his voice. "Are your connections still willing to fund more guns? They've spent a helluva lot already. Any chance of them backing out? I mean, after all, they are politicians."

It was Albert Perkins' turn to stare at the closed door. The mantel clock ticked. Luke swallowed. Somewhere outside a horse whinnied.

Al let out a stream of air, rubbed the back of his neck, then nodded. He looked at Luke. "Yeah. They're willing to back us. Look the other way, when those weapons disappear." He stood. "Just hate to come up with excuses. How long you think that'll fly?"

Until Quantrill kills me. "Not long, I guess." Luke rocked back and then forward, the movement stirring the nausea threatening to surface. This meeting needed to be over. Now. He groaned while he stood, then pointed toward the door. "Soon as I hear from the Iversons, I'll let you know. They're saying we'll get Springfields this time."

Albert stepped onto the porch and lit his cigar. "We may have to run them ourselves, Colton." His eyes rose to meet Luke's. "You ready for that?"

Luke knew the answer. He'd thought about it for months. "Yep."

CHAPTER FOURTEEN

September 1862

Luke stood in his barn and thought back to a meeting two weeks ago.

Quantrill hadn't killed Luke when he told him what'd happened. Instead of whipping out his Colt like Luke had imagined, plugging him full of .45s, that Partisan Ranger captain had chuckled. The chuckle turned into a full-blown guffaw, complete with snorts and teary eyes. Worse, Cole Younger and the two James brothers yipped like wild Indians and shot pretend arrows at Luke.

All that was downright embarrassing.

"I'll get you some more," Luke said. "Springfields this time."

"You do that." Quantrill nodded, reining his horse around.

"Watch yourself, Colton," Cole said. "This time it was your scalp. Next time them natives're gonna slice off your manhood." He saluted and rode off.

The laughter and jokes trailing after them still haunted Luke's dreams.

"Luke?"

Luke turned to the distant call. Leaning on the rake and peering out through the barn door, he shielded his eyes. The relentless summer sun reflected off the wall of his house. Heat waves shimmered across the patches of grass and weeds.

"Luke!" Sally raced across the wide yard toward the barn. Her skirts billowed like ships' sails. Wind today was fierce, but typical for early autumn. Luke hated this time of year in Kansas. The wind blew all the time. It put him on edge.

Waiting for her to reach the barn, Luke mentally listed all the things he hadn't done yet today. What would she nag about now? He worked as fast as possible, little time spent on cigar smoking out here.

Sally brushed a stray hunk of hair slapping her face as she stepped inside. Almost breathless, she surveyed the dark interior, wrinkled her nose at the pile of manure Luke was yet to muck out, and then gripped his arm.

"It's almost time, Luke. They're almost here. Another hour or so and the stage'll pull into town. You'll get to see your brother again. And meet Morningstar!" Sally glanced up toward the rafters. "Isn't that a beautiful name? Almost like poetry."

"Poetry, huh?"

"I can't wait," Sally said. "Aren't you excited, too? It's been so long since James left here. So much has happened—"

"All in good time. They've had a long trip. Give 'em a couple days to rest up before hammering them with questions. All right?" As much as Luke wanted to do that very thing the minute his brother's foot stepped onto Lawrence soil, he knew to wait. James had hinted at why he and his new wife were coming to visit, and so suddenly, but the story would come out. He and James were close, in an odd adversarial sort of way, and he looked up to James.

James was the brother closest in age, older by two years to the month. Even closer than Andy by a month or so. But more than that, James and Luke were alike. While their methods were different, their thinking was the same. Both rarely thought ahead before jumping right in. Both marched to the drummer in their heads, regardless of what people thought. And both fought for what they believed in.

Slipping her hand into Luke's, Sally stood on tiptoes to peck

Luke's cheek. "Wonder if he looks like he did when last we saw him." She probed his eyes with her wide blue ones. "Do you think he's changed? I mean, after being a captive of the Apaches and then in the army?"

Luke had certainly thought about it. A lot. He shrugged. "Don't see how he can't."

"You think we'll see his scars? I remember when Andy wrote and said there were some." Sally's shoulders slumped. "Think he'll talk about it? The capture? Should we ask him?"

"Don't know." He forced a tight grin. "We'll have to wait another hour to see."

Sally thought for a moment, then grinned. "Well, I can't wait." She moved toward the barn door.

Hanging the rake on the wooden peg, Luke kicked straw and manure off his boots. "Go get Adam ready, I'll clean up out here, and then we'll head to town."

Sally stepped outside, the sun framing her body. "He's ready, and so am I." She started toward the house. "Hurry. We don't want to be late."

Hugs, tears, handshakes . . . the roiling mob of well-wishers spilled off the boardwalk and onto the main street of Lawrence. Brigid Colton clasped James, embracing her son until her tears quit streaming. She let go only to extend her grip to Morning-star. They hugged and gushed, hugged again then swiped at tears tickling their cheeks.

Luke clinched his older brother in a bear hug. Damn, he'd missed James. It wasn't until this moment that he realized how much. Would James stay?

"My turn." A smile blossomed on Joseph Colton's face as he shook hands with James. "My God, son." His gaze trailed from James' boots to his hat. "You've become a man."

"I'll take that as a compliment, Pa." James pumped the hand.

"Let me see my boys again." Ma grabbed Luke's arm and positioned him shoulder to shoulder with James. Both parents stood back, their smiles wide and welcoming. New tears trickled down Ma's cheeks.

Luke reveled in the moment. But, were those tears welling in Pa's eyes? Were those tears for him or for James? Not wanting to think too deeply and spoil the moment, Luke chose to smile back.

Ma daubed her green eyes with an offered handkerchief and took a deep breath. "It's time to come home, everyone. We'll have a chicken feast!"

Luke hung an arm around James' shoulders, then took a close look at his brother's face.

Jagging across the left cheek ran a wide pink scar. Apache? Army? A souvenir from the livery stable?

As if reading Luke's thoughts, James whispered, "Apache."

Stomach full of chicken, mashed potatoes and Ma's fresh green beans, Luke pushed back from the supper table. Except for his son, everyone crowded around the table resplendent with dinner dishes, meal remnants dotting the bottoms, forks and knives crisscrossed over the tops. Conversations sailed around and across the table where hundreds of meals had been taken with his three brothers and parents. Luke soaked in family. While he still had Ma and Pa, he sure enjoyed this moment with James and lovely Morningstar.

She hadn't talked much. Maybe she couldn't squeeze in a sentence in all the commotion, or maybe she was usually quiet. Luke regarded this sister-in-law. Her high cheekbones, ebony hair, and skin glowing a light tan emphasizing her Indian heritage. He searched his memory for which tribe. Had James said? And did it matter? Another look at her and he realized why his brother had fallen for such a beauty—she was special.

Something about her eyes—she seemed to take in everything with one blink. Not only did he appreciate her face, but also her body, which filled out her dress just right.

As if sensing his examination, Morningstar turned her dark eyes to Luke, seated across from her. "I understand you haul freight for a living, Mister Colton."

Caught off guard, Luke stuttered. "Uh-huh." What kind of answer was that? He sat up straighter and played with the tines on his fork. "I've been hauling various goods for a couple years." Realizing the fork was a poor choice of toys, he replaced it on his plate. "And there are way too many of us to be called 'Mister Colton.' Call me, Luke. Please."

A chuckle shook her shoulders. She averted her eyes then returned the gaze to Luke's face. "Do you enjoy your line of work, Luke? And what's the oddest thing you've ever hauled?"

No way he'd tell her it was guns for the Bushwhackers. "I suppose I like my job as much as the next man, Missus Colton. And I haul just everyday supplies . . . building materials and foodstuff. Nothing unusual—or interesting."

She flashed a smile. "There are too many of us Coltons to be so formal. Please call me Star."

It *was* pure poetry. Luke blinked, swallowed then jumped at a rapping at the front door.

Pa stood before anyone else could get to their feet. He opened the door and there stood Elmore Gibson, looking to his right and left.

"Come in, Mister Gibson," Pa said. "I'd like you to meet my daughter-in-law, Morningstar, and you remember my son, James. They've traveled all the way from New Mexico Territory."

Morningstar nodded and smiled at the visitor, while James stood to shake hands. Pleasantries were exchanged, then Gibson turned to Pa.

"Could I speak with you outside?" He turned to everyone, his voice louder than necessary. "Boring freighting business, I'm afraid. But urgent. I won't take Joseph away from you very long."

Gibson and Pa stepped into the fading day, closing the door behind them. Within moments, the door reopened. Pa motioned to Luke. "See you a minute?"

More than likely Mister Gibson would want Luke to take extra freight somewhere. And probably for several days. Days that he'd miss getting to know Morningstar and spending time with James. And while he sure didn't want to go out of town, he was doubly sure he didn't want to lose his job. Jobs were growing scarce in Lawrence, all over, for that matter, and he had two other mouths to feed. He stepped into the waning light and closed the door.

"Luke," Mister Gibson said, "I've got some special freight I need picked up from Kansas City tomorrow." His gray eyes probed Luke's face. "It'll only be two days, there and back."

No slid to the edge of Luke's tongue, but stuck there when he looked at Pa. His face was tight, stern. Whatever this freight was, it was important. Nodding, he knew he'd regret such a quick decision, but he needed this job. And, Mister Gibson had already reprimanded him three times in as many weeks for being late.

Luke forced a nod. "Of course, Mister Gibson," Luke said. "You can count on me."

Mister Gibson shook hands with Luke, something he rarely did. "I'll see you first thing in the morning and give you directions." He nodded toward the house. "I know you have guests. Don't let me keep you."

Dismissed, Luke frowned at Pa who nodded. All right. They had old guy talk to do. Luke envisioned the molasses pie Ma had made this morning. Despite his distended stomach, he had room for dessert.

CHAPTER FIFTEEN

"Pa's sending me into town for supplies, Luke." James looked through the screen door on his brother's front porch, which shielded his body from the noonday heat. The sun and wind relentless for days, no rain had brought cool moisture to the parched prairie. "Need anything?"

Luke opened the door and stepped out. The screen slammed behind him. "More tobacco. Can always use more of that."

From inside, Adam whined. Sally scolded the little boy. Ever since he got back from Kansas City yesterday, it had been nothing but mayhem at his house. Luke snorted. "Think I'll go with you."

"Can always use the company." James thumped his brother's chest. "Give us a chance to catch up."

Luke hollered through the screen. "Going to town with James. Be back later." He didn't wait for an answer. Instead, he bolted down the steps.

After purchasing a pouch of tobacco and new matches, the brothers stood on the boardwalk of Massachusetts Avenue, the main street of downtown Lawrence.

Luke gazed through the storefront window of Otis' Mercantile. A new hat, a bowler style all the rage in the East, beckoned. He pointed.

"What d'you think? On me?"

"Might." James peered at the price tag. "Kinda costly. You

can buy a lot of beer for that price."

"Speaking of which," Luke said. "How about I buy you one . . . or two? We got time."

"We do." James nodded and licked his lips. "It'd taste good right about now. It's damn hot out here."

Dodging horses and wagons, Luke led his brother across and then up the street to Dulinsky's Tavern, a place that always made him happy. At least the beer did.

They found a table near the back and sat. A saloon hostess sashayed by, took their drink orders, then wiggled her way up to the bar. Luke stared at the retreat. Tempting. His gaze switched to his brother. James frowned.

"Got that look on your face, little brother."

"Which is?" Luke didn't like where this was going.

"You know what the hell it is." James leaned close. "You're married. Can't play around anymore."

"I ain't dead." Luke snapped at his brother's attitude. "Listen, if I want to look at women, I can. Hell, James, I'm a grown man now."

James held up a hand. "Whoa. Way too early to start a fight. I'm just saying—"

"Here you are, boys." The hostess set down two beer glasses. "That'll be fifty cents."

Luke looked up into her round face. "Put this on my bill, will ya?"

She flashed a smile and sashayed back to the bar.

"Gonna get yourself in a heap of trouble, Luke." James sipped his beer. "Women. Nothing but trouble."

What'd he know? He'd lost his first girl to some has-been sheriff. And this wife . . . who knew how he ended up with her. She was pretty, but why'd James marry an Indian when he'd been abused by them? Luke would find out. In the meantime, he'd change the topic.

"Don't get me wrong. I'm glad you're here." Luke sipped his beer, the cool liquid soothing his parched throat. "But why? And why not Trace or Andy?"

"Trace's busy being sheriff. And with Teresa and Faith, he can't just up and leave."

"Andy—"

"Works at Bergstrom's Stable horseshoeing and other hot work." James examined the palm of his right hand. "I been working there, too, but mostly driving freight wagons."

Luke nodded at his brother's hand, a raised red stripe crossing from thumb to little finger. "What happened there?"

"Apache." James closed it and then opened the fist. "Early this year, had a fight with one of Cochise's henchmen. I grabbed a knife meant to kill me. Sliced me pretty good." He flexed the fingers. "Isn't as strong as it should be."

Luke ordered shots of whiskey along with more beer. He studied James' scar. Looked like it hurt. "So why are you here?"

"Just to visit and spend time with my younger brother."

"Keep an eye on me?" Luke nodded at the waitress as she brought the next round.

James frowned at his half-full beer glass, a full beer glass and a whiskey shot glass in front of him.

"You drink like this all the time?"

That was it. Too much scrutiny. Luke slammed down his glass. Conversations halted while Luke ranted.

"It's none of your damn business how much I drink. Who I look at. Which side of this damn war I'm on." Luke dropped his voice and eyed James. "That why you came? To spy on me? See what I'm up to?"

"No." James grabbed Luke's arm. His words were soft. "But I'd like to get to know you better." James patted his brother's arm. "Hell, we're brothers. We back each other's play. I just wanna know who I'm backing."

That made sense. Maybe he was overreacting. And with James here now, maybe there'd be another gun hand to help with the cause. But he wouldn't tell him about Quantrill. Not yet.

Luke mulled it over, while everyone else went back to their own conversations and beer. James studied his glass.

Two minutes spread into three before James spoke. "All right, little brother. What's this all about? What's eating you?"

By the time Luke finished explaining, expounding on his political leanings, four empty shot glasses and two nearly empty beer glasses cluttered the table. James leaned against his elbows planted on the table.

"Unbelievable," James said. "Goddamn unbelievable."

"You gonna hate me, too?" Luke's eyes trailed over his brother's tense face. What was he thinking? Unlike Andy, James' demeanor gave nothing away. "Just say it. Lecture me like Pa does."

Instead of lecturing, James sat back, steepled his fingers and studied the pyramid they created. Silence hung over the brothers until Luke felt like screaming. And yet, there was a calmness, a part of him, glad he'd shared. He'd needed somebody to confide in and, whether James agreed or not, Luke was relieved.

Rubbing his stubbled face, James nodded. The movement was small, deliberate, as if he was thinking but not committing. Luke analyzed every motion.

"No, I'm not gonna lecture you. Fact is, we've done just about the same things," James said. "I got thrown in Trace's jail for two months. Charged with inciting a riot."

"You did?" Luke sat up straight. This was gonna be good. His older brother in serious trouble.

"Yeah. Mesilla's under martial law and I don't agree with it. People were hungry 'cause the army took all the food. That was no way to live and I tried to get the army to see things my way. At least get the people to rise up and be heard."

"Nobody did, I take it."

"One or two, but not enough to make a difference. Not enough for a real revolution. I went to trial, got sixty days behind bars, then asked to leave town. Trace and Andy were real sore at me. Barely even waved 'bye.' "

"Holy damn, big brother. Guess you're more of a Rebel than I knew."

James raised his eyes to Luke's. "You never cease to amaze me, Luke. Never." He swallowed the last inch of beer in his glass. "You know I fought for the Union. Me and Andy. Trace agrees with the Union, too. In principle."

"I know." That familiar knot grew in Luke's stomach.

"So I can't say I'm behind you on Bushwhacker thinking." James pushed the glass away. "Men can have their damn politics. North, south, east, west. I don't give a damn. But Luke, slavery's a whole 'nother issue. One I can't agree with."

Mellowed with the whiskey's effects, Luke decided to hear what James had to say. Maybe after much discussion, that hardheaded brother would change his mind.

Luke gestured to the barmaid for more beer and then turned to James. "All right, big brother. What's so wrong with slavery?"

A long pause, then James lowered his voice. "I've been one. Know firsthand what it's like." The brothers' brown eyes met. "It's a hell I wouldn't wish on anybody. Not even Lucifer himself."

Wanting to dispute and refute, Luke opened his mouth, but James continued.

"You saw this scar here." James ran a trembling finger across his left cheek. "Apache whip. Trying to whip me into submission, admit I was inferior. I was a captive. A slave." He touched his bottom lip. "These scars here? Knives and fists."

Bending nearer for closer inspection, Luke grimaced. Horrific, constant reminders.

James pushed up his long sleeves on both arms. "Here." He nodded at wide pink ribbons encircling both wrists. "Apache rope. Two full months being tied. All the time. Day and night." He rolled them down and pushed aside the hair hanging over his forehead. A pale pink stripe ran side to side.

Luke touched the scar hidden under his hair.

James allowed the hair to fall back in place. "Apaches tied wet rawhide around my head. It dried, squeezed my head until . . . well, I couldn't hear Trace scream anymore."

"What happened?"

James shrugged. "Cochise cut the binding, Trace says. Afterwards, I couldn't focus on anything for a day and the headaches made me throw up for a couple of weeks."

As much as Luke wanted to show off his own forehead scar courtesy of the Indians, he chose to let his brother finish.

"But there's more." James started to pull his shirt out of his pants, then stopped. "The rest I'll have to show you at home. I got sixty-nine more whip scars."

Luke's eyes flitted from his brother's face to his wrists and back. There was a helluva lot James hadn't said in his letters. A helluva lot.

CHAPTER SIXTEEN

November 1862

November ushered in cold, blowing snow that swirled around Luke's legs as he tramped toward the barn. Pa, being laid low with a nasty head cold, wouldn't be out in this kind of weather. And James had taken Morningstar to visit a former school friend of his. Since it was a ways out of town, they would be gone most of the day. So with Ma inside caring for Pa, everyone else gone, Luke took advantage of the situation. He'd sent word to his Cutthroats to meet today. Come in back through the ravine.

The barn inside wasn't much warmer than outside. Except for a couple of lanterns and one small kerosene heater, the only source of warmth was the animals. Pa's two horses waited in their stalls at the far end of the barn, emitting heat too far away for Luke to appreciate. And the dog—roaming free—made his bed wherever it was warm, usually near the horses, but out of reach of their hooves.

While he waited, Luke thought about Quantrill. That man was raiding down in Missouri and hadn't left anything for Luke to do. Just keep his eyes open, is what he'd said. So, that left Luke sending his Cutthroats on the road. This mission wouldn't fail.

Harvey Tillman was first to show up. His skinny frame looked thinner wrapped in an oversize wool coat, gloves and slouch hat pulled down to where it sat on his ears. Harvey had lost weight since the Kiowa attack, and those were pounds he couldn't afford to lose.

Luke and Harvey shook hands as soon as the barn door closed against winter's sting.

"Luke, glad you called this meeting," Harvey said. "With the fall harvest in, such as it was, Harry and me got nothing to do. Got our plow fixed, fences mended, wood chopped for Ma." He shrugged. "Long days and nights, my friend."

Luke shoved his hands into his coat pockets. "You and your brother take good care of your ma." He craved a cigar, but knew not to light one in here. "How's it going with the three of you under one roof again?"

"We get along fine. Ma still does the cooking and cleaning, Harry's got a job in town, so he brings in some money, and I do the chores that Harry don't." Harvey shrugged. "You remember. After Pa and Henry died? How hard it was on Ma?"

Memories of the funerals marched across Luke's mind. Two years ago. Tragic hunting accident. Harvey's pa mistook his son for a deer. Shot and killed him. Then finding out what he'd done, turned the gun on himself. Grief tugged on Luke's chest. No family deserved to lose a father and son together, like that.

Before Luke found the right words, the barn door creaked open, Albert Perkins, along with Smitty Jenkins, Billy Hopper, and three others pushed inside. Coat collars turned up, hats snugged down tight, they reminded Luke of bands of outlaws he'd seen pictures of in the newspapers. Scary, low-down rascals, just ready to kill. Then he rethought. We *are* outlaws!

Or gonna be outlaws.

Or want to be outlaws.

Whichever it turned out to be, Luke knew beyond a doubt that he and his Colton's Cutthroats would make a difference in this damned war. It was a vow he took seriously.

Luke waited for the men to exchange grumblings about the weather and the war before calling the meeting to order. Even though he knew Pa was laid up, there was always the chance he'd come out to the barn and find this group of misfits, plotting and planning how to get rifles and handguns behind enemy lines. Pa would not be happy.

"Men," Luke said. "We haven't been all that successful. After me and Harvey ran into those Indians, we lost the Enfields. But last month, the Iverson boys managed to get ten Springfields over to Albert." He nodded toward Albert Perkins, planted on a hay bale and rubbing his hands together.

"That's right," Albert said. "The boys and I got those rifles *and* bayonets to the men who asked for them. So that part went as planned." His eyes shone. "Now we've got bigger fish to fry."

"Not just bigger fish," Luke said. "It's a whole whale." Not wanting Albert to take over as he'd seen him do other times, Luke stepped closer to the men. "It's gonna be tricky, and timing is important. We can't let any of this out of this barn. Not a word." Luke looked from man to man. Each one nodded.

"Fine. Here's what we've got to do."

Luke flattened out a map and waited for the men to gather around. His cold fingers traced blue lines of roads radiating out from Lawrence. He started there.

"We'll leave in two days. Before first light." His gaze swept over the seven men, their faces frowning. "We'll stay off the main road as we head south toward Fort Smith, Arkansas."

Harvey whistled low. "That's a helluva long ways, Luke. How far you reckon?"

"Gotta be fifty, hundred miles," one of the other men said. "And I ain't never even been out of the county." He frowned and swiped his hand across his mouth. "I can't go clean down to Arkansas." He stood and wrapped his coat tighter around his body. "That leaves me out. I'm goin' home."

"Me, too," another one said as he grunted up to his feet. He tucked one hand under an armpit and blew on his other hand.

"Besides, it's too damn cold to ride around the countryside, looking for someone to give our guns to." He started toward the door. "Count me out, too. Come on, Sam, let's go."

Before Luke could persuade them to stay, the barn door opened and closed—the men gone. Luke knelt on one knee. "Anybody else not going?" He pointed to the map, his finger tapping on Fort Smith. "We gotta go there, they say. Turn the rifles over to a Confederate soldier named Hindman. Down at Fort Smith. Army says that's where the action's gonna be."

"Action?" Smitty Jenkins pulled in air that straightened his towering frame. "Hell, yeah, I'm ready for action. Tired of sittin' around on my hands, waitin' for a chance to show them Federals what we're all about. Hell, yeah, count me in." His wide brown eyes sparked. "Hell, yeah."

Luke grinned at Smitty's enthusiasm. However, this was war. Men died in war. He hoped Smitty and the rest of his Cutthroats would return to Lawrence in one piece.

CHAPTER SEVENTEEN

The next day, Luke found James in his barn showing little Adam how to lasso a hay bale. The rope swung left and right tangling around the two-year-old's legs. By the time Luke made his way over, James had picked up the boy and plopped him on his shoulders. James loped around the barn neighing like a horse. Adam's squeals of delight brought a smile to Luke's face. James was turning out to be one terrific uncle. He needed children of his own. Were some in the near future?

Right now he needed to get packed for his trek to Arkansas. Would James come? No, Luke knew better than to ask. There was no way James would change his mind and see the Bushwhackers were right, states needed to be able to choose their own destiny.

Spotting Luke, James giddyapped over to his brother, pulled back on imaginary reins, and set Adam on the ground. Adam pranced around the barn before running for the door. James smiled as his nephew whinnied his way outside.

"Great son you've got there." James caught his breath. "Wears me out, though."

Luke walked toward the stall where his horse stood, protected from the cold. He picked up a curry comb and then turned to face James, standing behind him.

Luke pointed toward his son galloping toward the house. "Are you and Star planning on kids? Or have you already started? She'd be a great ma."

Silence knifed its way between the men. James stared at his feet, then back toward the house, then over to Luke. His words started and stopped.

"James?" Luke was worried. Was something wrong? Maybe those Apaches . . . no, he couldn't bring himself to envision what he figured they'd done. He'd heard stories.

Another glance toward the house then James swallowed hard. "Nobody but Trace knows. Give me your word it won't go any further than this."

The seriousness on James' face made Luke frown as he nodded. "Promise."

James dropped his voice as if the horse would hear. "Apache abuse. Torture. A few days before it ended, I got married."

"To Morningstar?"

"No. Dark Cloud, a Pima girl, not more'n fourteen, fifteen. She was a captive, too. Cochise married us and forced us . . ." James' shoulders slumped then straightened as he looked away. "Anyway, I bedded her." His words turned into whispers. "They watched."

A knot caught in Luke's chest. His brother had gone through hell.

James sniffed and then blinked. "We were married three, four days until the Apache . . . took her into the desert . . . she didn't survive." James shrugged. "After that . . . even with Star as pretty as she is, I can't—"

"Understood." Luke held up a hand. "You try with anybody else?"

James' glare pushed Luke back a step.

Luke rushed his words. "I mean . . . is it Indians or you? Maybe if you weren't with—"

"It's *me*, Luke." James slammed his fist against the stall rail. "It's all me. And yes, I've tried with others." He picked up a nearby shovel, regarded it, then blew out air and set it down. "Slavery. Look at what being owned by somebody does to you."

CHAPTER EIGHTEEN

Luke rapped at his pa's wooden door, then pushed it open. "James? Pa? Ma? Star?"

"In here." Ma's voice carried from the parlor.

Luke tugged off his hat and joined his family, each holding a cup. Early-morning light streamed through the windows. Ma pointed her cup toward the kitchen.

"Coffee's on the stove. Want some?"

Luke shook his head.

"You're up bright and early, son." Pa sipped his coffee. "Pull up a chair."

"Thanks, no. Just stopped by to let you know I gotta go out of town for a few days." He nodded to James. "Thought maybe you and Star could keep Sally company while I'm gone if you don't mind."

"Of course." James narrowed his eyes the way he did when Luke was hiding something. Damn his brother. James knew him too well. "Expecting trouble?"

"Not a whit." Luke shrugged. "Just want to be sure my family's safe."

Morningstar produced a heart-stopping smile. "Where're you going?"

That bit of information he wasn't about to tell anybody. He fought for a mental map.

"Just up to Fort Leavenworth. Might take a few days, though." Luke backed toward the door, knowing more questions would be forthcoming if he stayed. "Gotta go. Thank you."

He fitted his black hat on his head and bolted for the door.

Each of his men carried two Springfield rifles tucked in bedrolls and five Navy Colts in leather bags on both sides of their saddles. Once the arms were delivered, the ride back to Lawrence would be lighter and easier—for men and horses. So far, the four-day ride had been long and arduous. Days traveling fast and quiet, nights spent camping close to streams and trees for cover. Luke knew the distance from Lawrence to Fort Smith was long, closer to two hundred and fifty miles, much farther than the fifty or hundred Sam had thought.

Luke studied the map with attention to detail, and knew right where they were this afternoon. Sager Creek, northwestern Arkansas. This time of year, late November, the sun would be setting within minutes. Then it would get cold. Damn cold. A place out of the icy wind would be nice tonight. He twisted in his saddle. Although he was young, just turning twenty, his vertebrae popped and snapped like that of a much older man.

Then, like a miracle revealing itself, between the trees—a cabin. No smoke spiraled from the chimney, no horses whinnied or children played. No wood being chopped. Just birds sitting high atop the Arkansas dogwoods, chirping their good nights.

"Stay here, men." Luke held up a hand to the four riding behind him. "There's a cabin I'm gonna check out. Might be a place to stay tonight."

The cabin was indeed empty, but only recently. Dishes were cleaned and put away. The single bed made, the quilt smoothed. A couple firewood logs lay stacked beside the fireplace, kindling nearby. A few food cans with various labels and jars of pickles sat on shelves in the kitchen, right next to the cookstove. Luke smiled. They would eat something good and hot tonight!

By the time the men took care of their horses and brought the pistols and rifles into the cabin, it was true dark. After eating and storytelling, the men rolled up in their wool blankets and moved closer to the fire. Within minutes, snores filled the one-room cabin.

CHAPTER NINETEEN

Early-morning gray spread across the room. Luke yawned, stretched, and then scratched his chest. Eyes opening, he took in the cabin's wooden walls, covered in newspaper to keep out the drafts. And this morning it was cold. Really damn cold. His breath spurted out in crystalline clouds as he pulled his wool blanket up around his chin.

Why hadn't somebody remembered to stoke the fire during the night? And, why was it so cold with five men inside this cabin? Luke rolled onto his side and peered across the room. Four other bodies lay rolled inside four blankets, like bugs inside cocoons. Since he was in charge, he'd have to be the one to get up and light the fire. Luke shivered, but set his mind on the task at hand.

Within minutes and with a few well-placed logs on the fire, Luke could no longer see his breath, and his fingers weren't so stiff and numb. It would take longer for his nose and ears to warm, but a good stiff cup of coffee should fix that.

Billy Hopper, second man up, was followed by Smitty Jenkins and Harvey Tillman.

Albert Perkins kept snoring.

Billy helped Luke stack more wood on the fire and then ventured outside for another armful of kindling. They had burned all the original wood and common courtesy required restocking the supplies. The cans of green beans and corn would be harder to replace. Maybe Luke should leave a note. On second thought, probably not. He didn't want anybody knowing where he and his men were. He'd just leave money. He was a gunrunner, not a thief.

By the time sunlight streamed through the narrow windows and flooded the cabin, the coffee was black and strong, all the men up, and bedrolls stacked neatly by the door. Breakfast, stew and beans, was cooking. Smitty and Harvey were outside tending the stock, while inside, Billy and Albert Perkins cleaned their weapons.

Before Luke could call the men in for eating, Smitty Jenkins and Harvey Tillman pushed open the door and stepped inside, blowing on their hands.

"You ain't gonna like this, Luke," Harvey said.

Luke looked up from over the pot on the stove, his spoon held midway in the air. "Like what?"

Smitty jumped in. "Hell and damnation. We're almost in the middle of the war, that's what."

Spoon and stew forgotten, Luke's long strides took him across the cabin. He stood within inches of Smitty and Harvey. "What? They're supposed to be miles from here." He turned to Harvey. "How'd you find out?"

Harvey rubbed his hands together and then across his sandpaper chin. He pointed over his shoulder. "Met a fella when me and Smitty took the horses down to the creek."

Billy and Albert joined the circle.

Smitty nodded. "He said there was Federals, those damn Yankees, headed this way, supposedly on their way down to Fort Smith, and we're right in the middle. Everybody in the town—"

"Town's just over that ridge, he said." Harvey cocked his head to the right.

Smitty shot Harvey a quieting glare, as he continued. "He said a brigadier general by the name of Blunt's coming from

Missouri. Gonna be passing right by here."

"Right here," Harvey said.

"Fort Smith, huh?" Something clutched the inside of Luke's chest. Well, here it was. What he'd been waiting for. What he'd been talking about. But he wasn't really ready yet. On second thought, maybe he was. Ready to confront the Union army and ready to hand over the rifles and Colts to the Confederate soldiers. But he wasn't ready to die. Did that make him a coward?

While Luke mulled it over, Billy Hopper picked up his bedroll and rifle. "We gonna fight them Yanks? I mean, they're just right there!" Part of a smile flitted across his young face.

Smitty Jenkins thumped Luke's shoulder. "Hell, yeah, we're gonna fight! Hell, yeah."

"That's fine, Smitty," said Luke. "But we gotta go. *Now.*"

The sun elbowed its way through the clouds, but failed to warm the air. One of Luke's hands found warmth in his coat pocket while the other gripped his horse's reins. Luke waited for the men's conversations to end and for them to turn their attention to him. "It seems to me, we'd have a better chance of getting through to Fort Smith if we split up." He licked his bottom lip, a light stew aftertaste played on his tongue. "They might catch one of us, or two, but more'n likely they won't get all of us."

He waited for the men to quiet. "We'll meet up in Prairie Grove. You all remember the map we looked at last night?" A glance over his shoulder revealed no soldiers marching toward him, but they couldn't be far away.

Harvey Tillman hitched up his pants and nodded. "South and east. Right?"

Luke nodded.

"How far you reckon it is?" Harvey asked.

Before Luke could answer, Albert Perkins gave a nose whistle at Harvey. "Don't you remember anything, Harve? It's about twenty miles . . . as the crow flies."

Thin mouth crinkling into a grin, Harvey chuckled. "Problem with them crows, they don't fly straight. They take detours."

"They sure do, Harvey," Luke said, matching his friend's grin. He grew serious. "Men, we'll meet up in Prairie Grove in a couple of days. If you reach the Boston Mountains, you've gone too far."

Smitty swung up onto his horse and adjusted his weight in the saddle. "See y'all down there." He leaned over to Luke still standing. "And if I get a chance to kill me a Blue Belly or two, I just may."

There was nothing Luke could do or anything he could say to change Smitty's mind. He didn't want anybody hurt, but each man knew the risk. Luke shook hands with Smitty. "Remember, these rifles ain't worth losing your life over." Luke regarded the other three men. "Each of you. If you have to, give 'em the rifles. You can come home in one piece."

Luke shook hands with each man, and then waved as one by one, they disappeared into the forest.

The ride south took Luke over creeks, down hills, and up onto tree-covered ridges. He pushed hard, knowing if he could skirt the Union troops and then meet up with his Cutthroats in Prairie Grove, they could possibly travel together again. According to the original plans and instructions, when General Hindman's forces gathered at Fort Smith, Luke would turn over the Springfield rifles and Navy Colts they'd brought and be done. They could all go home and wouldn't have to fight.

However, the farther south he rode, the more Luke realized he wouldn't be able to turn these rifles over as easily as he'd thought. With General Blunt's Union troops moving at least fifty miles farther south than first thought, most likely he and the men would be on the perimeter, if not in the middle of a fight.

Luke pulled in cold late-November air, thrust out his chest, and tilted up his chin.

By damn, I'm no coward. I'll fight those Yanks like the man I am.

The sun failed to warm the day, and by late afternoon it was downright cold. Luke shivered under his wool coat and wished he'd find another cabin like the last one, now twenty miles behind. Some place to get out of this wind. A white flake drifted past his face.

Damn, it was going to be cold tonight.

But he couldn't stop now. *Wouldn't* stop. He had to see this through.

Luke topped a hill and caught his breath. A ridge, perhaps eight miles long and maybe as much as five miles wide spread before him. Stands of ash, maple, and elm trees covered those hills. And pockmarking the forest carpet were squares of orchards. What kind he could only guess. Less than an hour of daylight left, Luke questioned his mission. Maybe there were easier ways to support the cause. Warmer ways to run rifles to the soldiers. Less tiring attempts to skirt blockades and enemies. His entire body ached from the cold and this endless venture.

To his right, a road ran between a few trees. Further squinting revealed it was well used.

In the distance—voices. Indistinct, but there. It didn't sound like a regiment of soldiers or masses of people fleeing Yankee troops. Luke stopped and listened hard. Yep. Just two people in friendly conversation. He dismounted and hid behind a stand of maple trees and waited. Within moments two men rode past, their horses walking at a steady gait. Could they be headed to town? Luke decided to follow and find out.

Using the trees and brush as cover, he led his horse and dogged the men until he spotted a white steeple jutting up from the canopy of trees. Had to be a church.

As luck would have it, the church backed against a stand of ash trees. Access was easy. And now as the sun was about to set, Luke hoped he would be unnoticed. He tied his horse to a tree, and then eased around the side of the church. A main street ran in front, but only a single buggy clip-clopped past, turned a corner and disappeared. The two men gone. Most likely at home getting ready for supper.

While the church windows were high—he couldn't see inside, even standing on tiptoes—Luke discovered the door was unlocked. A creak, a step and he found himself inside. Hat in hand, he wasn't sure whether to stay or not. But it was warm inside. Gone was the breeze that had brought bumps to his skin and made him shiver inside his coat.

A wooden cross took up most of one wall, the pulpit, in front of the cross, a foot or so off the floor. An organ, its ornate rows of curlicues dancing across the top, sat in the corner. Six, maybe eight pews occupied the room. Not much room for prayer, but then again, how much room was necessary? Luke imagined parishioners singing and praying, hoping for this cursed war to be over, for their men to come home—safely. Probably what Sally was doing right now.

But time was short. Tonight, would those Federals waltz into this little town, whatever it was, and start a fight? Most importantly, his rifles would fall into enemy hands and he'd most likely be shot as a spy. Or at least as the gunrunner he was. Neither title appealed to him. Where could he hide the rifles until morning? Getting darker by the second, he had to act now.

His gaze fixed on the cross. It sat on a riser, a box of sorts. Further inspection revealed there was enough room for his two rifles to fit inside the wooden box. The Colts would fit inside the pump organ. Luke rushed back to his horse, pulled out the weapons and within minutes had them safely tucked away. Until tomorrow. He would retrieve them at first light and be on his way south to Prairie Grove. Unless *this* was Prairie Grove.

Shafts of moonlight filtered into the room, giving him enough light to avoid running into a pew. He stepped down the aisle, thoughts on supper and where to sleep tonight. Then it hit him. Why not the church? Nobody was using it and he would be gone before people came in to pray—or whatever they did early morning in a church. Decision made.

After unsaddling his horse, swiping the saddle blanket across her sweaty skin, he grabbed his bedroll and jerky and made his way back inside. Grateful for the warmth, he shook off snow clinging to his hat and coat. He'd find a pew near the front that was comfortable, eat his supper, and then catch some sleep.

While he ate, his thoughts drifted home, to his folks, then to New Mexico Territory, a place his three brothers now called home. They were fighting their own war.

He remembered letters from oldest brother Trace, filled with worry about James and Andy who were in the Union army a few months back. Luke pushed down loathing for the Union and knew they'd had no choice which side to choose. Just this year, they'd been out in Arizona marching clear over to California—and then back to Mesilla, while Andy tried to keep James from killing himself over memories and scars left from his Apache captivity.

A hand on Luke's shoulder jerked his head up and his body to his feet. He spun around and crashed into a man. A candle illuminated a surprised face.

"I'm sorry, son. Didn't mean to startle you." The man's black collar and cross hanging around his neck clued his occupation. "I just came in for evening prayers and saw you." Kind green eyes sparked for a moment. His rounded face, shadowed by a light trimmed beard, lit up as he smiled. "Didn't mean to scare you," he said.

"Guess I was thinking too hard, Reverend." Luke picked up his dropped jerky.

"It's always good to be thinking." The Reverend stuck out a hand. "Giles Beckett, Reverend Beckett out of Fort Smith."

"Luke Colton . . . out of Lawrence, Kansas." They shook.

Luke chided himself a second time for not thinking fast enough to give a false name. And hometown. *Not much of an outlaw when I can't remember to be one.*

"Lawrence, uh?" Reverend Beckett's gaze traveled across Luke then up to the wood-planked ceiling. "Went to seminary school with a fella from Lawrence. Let's see . . . Burroughs. Yeah. Franklin Burroughs." Beckett's eyes snapped to Luke's. "You know him by chance?"

Of course he knew him. Even if he wasn't married to Frank's daughter, everybody in Lawrence knew Reverend Burroughs. And almost everybody went to his church.

Luke stalled as long as he could. "No . . . name doesn't sound like one I've come across, sir. Haven't been in town all that long." Would he get struck by lightning for telling lies in a church?

"Too bad. He was a fine fellow," Beckett said. "Been meaning to get up there and look him up." His eyebrows furrowed. "Wonder where he stands in all this free-state war mess." He moved in closer to Luke who smelled chicken soup on his breath. "Where do *you* stand, Mister Colton?"

CHAPTER TWENTY

Voices. Outside, voices grew louder. Closer. Luke rubbed his eyes open and frowned, unsure of his surroundings. He sat up, the wooden pew under him squeaking with the movement. Still in the church. Behind him, many voices now. He turned his whole body halfway and stared at the church door just as it flew open. People swarmed in, pushing Reverend Giles Beckett ahead. Luke bolted to his feet, his hand searching for his revolver tucked inside his waistband.

Luke stood facing the people. Judging from their clothing, townspeople. The good people of . . . Luke searched his brain. Last night Beckett had mentioned this village was Cane Hill, home to the famous Cane Hill College. But Luke had only half listened, his mind busy figuring out how to avoid probing questions.

"Don't tell us to stay calm, Reverend," one of the men said. His red nose matched his red cheeks. Flakes of snow dotted his shoulders. "Those Yanks'll be coming down here soon enough."

"And then what?" A man, his brown hat pulled down to his ears, his coat collar turned up to his ears, stepped forward, now within spitting distance of the Reverend. "We'll all be killed. You know that."

Reverend Beckett held up one hand. "Please, gentlemen. This is God's house, not a—"

"Who's that?" A third man pointed his finger directly at Luke. Beckett spun around like he'd been kicked. A tight grin replaced the frown and his wide open eyes flashed. He pulled in a deep breath, and then turned back to the people. "Luke Colton, out of Lawrence, Kansas." Beckett nodded. "Just passing through, needed some place warm for the night."

"And it was warm. Thank you." Luke's smile did nothing to ease the tension. He jerked his thumb over his shoulder. "Guess I should be heading out."

"Not right now you're not," the first man said.

"I'm not?" Luke's revolver sat warm against his skin. Would he have to use it? Against innocent townspeople? He hoped not.

Beckett turned back to Luke. "Someone spotted troops camped outside of town, down in Cove Creek Valley. They're saying Yanks."

Knots pounded inside Luke's chest. If need be, he'd break out the rifles and Colts and arm some of the town.

"Hell, yeah, it's Yankee troops," a man in the back of the crowd yelled. "I recognized Blunt's flag."

Luke and Beckett eased backward as more townspeople crowded into the tiny church. Luke estimated thirty men, maybe five women and a few teenaged boys occupying the space that fit twenty, twenty-five if they squeezed.

"They're coming! They're coming!" Someone outside pushed his way inside. He waved his arm over the sea of heads and pointed north. "Those damn Yankees are coming!"

Words flew around the room, bouncing off the wooden ceiling and walls. Concern, anger, fright and hatred ricocheted from the corners. Beckett took charge.

"Calm down, calm down. Panic won't help." He stood on tiptoes. "Those of you who can, go home and arm yourselves. Women and children should get to the basement in the college. They should be safe there."

Several people pushed their way outside into the winter morning air.

"The rest of you," Beckett said, "guard your farms or stores. Don't let the Yanks take anything they don't pay for."

A man, blond hair hanging around his shoulders, rushed back into the church. "Reverend. We got a Confederate regiment moving into town." He pointed south and turned frightened eyes on Beckett. "We're caught right in the middle."

"All of you." Beckett's voice rose above the crowd. "Go home. Take cover. The apocalypse is upon us. Hell's comin'!"

Before Luke could offer any of his Springfields, the townspeople scrambled outside, mumbling and shouting orders. Beckett raised both eyebrows at Luke. "You gonna stay and fight, Mister Colton? Or sit back and write your story?"

"My story?"

"Said you're a newspaper writer." Beckett gathered up Bibles scattered on various pews. "Figured you'd get the story of a lifetime."

Gonna be a short lifetime, Luke thought.

Then he remembered. He'd told Beckett he was a reporter from Lawrence covering the war. Another lie in a church. Luke glanced up as if God would strike him dead. Then he rethought. If there was a God, He'd be busy elsewhere in this war.

Beckett glanced around. "Hope they stay out of this church. Took all the money these people had to build it. Sure would hate to see it burn."

"I'll stay here to protect it, Reverend." Did those words come out of Luke's mouth? What the hell was he thinking? He didn't care about this place. Not really. It wasn't his church, or Frank Burroughs' church. Hell, it wasn't even in his own state.

"I shouldn't ask you to do that, Mister Colton," Beckett said. Arms full of Bibles, he darted toward the door. "But I do appreciate the offer, and I'll take you up on it. I'm going over to the college and help out where I can."

Before Luke could renege on his offer, or explain, Beckett

was gone. Luke stood, frozen, wondering what the hell had just happened.

Boom! A cannon roared somewhere behind the church. Luke ducked, his survival instincts on alert. He rushed up to the cross, uncovering the Springfields, then to the organ for the pistols. All safe and secure. After recovering the arms, Luke pulled out his .36 Colt Walker revolver and checked the chambers. Full with black powder and balls. He hadn't cleaned it last night, although he hadn't used it, but still, he hoped the powder hadn't gotten wet. The gun wasn't good for much other than cracking walnuts if the powder was damp.

He thought back to a time he and James had been hunting rabbits. James got his, but when Luke pulled the trigger, he got nothing. No flash. No bang. No dead rabbit. Nothing. Luke didn't want to die from stupidity. No time like the present to reset the loads. A scan of the room revealed no saddlebags, no canteen even.

Must've left them outside. Luke kicked himself for not paying more attention to detail. That fault right there could get him killed. Needing to tend to his horse anyway, he pushed open the church doors and eyed the road. A store he hadn't noticed last night sat across from him. "Johnson's General Store" blazed across the front in big white letters. The windows were shuttered, the door closed, probably locked. No supplies available if he needed them.

He stepped out into cold air, his muscles tightening, his breathing labored. People shouted from the distance. He couldn't make out the words, but guessed it was soldiers giving orders.

As if his feet were on fire, he sprinted to his horse still tied behind the church. She'd stripped half the leaves off the brush and pulled at her tether. Luke ran his hand down her neck. "It's all right, Maggie. We'll get you some water, find some oats, and we'll be fine." His horse was hidden in among trees and bushes, but still, Luke was uneasy about leaving her outside. Would a barn be better? Maybe not. Especially if they decided to burn it. No, better leave her here.

Luke located his saddlebags pushed under the brush his horse had munched on. Shaking his head at his lack of thinking, he searched the bags for gunpowder and balls.

Bang! Gunshots, rifle shots behind him. Close enough to make his ears ring. Smoke floated toward him. His eyes watered. Sniffling and sneezing, Luke grabbed the bag and bolted for the church. More shouts. More gunshots. More feet tramping.

A bullet whizzed overhead. Luke dove for the door and rolled inside. More bullets splintered the door, the doorjamb, and then sailed inside the church. He pulled the door closed, then using the pews as shields, Luke crouched as he zigzagged up to the front.

Gunfire surrounding him, Luke covered his ears. Loud, it was so damn loud he couldn't think. His ears rang and his eyes watered at the stench of gunpowder. Then screams.

Men wounded.

Men dying.

Luke crouched on the floor, wedged between the wall, the organ and the cross. He reloaded his black-powder revolver. "Please don't come in yet. Please." He kept one eye on the door, one eye on his project. "Please not now." He was a sitting duck and he knew it.

One cylinder packed. Five more to go.

Now four.

The church door burst open. A man dove in, rolled across the floor, then hunkered down behind the pews. Luke craned his neck for a better look at the uniform, hoping he wore one. Unfortunately, the man's coat covered his clothes. Working faster, Luke loaded another chamber. Hands cold and shaking, he fumbled a handful of balls. They hit the floor and rolled.

The man jumped up, his rifle pointed at Luke. "Who're you?"

Luke stood and swallowed hard. "Colton. Luke." That was all he could remember, and even that was a struggle.

"Get over here." The rifle waggled toward the side of the church closer to the man.

Hands up, Luke sidestepped closer. Knowing he had seconds to explain, he forced words. "I'm a civilian."

"Yeah, and I'm Abe Lincoln," he said. His shaggy brown hair swept his shoulders. As he stood, he cocked his rifle. "Try again."

"Luke Colton."

"From?" The man's brown eyes narrowed.

"Kansas?" Luke's voice caught in his throat. At that moment, he knew if he lived through this, he'd never be as scared as he was right then.

He lowered his rifle and moved closer. "What part?"

Before he could explain, the door burst open and two men stormed in, rifles ready. They trained them on Luke.

Silence. Luke's heart beat in his throat.

"I know him." The man's thin eyebrows lifted. "That's Luke Colton from Lawrence." He lowered his weapon. "He's one of us."

Silence hung in the church while gunshots and cannon fire rocked the building.

"Well, Luke Colton," the first man said. "This here's your lucky day. I'm Lieutenant William H. Gregg. I ride with Quantrill and run this outfit."

Luke recognized Cole Younger and then squinted at Frank James. While they weren't really what he'd call friendly faces, they weren't technically the enemy.

Luke shook hands with each man. He couldn't keep the air inside his lungs from escaping in full force. Time was short and he needed to get these rifles and guns into the proper hands.

He wasn't about to tell Gregg he had some rifles. They'd probably take them from him and claim them as their own. Give them to Quantrill and get all the glory. He'd pretend he was in search of rifles. He explained.

"I'm heading down to Fort Smith. Gotta meet up with . . . my family," Luke said. Maybe he wouldn't get caught in a lie.

"Your family?" Cole Younger glanced toward the door. "Thought they all lived in Lawrence."

"Got an uncle down there who's poorly. I promised to help out on the farm."

Lieutenant Gregg snorted and turned his back. "Piss-poor time to be visiting family."

Luke raised both eyebrows and nodded.

Fighting raged all morning. Occasionally, a man would fly through the door, begging for protection or prayer. With so many people using the church as refuge, Luke hoped no one would find his hidden weapons.

As luck played Devil, Luke stood at the door helping a man escape a bullet barrage, when someone near the front of the church shouted.

"Look, men. Springfields. Two of 'em!" Men rushed to the front, clawing each other for rifles. Before Luke could stop them, they found the Colts, too.

"The Lord must surely be watching over us," one of the men said.

And just like that, his weapons were gone. The only gun Luke had left was his own, stuffed in his pants' waistband. With his guns and ammunition taken, he wasn't sure what he'd tell the men at Fort Smith, but giving guns to the Rebels was what he'd set out to do, and dammit, that's what he'd done.

Smoke, like gray fog, hung in the cold, damp air. Luke, along with Gregg, Cole and Frank, had fought from inside the church, evidenced by bullet holes and chunks of white plaster clinging to the walls. The organ sported a few holes, as did the cross. Luke reflected, guess nothing's sacred in war.

Midday and Luke pushed the church door open for the first time. No matter how overcast, how dark, he couldn't miss the body strewn across the church steps. Luke recognized the lanky man, his face pockmarked with mud, shrapnel, and frozen blood. Those eyes, which had once turned to God for help and guidance, now stared wide open in disbelief and horror.

Reverend Giles Beckett.

On one knee, Luke bowed his head and said the only prayer he knew, one he had said every night before going to bed. His eyes glazed over the carnage. The swelling stench of death and sounds of frozen blood crunching under his knee turned his stomach. Out of the corner of his eye, he took in blood coating the buildings, dripping, hanging frozen like icicles from the eaves, and running slick down the street. The cacophony of death images brought up last night's supper. Finished, he wiped his mouth and stood.

Horses and mules jerked in death throes, some, their bodies on top of human bodies. No one wins, Luke thought. No one.

Sounds caught his attention. Small sounds. Incoherent sounds.

Was someone hiding? Someone who would put a bullet in Luke's heart? He crouched, his Colt Walker gripped, his heart pounding.

Groans. Something shuffling through frozen leaves. Then something like a body sliding down a tree trunk. A light thud.

"Help . . . please. Don't let me d—"

Luke's stomach twisted again. He had nothing left to bring up, but his body tried. From his knees, Luke drew in a long breath, swiped a dirty, trembling hand across his mouth, then struggled to his feet.

"War's messy."

Luke jumped at the man's voice in his ear. He spun around and stood nose to nose with Frank James.

"War's messy," Frank repeated. He lifted one foot and peered at the mud on his boot. "Boots're full of muddy blood." One shoulder lifted. "Hate to fight in the rain. Messy."

"Uh-huh." Was that all he could say? Luke fought to speak intelligible words, but nothing formed. War sounds, death images, gunpowder smells whirled around his body until Luke knew he'd throw up again. Luke smoothed his mustache and craved a smoke right now. Cigar, cigarette, even a good wad of tobacco in the cheek would be welcome. Maybe a couple of these dead soldiers would have some on them. Hell, they wouldn't be using it and he sure needed it.

As if reading Luke's mind, Frank James checked the gun on his hip then cocked his head toward the nearest soldier, one on his side, eyes open. "What d'you say we get us some fixin's, Colton."

Chapter Twenty-One

Luke, Frank James, Coleman Younger and Lieutenant Gregg rode into Prairie Grove, Arkansas, under a full moon. Eerie shadows and long silver light tendrils danced across the treetops. Cold. It was damn cold and Luke shivered despite his thick, wool coat. The tobacco tucked in his right cheek kept his teeth from chattering.

Luke leaned over his horse and spit. The brown juice crackled as it hit the mud, which resembled frozen concrete tonight. Up ahead he could make out the slouched figure of Cole Younger. It had been a long hard ride and no doubt he was tired. Hell, they all were. Luke in particular. But he sat up straighter in the saddle, ran one hand over his numb face, then switched the tobacco to the other cheek. Maybe that would help. Keep him awake and alert, on his toes.

Ahead of Cole rode Frank, and then in the lead was Lieutenant Gregg. None of the men spoke much. Too cold. Too tired. Too on the lookout for Yankees. A rider earlier in the day had reported that a regiment of Yanks was headed for Prairie Grove, which was south of where they'd been at Cane Hill. But Luke knew if they and the rest of the Rebels got there first, they'd have the distinct advantage of fighting from the top of the hill. Those damn Bluebellies would have to shoot uphill, and anybody who knew anything about fighting knew that was a disadvantage. This would give Luke and his fellow Rebels the upper hand.

Cole Younger slowed, then stopped. Luke did the same. Leafless trees rose like gray specters, their arms and fingers reaching toward the cloud-laden sky. Flakes, cold and hard, piled on his hat, on his shoulders, on his legs. Luke tugged off a glove and blew on his numb fingers, then shoved the entire hand under his armpit. Warm. Luke nodded. Maybe he'd get feeling back in those hands yet tonight.

While Luke waited next to Cole, Frank James and Lieutenant Gregg wheeled back to them. Gregg cocked his head and glanced over his right shoulder.

"There's a farmhouse up ahead," Gregg said. "We'll hole up in the barn. Stay warm. We'll check the house tomorrow in daylight. Don't want to run into any surprises tonight."

Frank James worked his jaw, then spit. "Then them damn, no-good Yankee scum gonna be running for the hills. Right back to the hole they clumb out of."

"That's right," Cole said. He leaned over and spit. "Got cha."

Luke fisted his stiff fingers and then spread them. Moving them proved tough. Just like other parts of his body, the fingers didn't want to move in this cold. He jammed the bare hand back into the gloves. "Let's go get warm."

The farmhouse, another mile down the road, stood reflected in the moonlight. Naked trees shimmied in the slight breeze, which brought bigger goose bumps to Luke's arms. What looked to be an orchard ran behind the house and a privy sat off to one side.

A barn, stone halfway up, then wood, loomed to his right. It was big. Big enough for all their horses for sure, and maybe three or four more. Luke dismounted, holding his hand over his horse's muzzle in case she smelled another horse in the barn. If she did, she'd whicker, and then they'd be discovered.

Luke pushed open the barn door.

"Who's there?" A thin voice shot out of the night.

In a heartbeat, Luke's gun grew hot in his hand. He crouched. "Who're you?"

"You tell *me*," the voice said. "I was here first."

Luke squinted into the dark barn. On the far side, an outline of a man squatting, holding a rifle chest high. Luke squinted harder. Billy Hopper? Why not? Billy was supposed to meet here in Prairie Grove. He and the rest of the Cutthroats.

"Billy? That you?" Luke caught his breath.

"Colton? Luke Colton?" The man lowered his weapon. "That you?" He stood and then held out a hand. "Damn. I'd recognize that scowl anywhere. Even in the dark."

Luke holstered his gun, walked over and shook hands with his friend. "Damn good to see your thick skin's still in one piece. No holes."

"Skin's too froze." Billy chuckled. "Them bullets just bounce off."

"Well, glad to see—" Luke glanced at sounds behind him. Bootsteps. A horse blew out air. Lieutenant Gregg led his horse into the barn, Frank and Cole on his heels.

Gregg slid to a halt and studied Billy Hopper. "Who're you?"

"Friend of Luke's here." Billy lowered his voice and looked side to side. "I run guns, too."

"Well, friend of Luke's, better get some shut-eye. There's gonna be fightin' tomorrow. I hear the Thirty-seventh Illinois and Twenty-sixth Indiana are headin' our way, and I guarantee you'll wish you'd stayed home with Mama." Gregg led his horse toward the back, followed by Frank and Cole.

Luke nodded. "Yes, sir." He lowered his voice. "Billy, you still got your guns?"

A stretch of silence from Billy told Luke what he needed to know. He raised both eyebrows at his friend. "That's all right. I gave out my guns, too. Didn't see any sense keeping 'em when others needed 'em so bad." He patted Billy Hopper on the shoulder. "That means we have less to carry now, that's all."

"And we can get more back home." Billy's smile blossomed.

"Sure can." Luke tugged on his horse's reins. "I best put her up and then get some shut-eye. Gotta be on our toes for tomorrow."

CHAPTER TWENTY-TWO

Bang!

Bang!

Luke jerked awake. Gray silhouettes of men and horses. He rubbed his eyes, his vision shrouded by clouds of his icy breath. Lieutenant Gregg and Frank James peered out through the barn door. Luke eased to his feet. A scan around the barn revealed no Billy Hopper. His horse was still standing in the stall, so Billy must've gone out back to the privy. Or to fight the Yanks.

Bang!

"We gotta get up to that farmhouse, Lieutenant," Frank said. "Rifle fire's still a ways off." He closed the doors and turned around. His narrowed shoulders made him look smaller than he really was. "Looks like a good place to take down those stinkin' Bluebellies."

Gregg pulled on his gloves. "I agree." He pointed his chin toward the house, a hundred yards away. "Frank, you and Cole get up there. Try for the second floor."

Frank tossed a sideways grin at Cole. He pointed one finger at the house, then squeaked open the door and slipped through with Cole Younger on his heels.

The lieutenant turned his brown eyes on Luke. "I spotted an orchard behind the house." He pointed to the right. "Head through there. See if you can spot any Yanks."

Luke nodded, the knot in his throat blocking any sounds

threatening to surface.

"Meet us in the house." Gregg peered through the wooden barn doors opened just wide enough to peek through, and then looked over his shoulder. "Question?"

A shake of Luke's head, and Gregg slipped through the doors. Luke pulled in frigid air. Any glamorous idea about war evaporated.

There was enough early-morning light for him to watch his boots plow through little snowdrifts. Everywhere he looked he spotted rifles. Men and rifles. Or were those trees? Men and trees? He squinted. No. Just trees. Where in the hell were the men?

Luke darted from apple tree to apple tree, crouching, listening for boots crunching frozen mud, rifles cocking, men breathing. An occasional gunshot in the distance punctured the silence. But nothing close. Satisfied, he gazed back at the barn, now shrouded in fog, then peered to this right.

Through the haze rose the farmhouse. Luke remembered that someone said the family who owned it was named Borden. Right now, its wooden clapboard siding glistened with icicles. Luke tiptoed to the back of the house, gripped the doorknob and pushed his way inside. The first thing to strike him was the smell, this kitchen had been used in the last day or so. Stew, rabbit maybe, clung to the air. And second, the quiet. The pall flooding this house brought goose bumps to his arms. He eased the door shut, cringing at the squeaking hinges. Why did hinges always creak at times like this?

His gaze swept the kitchen. To his left stood the stove, a pot of what he suspected was stew, perched on the cast-iron surface. A spoon, something brown and hard coating the end, lay haphazardly next to the pot. Luke sniffed. Definitely not rabbit. Chicken probably.

Against the opposite wall stood the sink, a few dishes piled in

117

the bottom and two glasses sitting on the counter. The kitchen was small, but comfortable.

But where was everybody? Luke knew at least Lieutenant Gregg and Frank James were inside, but the quiet was deafening. Pulling in a long draw of air, Luke plastered his body against the kitchen wall, then eased his head around through a doorway opening into the parlor. Empty. He licked his chapped lips and stepped fully into the room. Blue-flocked wallpaper covered the walls, setting off a dark-blue velvet settee against one side. If perfect fabric was any indication, then nobody ever used this room. And nothing appeared out of place.

A floorboard above him creaked. Heart thundering, his gaze flew to the ceiling, as if he could see through the oak and discover who walked over his head. Was it Gregg and Frank? Or a Union pig ready to kill?

Luke closed his eyes, a feeble attempt to calm his heart. His stomach clenched, but he knew he had to find out who was up there. He gripped his Colt Walker, eased out of the parlor and started up the stairs. One step on the first stair and it creaked. Damn that wood, he thought.

A second step proved quiet. Halfway up, he stopped to listen. Bootsteps coming closer. A breath pulled in then he bounded up the remaining stairs.

As he reached the top, a gray-suited soldier rushed him. Luke spun to the ground, rolled twice then careened into the wall. He shook his head and then focused on the rifle barrel and bayonet inches away from his face.

"Don't . . . I'm . . . not . . . ," Luke stammered, but damn, he was scared.

Too frightened to shake, he knew he should breathe, but even that movement might prove fatal. Instead, he forced words again. "On your side."

Dark-blue eyes, narrowed against rising sun flooding through a window, probed Luke's face. The man holding the rifle shifted his weight. "Talk."

"Luke Colton. Kansas. With Lieutenant Gregg. Frank—"

"James? Frank James?" The soldier leaned back and turned his head sideways to where he squinted out of one eye. "And Cole Younger?"

Luke couldn't nod fast enough. "Them, too."

The Rebel lowered the rifle and then offered Luke a hand up. "Cain't be too careful, 'round here."

Was that an Arkansas accent, Luke wondered? He'd heard so many different accents in the past few days that he hadn't taken particular notice. But this one was right here, in his face. And the face behind that accent was young. Hell, younger than himself. Maybe even younger than Andy who just this month had turned eighteen.

Luke picked up his Colt and glanced around the top floor of this house. What he guessed were three or four bedrooms sat on either side of the hallway. Rooms seemed smaller than what he'd seen from the outside.

"This way." The soldier jerked on Luke's arm and looked back to speak. "Name's Denton. Just Denton." He stopped and half a crooked grin slid up his pockmarked face, a three-day beard shading his cheeks. "But ya can call me Denny Joe."

He had to have cover if he was going to survive war. "Fine. Denny Joe, it is." Luke cocked his head toward the far room. "Let's use that room down the hall on the left to shoot from."

Denny Joe nudged Luke. "Good idea. That's where Lieutenant Gregg and Frank James are, anyway."

"What? Why didn't you say so right away?" Moron, Luke thought. Idiot. They're all idiots around here.

Luke zigzagged behind Denny Joe as they crouched their way down to the far bedroom. Lieutenant Gregg squatted next to one window overlooking the front of the house, Frank and Cole knelt by the other window, the view blocked by a tall tree.

The lieutenant squinted at Luke. "And?"

"All clear. Didn't see a soul. Blue or gray." Luke shrugged one shoulder. "Want me and Denny Joe to take this other room?"

Bang!

A bullet slammed into the side of the house, next to Gregg's window. Without further instructions, Luke sprinted toward cover in the room directly across the hall. He slid to a stop and peered out through the window, its panes dotted with frost. From this vantage point, the apple orchard stood lifeless, like frozen soldiers waiting for marching orders.

And then he spotted them. Gray-suited men, Rebels, rushing toward the orchard, their rifles in hand. They slid behind the trees and some knelt in what Luke guessed was prayer.

"Get ready, men!" Lieutenant Gregg's voice carried across the house. "Here they come!"

Could he squeeze his gun any tighter? Luke forced out air, then pulled in a slow chest full. No need to die because he wasn't thinking straight. He hollered as loud as he could. "Rebs down in the orchard, Lieutenant. We're safe now."

Before another word, bullets seemed to come out of everywhere, even the ceiling. Balls of iron slammed into the wall, the bed, through the window, even next to Luke's face. A splinter sliced his cheek and something warm ran down his chin. Hands shaking, Luke aimed out the broken window and fired to his left. Someone in blue on the ground below crashed to his knees. Was that from his bullet?

Shoot. Reload. Shoot. Reload. *Keep the head down* became his mantra.

Men screamed . . .

Shouted . . .

Ran . . .

Shot . . .

Cried . . .

Died.

The day melded into one long blurred haze of loading, shooting, reloading, running from Bluebellies when they swarmed the house, then retaking the house with Rebel reinforcements. The fighting had subsided enough to allow Luke to curl up in the downstairs parlor corner, his ammunition bag empty, and wait for the bullet that would end his short life. Had he slept while he crouched there? Probably not. But now as the creeping dusk turned the world gray, it was quiet. Deathly quiet.

Luke raised his head and looked around. Bodies. Three, no, four men sprawled out around him. No mistaking the way death looked. He swiped his blood-caked, gunpowder-blackened hand across his forehead.

Knowing that at some point he'd have to stand and see who was the victor, his mind flip-flopped between wanting to sit here a while longer, or to go see. Not be a coward. The blue-flocked wallpaper, which once had graced a proper parlor, was now splattered with red, and ragged holes. Luke pulled in a familiar smell. Definitely not stew. Smoke. Something was burning. On fire.

That brought him to his feet. A glance outside revealed the front littered with bodies, a few being dragged off, one a medic inspecting. But no raging bonfires.

Warm. It was warm in the parlor. Smoke billowed down the stairs radiating in all directions. Luke coughed. He bolted for the front door, then decided that Union soldiers would more than likely mow him down. He rushed to the kitchen door, but flames licked the wall directly above the door.

Deciding to take his chances with the soldiers, he raced back to the parlor, threw open the door and ran like the terrified man he was. Luke zigzagged around bodies, bolting between trampled bushes, rushing past men in blue and gray. Only a stray bullet now and then altered his path.

Up ahead, not more than thirty yards, Luke spotted the barn rising out of the smoke. If he could make it that far, he'd have a chance of surviving this. Would his horse still be there? Would any kind of safety? His boots plowed through mud, blood, and melting snowdrifts. The wind shifted directions, blowing smoke directly at him. Luke coughed, his eyes watered, blurring his vision.

At last, the barn was within reach. He slid to a stop at the closed doors. Were Yankees in there, waiting to shoot him to pieces? An ear pressed to the door and he had no answers, only silence. A mighty groan, timber crashed behind him. Luke spun around in time to see the house collapse in on itself, flames jutting to the moon, reaching for the stars. The entire house exploded, debris flying in every direction.

Men scattered, running, screaming, carrying the wounded and dying. All of this Luke took in, yet his hand remained glued to the barn door. Should he open it? One more decision was too much. War was too much. Life was too much. All he wanted was to be home with Sally and Adam. Maybe a beer, too.

The door pushed toward him, breaking the reverie. Before Luke could bolt for cover, he stood face to face with Frank James.

"Where the hell've you been?" Frank pointed at the house. "The Borden house's burning like a son of a bitch." A smile blossomed on his dirty face. "War's messy. But ain't it excitin'?"

Again, one too many questions. Luke couldn't sort out any of it. Frank's tight grip on his arm pulled Luke into the barn. He stumbled into dark, pockmarked with pools of light from kerosene lanterns. To Luke's right, Lieutenant Gregg and Cole Younger slumped on bales of hay and shared long pulls from a flask.

Frank James tugged Luke's arm again. "Your friend's over here." He pointed into a darkened stall, a horse lying on its side.

As he lay backed against a wall, Billy Hopper's eyes traveled up Luke's body and then rested on his face. Billy's lips parted, forming a twisted grin. His right ear hung in shreds nearly to his shoulder and blood coated his hair, dripping over his tattered shirt. Billy gripped his left thigh. Luke knelt and peered closer. Billy's lower leg was as shredded as the pants that had covered it.

"Just lie still there, Billy." Luke held his friend's shoulder, although what he wanted to do was run. Run screaming. Instead, he calmed his voice. "I'll find a medic, then you'll go home better than new."

Foam burbled from Billy's mouth. "No." He clawed at Luke's arm and managed to grip his hand. "I'm scared."

Billy's shaking hand grew still in Luke's. Luke closed his eyes and cursed the pressure building up behind them. Something wet dripped down his cheek. He brushed it away then closed Billy's eyes.

Luke knelt until his muscles shook—from cold or fright or fatigue. It didn't matter. Nothing mattered right now. Nothing except this damn war and putting a stop to it. This senseless killing, the pain and suffering had to stop.

Scrubbing his face with his tired hand, Luke pulled in smoky air and then stood. How could he, Luke Jeremiah Colton, stop this war? He turned to Lieutenant Gregg, still perched on the hay bale.

"Lieutenant." Luke plodded across the barn to Gregg. "Tell Quantrill I'll do whatever it takes to see the South win. Tell him to send me a note, or even stop at my house, anything. Gotta end this war."

CHAPTER TWENTY-THREE

Back at home, but stomach boiling, Luke fought his demons as he sat on a hay bale in his frigid barn, sucking on a poor excuse for a cigar. Something that passed for tobacco was rolled inside a leaf of suspect origins. Corn husk perhaps. The smoke curling around his nose and up into the barn reeked of old wet horses. Exhaustion replaced caring.

Exhaustion from not only memories, but from the new baby who seemed to delight in fussing as soon as he managed to get to sleep. Luke had been home less than a week before Sally delivered a little girl, Hannah. That was Sally's grandmother's name and one she insisted on using. Luke didn't have a better name in mind, so Hannah Patience Colton it was.

Luke struggled to keep his cigar lit. He needed this smoke, this time to think, this time away from Sally's endless stares. Those questioning glances, her eyes probing his. She wanted to know where he'd been, what he'd seen. She knew he'd been around shooting, but had no true idea of the hell he'd lived through.

After three long weeks of hard riding, north through Arkansas, Missouri, and into Kansas, bypassing both Union and Rebel camps, Luke's lower back and shoulders had taken the brunt of the perilous trek back home. He ached in places he had never used before. His "men," what was left of them, had ridden with him, each one uncharacteristically silent, breaking the vacuum only when necessary. It had been a long ride.

And how often had they dodged bullets that came out of nowhere? For all the risks he'd taken gunrunning, nothing but hatred, doubt, despair and nausea had come of it. And he'd lost a friend. Billy Hopper. His thudding heart crept up into his throat, clamping down on his breathing until he thought he would pass out.

What he'd seen, hell, what he'd *done* was beyond description. But what he had yet to do, was planning to do, was close to unimaginable. On that cold, miserable ride back from Prairie Grove, Luke had talked to enough people who knew Quantrill. Ruthless, crazy, driven, a man with a cause—all those words used to describe him. He liked the sound.

Luke sucked in a lungful of smoke and held it.

He thought back to headlines in the newspapers declaring William Clarke Quantrill a scoundrel of the worst kind. A man who thought nothing of slicing heads off innocent women and children. A man who gnawed on their bones for dinner. In fact, Lucifer was now declared a saint and one to be welcomed for Sunday supper in comparison. But how to explain to Sally what he was doing? He didn't need to tell her or get permission. His conscience told him what to do.

He shivered despite his fleece-lined coat. A drink would warm him up. Luke dug around behind a bale of hay and pulled out a half-full whiskey bottle. A long pull warmed him. The barn door squeaked open. Luke jumped, the bottle hidden behind his back.

"Sally said you were here." James pointed over his shoulder toward the house. "Need some help?"

Luke held up his cigar, not willing to share the whiskey . . . or admit he had it. "Don't need help with this. I know how." He pulled in an extra-long drag releasing the smoke into the barn.

James nodded toward Luke's back. "Got enough for two?" He sat across from Luke. "Ride over made me thirsty."

125

Luke eyed his brother. "Why'd you come?"

James shrugged. "You've been gone a while, wanted to catch up. Plus, Star wanted to see the baby."

"No. I mean . . . why'd you come back here. Home? And are you gonna stay?"

Words started and stopped. James looked everywhere but at Luke. "I don't know."

"Don't know what? Why you came or if you're staying?" Luke's voice edged with anger, harder than he had intended.

James stood. "Look. I didn't come here to fight. You don't wanna share your whiskey"—he shrugged toward Luke—"fine. Don't."

"Pa send for you? Ask you to babysit me?"

"What?" James frowned. " 'Course not."

"Then why . . . are . . . you . . . here?" Luke's temper boiled just under the surface.

Shoulders heaving with pulled-in air, James took off his hat and ran a trembling hand through his shoulder-length hair. When he didn't say anything, Luke stood and offered the whiskey bottle. James took a long pull, then faced Luke.

"Honestly? Pa asked me to come. He's worried about you. Hell, Luke, we all are." James regarded the bottle still in hand. "But I think he was as worried about me, too."

That was a turn of thinking Luke wasn't prepared for.

"Why?" Luke's anger dulled.

James picked up a rake and scraped it across the dirt. "Been having a helluva time putting Cochise out of my memory. I beat up people, including Andy. The townspeople hate me. They asked me to leave. Nobody but one gave me a job. Say I'm a crazy, Indian-loving white man. Star's more accepted than me. Hell, Luke." James turned his gaze to his brother. "I've been spit on. People cross the street when I walk by."

"You're not crazy." Luke stood next to his brother as James

drew the rake over the same patch of dirt. "You've just been through hell. Takes time to heal."

"Been long enough. I still jump at shadows sometimes, still run without thinking, still taste absolute fear . . . still hit." James stopped and regarded Luke. "I was a slave for a little over two months. Think about these people who've been slaves their whole lives."

"They're treated better than you were."

"Are they?" Propping the rake against the stall rail, James glanced over his shoulder and then moved toward the door. "You sure about that?"

Chapter Twenty-Four

January 1863

He recognized the bay who stood fifteen hands. Gunnar Iverson's horse and next to it, his brother's brown one. Luke wagged his head when he realized he'd forgotten that the Iverson boys had sent word they'd also be meeting Quantrill. Too many things on my mind, Luke thought. Too many.

If battle had taught him anything, it was to keep his head down and stay out of sight. And to keep his gun loaded. At least half of those lessons he was following now. His .36 Colt Walker was packed tight with fresh powder, but out here on the prairie with only an occasional stand of trees, it was hard to stay out of sight. He made a big target and he knew it. Dismounting, he used his horse as a shield while he picked his way over to the Iversons. He could never be too careful. A long survey of the gentle rise of the land revealed no Quantrill. At least he wasn't showing himself right now.

Before Luke reached the other horses, his own gave a snort and whicker as a greeting.

Gunnar and Tobias Iverson stepped out from behind the bushes. They nodded and shook hands with Luke.

"Good to see you again," Luke said. Their smiles were wide and genuine. Luke took in their muddy boots, patched wool pants, coats in need of mending, and faces tense with anticipation. Except for the coat, he probably looked a lot like them.

Gunnar's blond hair stuck out from under a narrow brimmed

brown hat and hung at his shoulders. Neither brother had bothered to shave for several days, which, with their light beards, made their faces look furry. Like a cat's. Luke returned their smiles. Damn, it *was* good to see them.

Tobias broke off a twig and snapped it into little pieces. "Think this's a good idea, Luke? I mean . . ." His eyes trailed left then right. "Well, hell, Quantrill's the meanest son of a bitch around. And we're thinking of riding with him?" He tossed the tree parts at the ground, and then turned concerned blue eyes on Luke. "What the hell're we doing, anyway?"

Tobias Iverson, at the age of seventeen, asked questions no one should have to. They were good questions, ones he'd asked himself a million times on his four-hour ride here. Here—in the middle of nowhere. Nearest town four miles farther was Osawatomie, former home of a revolutionary preacher, John Brown, a man claiming to have stirred things up preaching against slavery. Looks like he did just that, Luke thought.

It had only been three weeks since Abraham Lincoln had declared all slaves free. And at what price? If they're free, where would they go? Many had never gone farther than five miles from their homes, most didn't read or cipher numbers, few had job skills. Freedom sounded more like a death sentence.

"I've been telling Tobe here," Gunnar said, "that we can do more good by riding with someone who's getting things done, making a difference, than just handing out guns a few at a time."

Memories took control. The stench of gunpowder filled Luke's nose. Sticky blood coated his hands. Cannons boomed next to his ear. Luke flinched, ducking from the battle raging all around.

A hand on his shoulder brought him back.

"Luke?" Gunnar frowned into Luke's face. "You all right? You're shaking."

Surprised at the voice in his ear, and then startled by the

pounding hoofbeats from behind, Luke wheeled. Clouds of steam erupted from the horses' muzzles as they slowed and then halted yards away from Luke and his friends.

Luke had less than a minute to explain, to come clean. He looked from Gunnar to Tobias. "I've wanted to tell you. I've been riding with Quantrill. Like you said, he gets things done."

"How long?" Gunnar's blond eyebrows disappeared under his hat.

"Several months."

"And you never told us?" Tobias frowned.

"Meant to," Luke said. "I'm sorry. Just . . ."

Before he could explain further, Quantrill reined up next to Luke.

"These your friends, Colton? Ones you told me about?" Quantrill's Roman nose stuck out between two dark eyes.

Luke pulled in as much cold January air as he could, threw his shoulders back and nodded. "Yes, sir. Gunnar and Tobias Iverson. They're good men."

A quick survey of the four riders. Two he recognized. Frank James and Cole Younger.

Luke probed his memory for the last face. Jesse from the first time Luke had run into Quantrill. He wondered again if this was Frank James' younger brother.

Quantrill, remaining in his saddle, fixed his gaze on Gunnar. "Why is it you want to join up with my Raiders?"

"Well, sir," Gunnar said. "Me and my brother here are runnin' guns and feel like we ain't making one diddly damn difference with this war. We're tired of seein' our friends die . . . and for what?"

"That's right," Tobias said to Luke.

"For nothing!" Gunnar Iverson stepped next to Luke. "We got men in town supplyin' us guns, but unless we can stop them Jayhawkers from comin' in and helpin' themselves to our supplies, to our whiskey, our—"

"How do I know you two ain't Jayhawkers spying on me and my boys? How do I know you're loyal Rebels?"

Icy wind snaked down inside Luke's coat. He shivered. Quantrill raised both eyebrows as his gaze trailed across Luke's face, then Gunnar's and finally Tobias'. He sat up straight, sniffed, then ran a sleeve under his nose.

Swinging down out of his saddle, Frank James stuck out a hand to Luke. They shook.

"Good to see you again, Luke." He turned to Quantrill. "Him and me and Gregg . . . and Cole here, fought at Prairie Grove."

Quantrill snorted. "Helluva battle from what I heard."

"Yes, sir, it was." Cole shook hands with Luke. "You're a damn good gunhand."

The horse under Quantrill shifted its weight and pawed at the ground. He pulled on dry grass, munching as the men spoke.

Quantrill frowned, his eyebrows pulling together while regarding the Iverson boys. "I don't take nobody in my group who ain't been done in by those Jayhawkers. Nobody who don't want revenge." He paused long enough for Luke to hear a far-off mockingbird whistle. "What's your story, Mister Iverson?"

Gunnar studied the ground, then glanced at Tobias. "Our daddy went to war, didn't come back. Our brother . . . same thing." He swallowed hard. "Them Jayhawkers took my family, Mister Quantrill. All's I got left is Tobias."

"Stinkin', lousy Jayhawkers!" Quantrill spit. "If you can stomach killin', ain't afraid of dyin', then you're welcome to ride with me. But if you ain't got the heart"—he balled his fist—"then you need to ride off right now. I don't take nobody who ain't got heart, the fire searing in your guts to do what's right, kill when necessary. To turn those Jayhawkers around and drill 'em in the ass."

Quantrill was worked up and Luke's passion was stirred.

Hell, yeah, he'd fight again. Maybe even die for it.

Gunnar and Tobias nodded.

Words much softer, Quantrill asked, "What is it you do, Mister Iverson? To make a living, that is?"

"Well, sir," Gunnar said. "Me and my brother do odd jobs, here and there, for folks. Right now, we're helpin' to build a barn up around Parkville."

"So, you're good with your hands, is what you're telling me?"

A partial smile blossomed on Gunnar's face. "Yes sir, we are. Pride ourselves on it, we do."

"They'll be good men to have," Luke said. He meant it. There had been more than a couple times when he was glad to have them at his back. He also felt good about Cole and Frank. His gaze rested on Jesse James. Maybe not him.

He'd have to watch him. There was something about that kid he didn't trust. Even at fifteen, he could do a lot of damage, a lot of killing. And if he and the Iverson boys ended up riding with Quantrill, Luke would keep a sharp eye out for knives hurtling toward their backs. Something about Jesse, maybe his eyes, Luke didn't trust.

"Listen, Mister Iverson—both of you," Quantrill said, "it's getting damn cold out here. Tell you what. You and your brother. You can ride with us."

"Thank you, sir. It's an honor." Tobias reached up and shook Quantrill's hand. Gunnar followed him.

"Here's what I want you three to do." Quantrill pulled his coat collar up. "A couple farms over in Vernon County, Bushwhacker farms, got raided a few days back. Three good men killed. Now I don't take kindly to anybody riding into Missouri and killing some of my Partisan Rangers."

"They also carried off livestock and two slaves," Frank said. "They had no call to take what ain't theirs."

Quantrill nodded. "So we're heading over to Franklin

132

County, here in Kansas. There's a couple farms of Union sympathizers, and a way station and trading post owned by a fella named Jones, John Jones, that needs . . . um . . . setting straight of their wrongful thinking."

Frank James raised a shoulder. "And if we have to torch the place to convince 'em, then—"

"I'll light the match," Jesse said.

"But Mister Quantrill," Tobias said, "what about the women and kids? I ain't in agreement with hurting them."

"If they stay out of the way, no harm will come to their person." Quantrill jerked his head toward Cole. "Let's go." He waited until Cole and Frank were again mounted. He moved in close to Luke. "You and your friends here. I want you to join Cole, Frank and Jesse, and show these Jayhawkers we mean business."

Swept up in the furor, Luke's chest swelled with pride. Finally an assignment he wouldn't lose. "Yes, sir. We'll be happy to ride with you. You can count on us."

"Good," Quantrill said. "Two days. In two days meet us at Jones' house. It's right on Tauy Creek and the Fort Scott road. Can't miss it." He waved, then reined his horse around, spurred, and galloped east. Jesse and Frank James, Coleman Younger on Quantrill's heels, followed.

Pellets of round ice bounced off Luke's hat. Storm clouds, steely gray, blocked blue skies. It's gonna be a long four-hour ride home, he thought. And judging by the frown on Tobias' face, he felt the same way. But they had farther to go than he did.

"What d'you think about staying with us tonight?" Luke headed for his horse. "It's gonna get nasty cold and we've got fire and food. Sally won't mind setting two more places."

CHAPTER TWENTY-FIVE

The ride back seemed twice as long as the ride out. Sleet pelted the three men while they galloped over the windblown prairie, flat, broken up only occasionally with treeless swales. A creek here and there challenged the landscape monotony. Before full dark threatened to erase the road, Luke spotted lights of the town less than a mile ahead. His white-clapboard house stood on the south side, and with few neighbors, Luke figured people wouldn't spot him and his friends riding in so late. Sally would explain he'd been working if anyone was up at this hour to see them ride in.

As Luke rode closer to the house, he spotted a familiar buggy parked on the side. His in-laws. What would the good Reverend and Missus Burroughs be doing out here, at dark, in the cold? Probably playing with the baby, Luke mused. New grandparents were like that, always fussing over the baby.

After rubbing down their horses and giving them a good helping of grain and water, Luke and the Iversons trudged toward the house, careful to stomp off as much mud as possible. The men wiped their boots, then stepped inside. Expecting a house full of cooking smells, instead Luke was greeted with quiet.

"Sally? Mister Burroughs?" Luke frowned toward the kitchen. "Missus Burroughs?" He shrugged at his friends. "Wait here. I'll see what's going on."

Before he took a step, Missus Burroughs, her hands clutching a towel, rushed from the bedroom. Her dark-brown hair, swept up in a bun, pulled tight against her face. Her pale cheeks were set off with dark pink, but her brown eyes lit up when she spotted Luke. "Glad you're back."

"What's wrong?"

"It's Sally. She's come down with a fever." Her trembling hands clutched Luke's. "I told her it was too early to be up and about, after the baby and with you gone and all . . . but she wouldn't listen to me. And now look."

Much shorter than Luke, Missus Burroughs still commanded a presence. In her mind, she knew right from wrong and never hesitated to tell people exactly what she thought. Luke often privately chuckled at her. But not tonight. Like her mother, Sally was a strong girl, so Luke rarely gave her health a second thought.

He nodded at the Iversons. "Missus Burroughs, this here's friends of mine. Gunnar and Tobias Iverson." A tilt of his head toward his mother-in-law. "Missus Sarah Burroughs."

"Ma'am." Both brothers muttered in unison, then yanked off their hats, and clutched them in their hands.

"Gentlemen," Sarah nodded. She turned her eyes on Luke. "James and Morningstar's been here most of the day. Her pa's a doctor, you know. She knows what to do. Adam's with your folks, and the baby is over at Missus Jenkins'. She's a wet nurse, you know."

Feeling his cheeks warming, Luke excused himself. "I best go see Sally." He hated himself for not thinking of his wife. What kind of man was he?

Sally didn't make a very big lump in the bed. Maybe five foot two, she didn't weigh more than a couple sacks of grain. But she was bull strong, something Luke loved about her. And her iron will added depth to her character. Something else he loved, but hated at the same time.

Luke eased down to the bed and met Sally's glazed stare. Beads of sweat dotted her ashen face, one that just yesterday was full of life and love. He took her hand. Clammy.

"How you feeling?"

"You came back." Sally's soft words floated around the room.

" 'Course I came back." True concern pressed against Luke's chest. Was she dying? What would he do if she did? " 'Course I came home. I love you."

A cough made Sally roll toward Luke. He grabbed a water glass from the table and held her head, something he never thought he'd ever have to do. "Here. A sip. You'll feel better."

Two sips, then Sally rolled onto her back and closed her eyes.

"Sally?" Luke's panic brought all sorts of images to mind. Soldiers dead on the field, parts blown off, freezing in the mud. He pushed them away. "Sally?"

A sigh, then she opened her eyes. "Love you, too, Luke."

A hand clamped on Luke's shoulder. Missus Burroughs stood beside him. "She's doing better than this morning. She needs rest now. The doc gave her some powder to keep the fever down."

This morning? Luke stopped listening at that. He'd been here this morning. True, he'd left while it was still dark, but shouldn't he have known Sally was sick? And why didn't she tell him? She was independent and keeping that to herself was just another way of aggravating him. She should've told him before he left.

When Luke walked into his living room, he shook hands with his father-in-law who was busy piling cut wood by the fireplace. Tobias stood just inside the closed door, arms loaded with more wood. Gunnar stuck his head out from the kitchen.

"I'm making stew. Hope everyone's hungry."

Nobody cooked today? Maybe Sally really was sick.

Within an hour, Gunnar had supper on the table. Stew in bowls and biscuits on a plate filled out the small wooden table.

It was normally big enough for Luke and Sally and now Adam, but to seat five grown people was tough. Elbow to elbow they ate.

Talk centered around Sally, the weather, the Iversons, Morningstar's help and church. Tobias cleared the table with Gunnar agreeing to wash dishes. Both men disappeared into the kitchen.

Reverend Franklin Burroughs turned his saintly eyes on Luke. "I expect you'll tell Mister Gibson you'll need a couple days off to take care of Sally." The gaze held steady. "With this weather, I can't imagine he'd be sending you very far."

"And the doctor says she should be up and about in five or six days," Sarah Burroughs said.

"Five or six . . . ?" Luke frowned. "Can't Star come and stay?" Hell, by then, those farms would be raided and burned, and I'll be one of Quantrill's Raiders for sure, Luke thought. A couple more attacks on Jayhawk farms, maybe I'll become one of his lieutenants.

Screeching chair legs against wooden floors brought Luke's attention back. Both of his in-laws stood, coats in hand.

"Your wife's your responsibility, Luke, not your sister-in-law's." Missus Burroughs huffed. "I've left the medicine. Directions are written next to the glass." She threaded her arms through her coat. "We'll stop by tomorrow."

"Good night, Luke." Franklin Burroughs shook his hand.

After seeing his in-laws to their buggy and muttering goodbye, Luke stood in the cold and considered.

Two days before he needed to be at the Jones Trading Post. Five days with Sally sick in bed. Which should he give his time to? Which was more important? His country or his wife?

CHAPTER TWENTY-SIX

Luke paced. Door to window. Window to couch. Dawn would break within moments and before the Iversons got here, he'd have to make up his mind once and for all. He had to burn down those farms. Had to. How else could he prove himself to Quantrill and become respected and, yes, feared? Because he sure hadn't proven anything yet. A failure was more likely what Quantrill was thinking Luke was. But this would be different. He'd show the greatest leader of the Bushwhackers what Luke Jeremiah Colton could really do.

Those Kansas Jayhawkers had to be stopped. Those farms, and the John Jones house, that trading post, were close enough that the repercussions would be felt this far into Lawrence. Yeah, he'd make an impact and it would be on those men who fought against him. Men who felt being one with the Union, allowing the government to dictate rules for everyone, was right.

It had been two days and Sally's fever was down and she ate. Soups mainly, but her mother, along with Luke's, kept her fed. Kept him fed, too. Adam spent his daytime at home, helping with the few chores he could handle, but stayed nights with James and Morningstar at their parents' farm. And little baby Hannah was content to be fed elsewhere. Luke had only seen her once these past two days.

Luke jumped at a tap on the front door. He opened it to Gunnar and Tobias and welcomed them in. After exchanging pleasantries, Luke got down to business.

"You both going?" Luke eyed Gunnar then Tobias. Their hard mouths set in thin lines gave him the answer.

"Are you?" Gunnar glanced toward the closed bedroom door.

Of course he was. How could he not go? But how to tell Sally and his folks? No way in hell he'd tell Sally or his in-laws, or even James for that matter, what he was doing. He and Reverend Burroughs certainly didn't see eye to eye on most topics, and this one was just capital. If the Reverend ever found out, Luke would more than likely be disowned, and maybe Sally would even divorce him.

On the other hand, if he became the war hero he envisioned, Sally would love him even more, and her father would have to be proud. Would his own pa be proud?

Luke's chest expanded under his wool shirt. "Wouldn't miss this for anything. I've asked my ma to stay with Sally while I'm gone. She should be here any minute now."

Tobias pushed scattered newspaper, a plate and two unwashed socks to the end of the sofa, unbuttoned his sheepskin coat, and then sat. "How long you think it'll take to burn—"

"Keep your voice down." Gunnar frowned toward the bedroom. "Nobody should know where we're going. What we're gonna do." He inspected each glove as he pulled them off. "Hell, I don't even know exactly what we're gonna do."

"Take down some damned Jayhawkers is what we're gonna—" Luke turned as the front door pushed open.

James Colton stepped inside closing the door harder than necessary. His eyes flitted from man to man and then rested on Luke. He nodded to Gunnar. "I'm James. Luke's older brother." He flashed a quick smile. "Well, one of them."

"Pleased to know you." Gunnar and then Tobias shook hands with James.

Awkward silence filled the room. Luke cleared his throat.

"James, my friends stopped by to see how Sally's doing."

James nodded. "Ma's on her way over. How *is* she doing?"

"Better. She'll be up and around today." Luke knew his brother hadn't ridden all the way over just to ask about Sally. Morningstar kept him apprised of her condition. James knew probably better than Luke how Sally was doing. So, why was he here?

Gunnar and Tobias shuffled their weight. Gunnar pointed toward the door. "We'd best leave. Glad Sally's doing better."

Tobias nodded as they eased toward the door. Once it closed and Luke and James were alone in the living room, James took a deep breath.

"This isn't my place to say, little brother. But . . . what the hell're you doing?"

"What d'you mean—"

"This running all over God's creation. Leaving your wife and kids behind. Hell, Luke, you got a tiny little baby that needs her pa, a son who adores you, and here you are gone half the time." James lowered his voice. "What're you really up to, 'cause I know it can't all be hauling freight."

Luke ran a hand over his face hoping to stall long enough to find the words to say what he felt. He nodded. "First of all, you're right. It's not your place to say. But since you did, I'll tell you." Luke stared out the window watching his pa and ma drive up in their buggy. Adam sat like a prince in the back.

James lowered his voice to a whisper. "You're running with Quantrill, aren't you?"

"What?" Luke spun around and then stepped back. Caught. "No. Why'd you say, even think that?"

"Because you're stubborn enough to do whatever the hell you think is right." James pointed a finger at Luke's chest. "No matter who pays the price, Luke Colton has to be right. And I'll bet Quantrill's got you by your . . ." James glanced at the closed front door. "I hope to God you make the right choices. Just know I'm watching you."

"Papa!" Adam charged through the door, then slammed into Luke. He wrapped his two-year-old arms around Luke's legs. The impact about bowled him over.

Once he had his feet under him again, Luke swept Adam up and pulled off his hat. "Hey, little man. You been a good boy for your grandma?"

Adam nodded as he wiggled out of Luke's grip.

Ma Colton untied her hat and unbuttoned her coat, hanging them both on a coat tree by the door. "I don't know, Luke. I just don't understand why Mister Gibson would send you out in weather like this." She helped Adam out of his coat. "That man has no sense. No good sense at all. Why, you'll catch your death a cold." Her brown eyes trailed up and down Luke's body. "Be sure to bundle up."

"Yes, ma'am."

Ma bustled toward the kitchen. "You have food packed? Enough? And water? Plenty of water?"

He nodded after each question. After a quick kiss on the top of her head, he said, "It'll be after dark before I get back. Don't know how long it'll be, but I'll be back."

He knew in his gut it would be well after midnight, and that was assuming things went according to plan. He held out little to no hope of that happening.

James picked up Adam who waved to Luke. James flashed a concerned smile. "I'll take care of your *family* while you're gone."

Outside, Luke waved to Pa checking a leather strap on the buckboard harness. Luke's long strides took him to town within moments.

Surprisingly, it was tougher for Luke to ride off than he'd imagined. James' words tore into his soul, stabbing at unvoiced doubts. Family strings tethered him in ways he would never have thought possible. What was wrong with him? He was a man. And in time of war, he was doing more than just providing for the family. Dammit, this task was bigger—he was providing for his country's future.

Some day, they'd thank him for his sacrifices.

CHAPTER TWENTY-SEVEN

They rode half the day, due south, the thirty miles eaten away one step at a time. Halfway to the meeting place, they stopped for a quick break sheltered by a twenty-foot patch of wild cherry bushes. The bacon, biscuits and cheese Luke had packed for the three of them did little to fill his stomach. His nerves occupied the extra room.

Try as he may, he couldn't shake James' voice nagging his brain.

So far the weather had been cold, but it hadn't snowed. Clouds on the eastern horizon hung low, almost threatening as if they were waiting for torches to be set to the house. Then, snow-filled clouds would swoop in to extinguish the flames.

Back in the saddle, the men spoke in grunts and gestures. Each, Luke figured, was playing out the scenario in his head. He knew he was. He'd grab women and kids, slaves if he could. Get them out of harm's way, then torch the trading post. These Jayhawkers would learn not to mess with the Bushwhackers. Not to get in the way of what the Southern states wanted— more land and the right to decide their way of life. And if that included owning slaves, then so be it. Slaves were important to the well-being of the South, their agricultural way of life, and no damned government had the right to come in and run their lives.

By the time he spotted Tauy Creek, Luke had worked himself up into a rage. Sun slightly west, Luke decided to stop at the creek, walk his horse downstream until he spotted the John Jones house, which doubled as a trading post, about two hundred yards farther south. How long they'd have to wait, he didn't know, but getting down off that horse felt good. Luke stretched and then rubbed his backside. He wasn't used to so much riding. Usually, he drove a wagon.

Tobias squatted by the creek and tossed in pebbles, a few skidding across icy patches. Gunnar stretched out on the ground beside his brother, closed his eyes, and snored. Luke paced. One eye on the house, the other on the road twenty yards away. Where were the James boys? Cole Younger? What in the hell was keeping them?

Luke allowed himself a long look at the house. The one he was about to destroy. Two stories in fine cut stone sat prominently on top of a hill that sloped off in all directions. The house was sizeable. More than likely it had lots of rooms, pantries, wardrobes and hallways. Trees shaded its west side. Back a ways stood the barn, one big enough to hold ten horses. Three of those horses stood in a corral attached to the barn. Two granaries, an icehouse, smokehouse, chicken house, blacksmith shop, cattle shed, three cisterns, and an orchard of fruit trees dotted the property. It was a fine place. And one, no doubt, in good condition because of the slaves.

More pacing. Luke couldn't sit. Small talk with Tobias did nothing to calm his nerves. The rumble of horses' hooves spun Luke around. He squinted south along the Fort Scott road. A company of about fifteen soldiers, their blue uniforms standing out against the brown of the prairie hills, rode closer. Small puffs of dust danced around their horses' hooves.

This brought Tobias and Gunnar to their feet. Before Luke and the boys could formulate an explanation as to why the three of them were there, the riders were on them.

The lieutenant in front raised his hand and his men drew up.

He peered down, his eyes scanning first Luke, Tobias, then Gunnar. He took his time and then returned his hard-eyed stare to Luke.

"Who are you, sir? Please state your business here."

Luke had had just enough time to figure out a name. "Burroughs. Franklin Burroughs."

He extended his hand. "Reverend Burroughs from Lawrence." Maybe if he could disarm this soldier with the Colton family charm, they'd leave him and the Iversons the hell alone. "I hold fine church services five nights a week. Each one only a short four hours long. You and your men are more than welcome to join us. To pray for peace, that is."

Ignoring Luke, the lieutenant swung his gaze to Tobias. "You arc . . . ?"

"I'm . . ." Tobias' eyes darted from Gunnar to Luke and then back to Gunnar. "I'm—"

"Embarrassed, sir. And ashamed." Luke said. He lowered his voice to a loud whisper. "He and his brother here, are . . . *were* derelicts, down-on-their-luck orphans, drunks I recently rescued from the dark recesses of locked iron bars. I'm guiding them to church where they'll be saved and take their vows."

"Vows?" The lieutenant's bushy eyebrows rose.

Struggling to remember any kind of church-related verbiage, Luke glanced Heavenward as he scrambled for something that made sense. "Of course. Vows of worship. Vows of service. And most importantly, vows of celibacy."

"What?" Tobias and the lieutenant spoke in unison.

"No flesh on flesh," Luke said. "It makes men weak."

Gunnar put his hands together as if in prayer. "Amen. But it'll be difficult."

"I know, brother, I know." Luke laid a hand on Gunnar's shoulder. "It seems like a great sacrifice now, a trial unlike any other, but you'll receive your reward in Heaven because of it."

He spread his arms wide to include the entire troop. "You, my fellow men, must give up your fleshy wanton ways to truly be at peace with yourself. To find harmony in nature. And to follow in my footsteps." Luke moved in close to the officer. "Come with us. Give yourself and your soul over to me in my church, and you'll be forever anointed. Just—"

"No need, Reverend." The lieutenant leaned as far back from Luke as he could without falling out of his saddle. "I'm sure your boys will appreciate being saved. Leading the good life." He jerked his bearded chin up. "Sorry to have bothered you."

A smile stretched Luke's cheeks as the last stinkin' Bluebelly rode past. Maybe Luke should rethink his stand with the church. He turned to Gunnar. "I'd make a dandy preacher, don't you think?"

Eye rolls from both brothers and a thump on his back from Tobias. That had been fun.

Luke spotted four riders on the road from the south. A closer look and he recognized Coleman Younger, Frank and Jesse James. The fourth man Luke had never seen. The men reined up and then dismounted, allowing their horses to break the ice on the creek and drink.

Luke nodded to Frank. " 'Bout gave you up. What kept you?"

"Damn no-good Bluebellies." Frank spit, moving his boot just out of glop range. "Had to hide out till they was far enough ahead." He spit again. "Damn Bluebellies."

"I'd shoot 'em right 'tween the eyes, if they was here," Jesse said. He pulled his Colt from his waistband and aimed toward the receding soldiers. "Stinkin' Bluebellies." Sighting down the barrel, he pretended to shoot. "Stinkin' soldiers. I hate soldiers."

"Hell, you hate everybody, Jesse," Cole said. "Put your shooter away and let's figure out how we're gonna come callin'."

Luke eyed the silent man swinging down from his horse. Standing less than Luke's height, this man stepped in close to the Iverson boys. His cold gaze traveled up and down Gunnar. "You a foreigner?"

Gunnar shook his head. "No."

The man snorted then glared at Tobias. "You?"

"No."

Frank James moved closer to the man. "This here's Clarke Blackhorn. He's a cousin of Quantrill's and he don't take to strangers."

"I can talk for myself, Frank." Clarke tongued a wad of something pushing out his cheek to the other side. He swiped a coat sleeve across his mouth, a swath of brown left behind. "Hate foreigners. Got too damn many in this country as it is. Saw your blond hair." He pointed at Gunnar's head. "Figured you for a Dutch." He spit. "Stinkin' Dutch."

Gunnar's left hand fisted. Luke stepped next to his friend and offered his hand to Clarke. "I'm Luke Colton from Lawrence. This here's my friends, Gunnar and Tobias Iverson." Luke and Clarke shook hands. Luke raised both eyebrows at Clarke. "What say we save our fighting for the Jayhawkers?"

A long look at Gunnar and Tobias, then Clarke nodded.

Squatting in a circle, the men agreed to swoop down on the house, each taking a side or outbuilding. Luke and Cole got the privilege of heading straight inside, right through the front doors. They were assigned the task of removing the women, children and slaves, and moving them to some form of safety, or at least outside. Jesse and Tobias were to put a torch to the barn and corncribs, chicken houses and anything else that would burn. Frank, Clarke and Gunnar would set fire inside the main house, shooting anybody who resisted.

The horses would be taken, along with any other livestock the men could wrangle.

"How do they know who did this?" Luke asked. "Who gets the credit?"

147

Frank snorted. "They'll know." He nodded toward Cole. "They just know."

Was Luke doing the right thing? What happened if people died? Did he really want to be responsible for someone's death? No. But then, he'd shot and killed several people a few weeks back. Luke's second thoughts about this adventure chilled him.

The difference was, these weren't soldiers shooting at him. These were people living in their home, running a trading post, doing the best they could in these trying times. Right now they weren't shooting at him, so how could he barge in and fire his gun?

He hated this conscience that seemed to have developed once he got married. Sally was a bad influence. Luke pushed aside doubts and focused on final plans. If separated, they were to meet at the tiny town of Palmyra, about ten miles north, at a saloon Frank knew. The Bon Ton, he said. Luke had no plans to get separated.

"Questions, men?" Cole stood and reset his hat.

Luke had none that were answered easily. On the surface, he knew this was right. It had to be done to show those damn Jayhawkers they meant business. Luke's gaze traveled over Gunnar and Tobias' grim faces, their mouths turned down and eyes narrowed. He knew them well enough to know they were worried. They probably felt like he did. Yet, no one spoke up. No questions.

"Good," Cole said. "Let's ride."

Chapter Twenty-Eight

No words were spoken the entire return ride. Questions pushed their way into Luke's mind, crowding out the desire to block out what he'd just seen. Hell, what he'd just *done*. Fatigue, deep down, bone-chilling fatigue had attempted to push him out of the saddle, but thoughts of home had kept him in.

Bloody and bruised, shivering from cold and spent energy, Luke convinced the brothers to stay the night. They walked their horses into Luke's barn and uncinched the saddles. Luke's horse hung her head as he guided her into the stall. All done in. After a quick swipe of their blankets over the horses' sweaty backs, Luke and the brothers latched the stalls' gates, then extinguished the kerosene lantern.

Now he was home, safe and somewhat sound. He forced his legs to carry him into the house. Gunnar and Tobias followed.

A single lantern burned in the kitchen, its glow casting eerie gray shadows over plates on the counter and a pot left on the stove. Pulling up his shirt, Luke used the low light to inspect his throbbing, burning side. He'd held that wound most of the ride back, and the jostling hadn't helped. It hurt worse now than when it'd first happened.

Closer inspection revealed an angry red slash, several layers of missing skin. But the bullet hadn't done any major damage, and he'd stopped bleeding an hour ago. A look at the Iversons. Both faces blotched with soot, blood and shock, stared at him. Reflecting on their recent foray into bushwhacking, Luke knew the three of them were damn lucky to have escaped unharmed. He sure couldn't say that about Mister Jones or Cole Younger.

Cole had about died when that slave came after him with a shovel. Cole undoubtedly lost some hearing in his left ear. And it had taken a few minutes for him to wake up after being clocked by that little old black man. If it hadn't been so deadly, the whole thing would have been funny.

And Mister Jones? Luke hadn't seen exactly what had happened, but word was the man had been killed, shot and then run through with a sword. Part of Luke was glad he'd missed it. Shooting somebody was much less personal—no sure way of knowing your bullet hit its target and besides, you're farther away. Stabbing . . . well, it was much too close.

Luke brought his thoughts back to the present. Quantrill would undoubtedly praise him and the Iversons for this raid. Despite his sore ribs and wound, his chest swelled. Doing what he knew was right. .

He nodded at the basin in the sink. "Wash up here. I'll get blankets."

The house was quiet as Luke navigated the living room. Tiptoeing to the bedroom, he took two blankets and pillows from the chest. Before making it to the front room, Sally turned over and sat up.

"Luke?"

"I'm back." He nodded at his armful of bedding as if she could see what he was holding. Scant moonlight filtered through the single window. "Hope you don't mind. The Iversons are staying the night."

She lay down and mumbled. A snore from the other side of the house surprised him. Not Sally's. Ma? In all the commotion, he'd forgot his ma was staying until he got back.

Luke handed a blanket to each Iverson. "One of you take the couch, the other the floor. At least it's warm. Here's pillows."

Once his partners were settled in the front room, Luke headed off for bed. As tired as he was, but with his side still throbbing, he wondered if he would sleep.

He crawled into bed next to Sally and squeezed his eyes tight. Sleep refused to come.

Women screamed. A child sobbed. Horses thundered past. Flames shot up in all directions, the heat terrifying. Luke watched . . . felt . . . relived the raid until the room lightened enough for him to see Sally next to him. Ma must be in Adam's bed.

Get up or try to sleep? Get up. His ma or Sally would be stirring any moment and he might as well get up, light a fire and push the cold out of the house. Before swinging his legs over the side of the bed and easing upright, he draped one arm across his eyes. Luke pulled in air.

"Luke! Luke!"

Someone shook his shoulders.

"I smell smoke." Sally's voice in his face. She shook him full awake.

Luke sat bolt upright, making sense of his world one piece at a time. Sally's blue eyes grew wide. She was breathing hard and pointing behind her. He blinked and rubbed his head. "Where?"

Sally moved back allowing him room to wobble to his feet. "I'm not sure. But the whole house smells like smoke, especially the front room. Come see." She tugged his arm. "I've looked all around, but can't find anything. Adam and your ma are safe outside."

Before they got two feet toward the living room, Sally stopped and frowned at Luke. She sniffed him. Narrowing eyes trailed up to his face. "It's you. *You* smell like smoke." She ran her fingers over the side of Luke's face. "You got something black there. Looks like . . . soot."

151

More awake now, Luke's thoughts jelled. He pulled Sally into his embrace. "Sorry. I ran into the Iversons out aways on the road—they're headed for a job—and that smoke's from our campfire. Guess it got bigger'n we'd planned." He looked over her head into the living room. "They up?"

"That's what it is. All of you smell like smoke." Pulling out of his grip, she turned around and spoke over her shoulder. "Your friends were up, dressed, and gone before I got up."

"Gone?" Luke followed her into the front room. "Why didn't you wake me? Did Ma talk to them? Were they all right?"

Sally spun around, hands on hips. "Now why would you ask such a question?" She cocked her head. "Didn't you just deliver supplies over to Palmyra? And if they're just passing through, why wouldn't they be all right?"

Luke had no answer. He still wasn't thinking straight, and this wasn't one of his better mornings. Something. He had to think of something quick. "We . . . they—"

"Did you three go out drinking?" Sally sniffed at him again. "And why'd you stay gone so long? Your ma fretted about you all night."

That was it. He wasn't about to stand around being questioned by his wife. Good God. "Look. I'm sorry about the smoke smell. It kind of followed us home. I'll get these clothes washed in town. All right? That make you happy?" What felt more like a hangover invaded Luke's body. He ached head to toe, his temples throbbed, his side burned, even his feet hurt. Maybe a good warm soak in a tub down at "Ernie's Washateria" would help. At least there, he wouldn't have to put up with women nagging him. He couldn't wait to hear what Ma had to say.

But she didn't say anything. That icy stare said more than words ever could. Only little Adam was glad to see him. Luke bounced him on his knee, letting him play horsey while he sipped cold coffee. Not only was it bitterly cold outside, it was damn chilly inside.

Down at Ernie's, Luke closed his eyes as he soaked in the big oaken barrel, water armpit high, and pulled in a drag on his cigar. Its smoke danced in front of him, then curled around his head on its way to the ceiling. Warm water, bordering on hot, sucked the aches out of his body. Even his side felt better. Could he stay here all day? He nodded to Ernie who brought another bucketful. It cascaded down Luke's back, washing off the few suds left from the shampoo.

Someone shook Luke's arm.

"Time to get out, Mister Colton. Two hours's the limit." Ernie handed a towel to Luke.

He had already paid the half-dollar in advance, which in his estimation was worth every single penny, then tipped Ernie a nickel. He may have to come back again real soon, and Luke liked being treated this well.

Next on his list was a shave, maybe a haircut. That should take some more time.

After the barber's, Luke, sporting a new hairstyle—parted in the middle and slicked down on both sides—and smooth cheeks, surveyed Massachusetts Avenue. A stroll down this main street of Lawrence might clear his head.

On the west side at the end of the avenue, he passed the brick Eldridge House, a hotel noted for its fine accommodations, and the fact it sat on the highest hill of the town. Its guests, sherry glasses in hand, Luke had heard, spent the sunset hours mingling in the hotel lobby, trying to impress each other. Luke had been told that, viewed from the top-story balcony, the Kansas River looked just like a silver ribbon. How many business deals had been conceived there, he wondered. He'd heard also it was a "Free State Fortress," often the central meeting place for Senator James Lane and his followers. They were Jayhawkers and Luke hated them and the Eldridge.

Next to the Eldridge sat Reverend Burroughs' Methodist church. Brick. Imposing. A two-story monument to piety. He shielded his eyes while he studied the top of the steepled roof. A wooden bell tower housed a bell brought by train and then mule team from New York. That darn bell rang every Sunday morning and could be heard across town. With its close proximity to the Eldridge House, was Franklin Burroughs a friend of James Lane and his cronies? Luke hadn't really thought about it until now. Politics and religion. Terrible bed partners.

He turned to go.

"Luke? That you?"

He recognized the voice. Reverend Burroughs on the steps. Luke considered ignoring the man and walking away, then thought better. A quick superficial conversation and he'd be gone. Luke extended a hand.

"Frank. Didn't know you'd be here."

Burroughs glanced side to side. "Around here, better call me Reverend." He shook hands with Luke.

Luke squeezed the hand harder than necessary then let go. "Sorry, sir."

"No harm done." Burroughs brightened. "You came just in time. You'll be the first to see our new stained-glass window. Come all the way from Italy. Bobbed over the Atlantic, then freighted by mule the rest the way. Arrived this morning, not a scratch on it." He patted Luke on the shoulder and pushed him inside.

The dark sanctity sat on Luke's chest like a sack of grain. How could people stay in here day in and day out? As he marched up the aisle, the same aisle Sally had used when they married, his hands grew sweaty and his breathing shortened.

Would he pass out before reaching this hallowed window?

Finally, he spotted it leaning against the wall. At least eight feet by ten feet, it depicted a man bathed in golden light. Luke admitted it was elegant and would certainly enhance this cavern of a church.

"You must be proud, Reverend," Luke said. "It'll look nice."

"Nice?" Burroughs bellowed. "That all you can say? Well, my son, it'll be righteous. Awe-inspiring. God-loving. Spreads the message of God. What He tries to tell—"

"Yes, sir," Luke said, backing toward the door. "I'm sure it'll be *all* of that." He nodded at the glass. "All."

"Didn't mean to sermonize." Burroughs walked with Luke. "I know this window will stand the test of time. It'll be a tribute to those who've given so much just so Lawrence can grow and prosper." He paused, gazing at the glass. "I just get so . . . so . . ."

"No apology necessary." Luke thumbed over his shoulder. "But I do really have to go."

Luke left his father-in-law standing in the aisle mumbling, as he pushed into bright sunshine and sweet freedom. He rushed up the street, distancing himself from the church as quickly as his legs and the crowd would allow. At long last he slowed.

To his right and down the street, on the opposite side, Luke spotted the Palmer Gunshop. Mister Palmer, if he remembered right, was a founding father of Lawrence. He'd been encouraged, *bought* Luke figured, to come west to Kansas. A man of his wealth, political ties, and keen eye for fine weapons was just what the so-called Massachusetts Emigrants Aid Society had wanted. Hell, Luke thought, it's what had enticed his pa to come. The opportunity to get in on the ground floor of creating a town. To build something. To make a better life for his family.

Family. A knot fisted in the middle of his chest. Maybe he should check on his pa, thank his ma again for staying last night. Maybe she'd be speaking to him by now. Luke tipped his hat to a couple of women sashaying past. He spent more time and effort gawking than he knew he should. They were fine women. Probably staying at the Eldridge. They turned a corner, and disappeared down a side street.

CHAPTER TWENTY-NINE

While the family farm sat south of town, close enough for Luke to visit often, he usually found excuses not to. Reflecting on the death and destruction from his recent raid, the permanence of death, he realized he needed to change that way of thinking. He caught up with Pa in his barn.

Joseph Fredrick Colton wiped his hands on his pants before shaking with Luke. "What brings ya this far out in the woods, son?" He raised one full eyebrow. "It wouldn't be to come lend me a hand now, would it?" Pa wiped his forehead with his sleeve.

Why had he come? Luke wasn't sure, except he owed his Pa for all the times he'd come over and helped with Luke's chores. It was only fair he help Pa once in a while. And now with James around, he and Pa rarely were alone. Which was usually fine with Luke.

Luke shrugged out of his coat. "Didn't want you having all the fun mucking out them stalls. Thought I'd join you."

Pa's brown eyes traveled from Luke's boots up to his hat, then rested on his face. Half a smile pushed up one of his cheeks. "Sally's mad, huh?"

Luke looked at the barn door.

Pa smacked Luke on the shoulder. "Good. I can use the help." He tossed a shovel to Luke who caught it within inches of his face.

The men raked, shoveled, added fresh straw to the stalls, refilled the coal oil in two lanterns, checked the leather tack for cracks and worn places, then piled flakes of hay in each stall. Tired, sweaty, Luke held his rake and surveyed his efforts. Despite the aches and pains from the raid yesterday, and the work today, he felt good. He and Pa hadn't argued even once. That was a record.

Pa leaned on his shovel and looked at Luke, then looked at the stalls.

Luke pointed with his rake. "Ma's fried chicken would sure go down good right about now." He could already taste it. While she usually made fried chicken only on Sundays, maybe she'd made an exception and had cooked it today. "Think she made some?"

Sniffing toward the house, Pa cocked his head. "Could be, but smells more like regular roast."

Luke considered. "Regular roast would be fine, too." He hung the rake between two pegs, then glanced to his left. Fresh straw sat mounded against the back of an empty stall, left alone when Pa worked that area. It wasn't doing the horses any good there. Luke retrieved the rake and headed for the pile.

"Just leave it be." Pa wiped his forehead with his bandanna. "I'll get it tomorrow. You've done enough for today."

"Just take a minute." Luke's rake plowed into the far side of the straw.

Pa grabbed Luke's arm. "I said I'd take care of it tomorrow."

The men stood, shoulder to shoulder. A close look at Pa revealed a set mouth, hard eyes, a firm grip on Luke's rake.

"Pa? What's going on?" Luke pulled out of his grip and raked at the straw.

A door, short and narrow, sat behind the pile.

A door? Why? And what was behind it? None of it made sense.

"Get away from there." Pa gripped both of Luke's shoulders and pulled. The men flew backward, thudding to the dirt floor,

158

Luke on top.

Luke rolled off, found his knees then crawled to the door.

"No, son. Don't." Pa's demanding tone made Luke more determined to see what it was.

Luke pried open the door and peered inside. Ragged breaths behind him and he knew Pa had something to hide.

Slats of setting sun gave off enough light for Luke to make out three huddled forms in the corner of a space no more than three by six feet. Eyes blinked at him. He blinked back.

Luke scrambled back and met Pa's glare. "What the hell?"

"Told you not to open that door." Pa tugged Luke's leg. "Now get the hell outta there."

Rustling from deep inside.

"It's all right, Miss Georgie." Pa peered over Luke's shoulder. "This here's my son. He won't hurt you." He glanced at Luke. "Will you?"

"Escaped slaves?" Luke whispered. More blinks. "They're . . ." He backed out of the door while Pa closed it, mounding more straw in front.

"I can trust you, can't I?" Pa turned fully to face him.

Harboring runaway slaves stepped over the line. Pa didn't understand. Slaves were needed. Giving them their freedom was helping destroy the South. But would Luke rush back to Quantrill and tell him? No, he wouldn't.

"Luke?" Pa's voice in his ear.

Shaking his head, Luke heard his words, like someone else uttered them. Someone far off, in a can. "I'll keep your secret safe."

And he would. Luke wouldn't tell anyone, but he'd have a lot of thinking to do on the ride home. He wondered how he'd never noticed the extra width on the outside of the barn. This addition wasn't here last year. However, three feet wasn't much in a barn this size.

Pa finished piling straw and hay in front. No wonder Luke had never suspected. The hideout proved impossible to detect even from five feet away. Pa was clever.

Luke stood, staring at the stall, now transformed from the gateway to safety back to a horse home. Grabbing his coat from a stall rail, he slipped into it and stormed outside. Pa stopped him just as a blast of frozen air hit Luke's face.

"You'll keep quiet about this?"

Pa's words hit Luke like the ice pellets slamming into his hat.

"Gave you my word, didn't I?"

CHAPTER THIRTY

March 1863

Luke rode side by side with Frank James and Cole Younger. With the days longer and a bit warmer, even though it was just March, their forays into small towns were more frequent. Luke was away a day or two a week when he wasn't driving for Mister Gibson.

Raiding was much easier when they were not fighting blizzards, too. In fact, tonight had been especially easy. The town, Hickory Point, had given up with just a few shots fired and only two people killed. As much as Luke believed in these raids, he still cringed at times when men died. He'd watched Quantrill knife more than a couple, and each time the splattered blood twisted Luke's stomach. He chided himself for turning away, but the stench of blood and bile was too much.

But now, at the same time as Luke and his partners were heading northeast toward Lawrence, Quantrill and his other men were heading south, driving the slaves gathered from the raid. There were people in the border towns in Missouri who would make sure the "colored folk," the polite term Luke had heard them referred to, would be returned to their rightful owners. And, he'd heard, the owners would be glad to pay for their return.

Slaves were a valuable commodity for the South, and Luke was determined to keep it that way. He didn't care what Pa and James . . . the entire North for that fact, had to say. Nothing

161

would change his mind.

Stars glowed overhead as he listened to his horse's rhythmic gallop. She'd been put to the test tonight, with the burning and looting, but even under fire, she hadn't bolted and run off, leaving him stranded. No, she'd waited by the trees, and munched on bits of grass she'd uncovered through the thin mantle of snow. She was a good horse, a treasure disguised as animal hide.

"How far now you figure?" Cole Younger yawned. "I could use a hot bath, whiskey, and a woman."

"To hell with the bath and whiskey," Frank said. "All this shootin' and burnin' gets me all fired up."

Luke thought. If they stopped over in Franklin, he could still get home by daybreak. Then he'd slip into Sally's bed, and she'd never know any different. He sniffed his coat. Didn't smell like smoke tonight. Only one house at Hickory Point had burned, and Luke had stayed upwind most of the time.

"What about you, Luke?" Cole said. "Whiskey or women?"

There was a time he wouldn't have had to think about that for even a second. But he sure as hell wouldn't let on he'd changed his mind. Luke shot a look at Cole. "It's gotta be damn fine whiskey to get my attention."

CHAPTER THIRTY-ONE

"Look here, Luke." Sally held up a folded newspaper. "Look what it says right here. Can you believe it?"

"Believe what?" Luke reached across the kitchen table and tried to look concerned. He frowned and pinched his eyebrows. Too early. The sun had just come up and he'd been home only an hour or two. How would he make it through the day? His boss was sending him clear over to Independence, fifty miles away, and Luke wasn't sure he could stay awake on that trip.

He unfolded the paper, the words blurred. Luke gulped coffee and refocused. Something about a new law office opening up. It didn't make sense.

"Those border ruffians." Sally turned the paper over and pointed. "It says they burned down Jones Trading Post over in Vernon County a couple weeks back. Killed Mister Jones and another man, scared poor Missus Jones half to death. They even took the black folks and run off the horses." She tsked as she wagged her head. "How could somebody do that, Luke? How could somebody burn down another man's house, just because he didn't agree with their politics? How?"

He didn't want to get into it right now. That was a much larger discussion, one they'd had many times. Sally always ended up mad and then in tears. Then she'd give him nothing but supper and silence until she got over it. He wasn't up for it today.

"I don't know. Some people can't leave well enough alone, I

guess." Luke drained his cup, stuffed ham into his mouth, and spoke through it. "Gotta go soon."

"You know," Sally said. "If I were riding with Quantrill"—she handed Adam a small biscuit and then turned her narrowed eyes on Luke—"I'd be very careful. I'd watch my back all the time."

Fully awake now, Luke took in his wife's face. Mouth set in a tight line, shoulders pulled back. "Why d'you say that?"

"Haven't you been reading about him? He's ruthless, a cut-throat, the leader of those border ruffians. I hope God smites them all."

"Smites?" Luke wanted to chuckle but thought better of it. "Isn't that what Quantrill's doing now? That'd make you just like him."

Just as the last word was uttered, Luke regretted it. Sally launched into a tirade about proper and improper smiting, and how the North was trying to keep America together and the South, with all their Bushwhackers and border ruffians, kept the United States from coming together and living in peace. Luke munched on what was left of Adam's biscuit and scanned the newspaper. Sally took a breath.

Before Luke could explain, Sally continued.

"And Luke, I don't understand your boss. First he has you going to Hickory Point yesterday, and then turns right around and sends you the other way to Independence. It's too much for you."

"Hickory Point?" Luke perked up at that. Hadn't he told her Lecompton? Would she find out that Hickory Point was ransacked? Their slaves stolen?

She aimed a spoon at Luke. "That's where you said you were going yesterday." One fisted hand on her hip, Sally glared. "You didn't?"

Damn. If he told her yes, she'd hear about the raid eventually, and put two and two together. She was smart. If he told her no, then he'd have to say Lecompton, and the other freight driver *always* took that delivery.

"Luke?" Sally picked up the baby, now fidgeting.

"Sorry. Not Hickory Point. I went to . . ." *Where the hell did I go?*

Hannah Patience Colton squalled. Her little fists bobbed in the air, her round face turning pink. Sally picked her up, bouncing the baby on her shoulder.

"She needs to be changed and then fed." Sally pointed at the bedroom. "Star and I are going shopping today. Your brother's agreed to babysit. Imagine."

He couldn't. Why in the hell would James agree? Must be a glutton for punishment, as they say. Or maybe it was his way of keeping an eye on things. Watching him. Just like he'd said. Then it hit him. James wasn't babysitting Adam. *He's spying on me, using my son.*

"I gotta go." Luke pushed aside the dish and paper, standing as he ruffled Adam's hair. "Be a good boy for Uncle James today."

Adam gripped Luke's leg, holding on while both made their way to the front door. Luke buttoned his coat and then picked up Adam. "I'll be home tomorrow night."

Sally waved a kiss from the bedroom. "Be safe, Luke. We all love you."

Luke stepped into early-morning cold.

The wagonload of barrels of nails, screws and assorted building material, plus boxes of dried meat, potatoes, flour and canned vegetables, bounced along as Luke bounced, too. At least the movement kept him awake. The day was turning out to be colder than he'd planned; his coat not enough to keep him from shivering. Another couple of hours and he'd be in Independence, unloaded and then bedded down for the night at the Empire Exchange Hotel.

He liked the Empire. A dollar bought a bed, clean sheets, a washstand with fresh water, and for another dollar, the Independence Opera House would supply entertainment of the soft, feminine kind. He'd save his dollar tonight. He had Sally waiting at home.

Morning came much too soon. Luke pulled back the curtain, his view looking straight into another hotel. A man in the room opposite yanked his curtains closed. For a brief instance, Luke thought he recognized the face. But who? He brushed aside conjecture and went downstairs to the restaurant. Their breakfasts were plentiful and inexpensive.

Luke ordered flapjacks, sausage, biscuits, eggs and coffee. Lots of coffee, the blacker, the better. Maybe it would jolt him awake. He hadn't had much sleep the last few nights, and even though he was only twenty years old, he was tired. Bone tired.

The restaurant decor reflected that of the hotel rooms. Clean, neat, orderly. Wallpaper, designs with what Sally called *"floor de lees,"* covered the walls making this room, with ten tables and wooden chairs, somehow homey. Luke glanced at the newspaper he'd picked up. More Jayhawkers killed. This part of Missouri catered to Jayhawkers, so he knew not to gloat too loudly. If he said something, more than likely he'd be run out and over by stampeding horses, and he sure didn't want to die like that.

Attention on the newspaper and mouth full of sausage, Luke jumped at a voice in his ear.

"Howdy, Colton."

Jesse James. The face Luke had seen earlier in the hotel window.

Luke swallowed and then pointed to an empty chair at his table. "Jesse. Good to see you. Have a seat."

Jesse motioned to a waitress, and then sat. He leaned back

after ordering coffee. "What brings you out this way?"

"Business is all. I-I deliver freight for a company in Lawrence." Why was he stuttering around this fifteen-year-old? Maybe because of what he'd heard. Murder, pillage, rape. Luke held his cup between them like a shield. "And you?"

Jesse cocked his head. "Been home takin' care of Ma. She's been poorly and I thought I'd lend a hand." He drained his cup and plopped it on the table. "She's better now, so I'm headin' over to find Frank. You seen him lately? Know where he's at?"

Luke related their last great foray, and where he figured Frank had headed, other than up the stairs with Betsy. Frank hung around Lawrence, but where exactly was anybody's guess. And Luke liked it that way.

As Jesse stood, he glanced side to side, tapped the newspaper, and then lowered his voice. "Be careful 'round here. There's Jayhawkers everywhere." He chuckled, reset his hat and strolled out of the restaurant.

Since Jesse hadn't left any money for coffee, Luke tossed an extra dime onto the table.

Bright sun and brisk air lifted Luke's spirits. However, something about Jesse James set wrong with him, and he struggled to figure out why. The kid had done nothing to earn the feeling. He hadn't tried to kill Luke, or his friends. Hadn't stolen anything that he knew of. Hadn't even run from that burning trading post when the flames got unbearably hot. No, Jesse James didn't deserve Luke's distrust.

As Luke bounced along the road, heading west, his thoughts turned to the barrels secured in the back of his wagon. The Independence store had offered to pay him extra to take these four full flour barrels back to Mister Gibson's business. He shook his head. Hadn't he taken flour *to* the store? Seemed silly to bring some back. He shook his head again. Business. These people made no sense sometimes.

Ahead lay the area where he'd first encountered Quantrill and Jesse James. To his right glinted the wide Missouri River, this time of year more mud than water. Stands of wild cherry bushes hid the view until he crested a low hill.

Bang!

Luke ducked as a bullet whizzed past his ear and splintered the top of the wooden seatback next to him. He slapped the reins over the horses' rumps. They sprinted.

Bang!

The bullet skimmed across one horse's neck, drawing blood. She reared and then galloped, Luke desperate to hang on. Horses and wagon zigzagged crossing the road twice, around another stand of bushes, then headed straight for the river. Before Luke could get them stopped, both horses and he plowed into the water. The wagon overturned after ricocheting off a boulder.

Mud, water, small rocks smashed into Luke's face as he struggled to clear his head. He stood. First things first. He inspected the stock. While one was nicked, the wound wasn't life threatening, which was good, because he sure didn't want to walk all the way back home. But the wagon was a problem. And who was shooting at him? He hadn't seen a sign of anybody. No wagon tracks, no hoofprints, no droppings . . . no nothing.

He pulled his Colt out of his waistband. Dry enough to use.

"Drop it!"

A voice boomed from the riverbank. Luke spun around. Two men stood, shotgun and pistol aimed at Luke's chest. He tossed his gun onto the bank. It *thwucked* into the mud. Arms above his head, Luke struggled to recognize the two. One was considerably shorter than the other, the taller standing not much above the horse's ears, but their weapons more than made up for their lack of stature.

"Get up here where we can see you, boy." The shorter man,

dressed in a narrow-brimmed hat and homespun clothes, waved his pistol at Luke. "Hands out where we can see 'em."

Luke did as told.

The shorter of the two men glared at Luke as he spoke to the other one. "Check 'im for another gun."

Patted down, Luke stood, hands still up, questions raging through his head. He chose silence, instead.

Shorty squinted against the overhead sun. "You Luke Colton?"

Luke frowned.

The bandit nodded. "Thought so." He waved his gun at the wagon. "Get down there. Turn it upright."

How did they know his name? Luke pondered on it until a shotgun barrel pressed into his chest.

"Move, Colton. You got work to do."

Shotgun and pistol aimed at his back, Luke marched down through knee-high water and mud. He put his back against his wagon and pulled up. The horses tugged, wood squeaking and groaning, but the wagon remained stuck sideways in the mud.

"I'll help." The taller man waded into the cold water and mud, and then also backed against the wagon, and the wagon groaned upright.

Luke took a moment to study this man. Early thirties, hadn't shaved in a day or two, pockmarks under the whiskers, bulbous nose, possibly broken a time or two, two beady watery blue eyes, and really bad breath. Luke stepped back when the man spoke, rotten garlic odor roiling from his mouth. Must be a real treat for the ladies.

Before Luke could pull his feet out of the muck, the taller outlaw scrambled into the wagon seat, snapped the reins, and drove the wagon up the riverbank and onto dry land. Luke followed. So far he knew nothing. No names, no reason.

Shorty climbed into the wagon bed and pried off a barrel lid.

Luke stood next to the wagon and shrugged. "Nothing but flour in there. I'm hauling it back to Law—"

"Just what we ordered." He held up a Springfield rifle.

"How many in there, you reckon?" The taller outlaw turned on the wagon seat.

Shorty peered into the other three barrels and then spoke over his shoulder. "All of 'em."

How can a day that started out so right, get all shot to hell? Not only was Luke most likely hauling stolen rifles, but also he'd more than likely have to walk all the way to Lawrence, or worse, back to Independence and tell the grocer Luke had lost his "flour." And it wasn't his fault it got lost. Hell, not lost, stolen.

And why in the hell was he hauling stolen rifles? This wasn't going to be good.

After replacing the lids, Shorty jumped down and then nodded to Luke. "This is your lucky day."

"How's that?" Luke couldn't keep questions contained any longer. He was shivering—cold, scared and now wet.

"Ain't gonna kill ya."

"What?" Taller outlaw blinked at Shorty. "But we agreed—"

"I know, but what I got in mind's better." A cackle erupted from his mustached face. Shorty waggled the pistol at Luke's feet. "Boots. Off. Now." Another cackle. "Socks, too."

Not his boots. And not without a fight. He fisted both hands and then chose to plead before punching, the odds not in his favor. "Look. You got both your horses and now mine. Let me have one." He turned what he hoped was a pathetic look on both men. A lie popped into mind. "Today's my little boy's birthday, and I promised him I'd be home. We're having a party as soon as I get back."

"A birthday party?" Shorty said. "Ain't that nice."

Luke pulled out all the stops. "And my wife's expecting our

next baby any day, and if I'm not home for her time, well—"

"Shoulda kept your parts in your pants. Then you wouldn't have no party to miss." The shotgun hammer clicked. "Boots. Socks. Now."

Luke swung at the shotgun, knocking it away. Fists up, he turned toward Shorty.

Stars flashed.

Blackness swallowed him.

CHAPTER THIRTY-TWO

"Luke? Luke?"

Something nudged his shoulder. A voice in his face.

"You sleepin' or . . . you dead?"

Now it shook him until he forced his eyes open and focused. Within inches loomed a face. Rounded with close-cropped wavy dark-brown hair, worried brown eyes, like coffee. Luke put a name with it. Albert Perkins. From Lawrence. One of his band of "Cutthroats."

Albert's strong grip pulled Luke upright. Sitting on the cold ground, Luke ran his hand through his hair, across his face, and then over his chest. Alive and no holes. However, his feet were numb. No boots, no socks, and now that he looked around, no coat. Hat on the ground.

The part-time accountant straightened, offering a hand up for Luke. "What're you doing here?" He looked right and then left. "I mean, you're out here in the middle of nowhere, without a horse, and . . ." He waved at Luke's feet. "I mean . . . ?"

"Got robbed. Held up and stinkin' robbed." Luke stood, massaging the lump on the back of his head, the goose egg throbbing. "Dammit."

"What'd they steal?" Albert plucked a canteen wrapped around his saddle horn and handed it to Luke.

"Flour barrels."

"Flour?"

"But it wasn't flour."

"It wasn't?" Albert frowned.

Luke drank half of the canteen's contents, then handed it back to Albert. "Guns and rifles. It was guns and rifles in there." Now shivering so hard Luke knew he'd fall apart, he took the liberty of friendship and searched through Albert's saddle and packs.

"Guns. Hum." Albert shook his head, his eyes trailing across the river as if he could see clear to Lawrence. "Anybody else in on that?"

"How the hell should I know?" Luke dug into the right saddlebag and under a can in the bottom, he located a pair of wool socks. He slipped them on, grateful for the little bit of warmth. "Got any more? Like a coat in here?" He pawed deeper but found nothing useful. "And why're you out here in the first place?"

Albert shrugged. "Boss sent me on business. Got a couple accounts over in Independence."

Luke glared over the back of Albert's horse. "You know what really chafes my ass?"

"Losing your boots?"

Luke gave an annoyed shake of his head. "Those damned outlaws knew who I was. That's the scary part. How'd they know me?"

"You know them?"

"Never seen 'em before."

Albert followed Luke's gaze west, toward Lawrence. "Somebody told 'em. They knew you were going this way, gonna be here today." Albert frowned. "How's your head? You're lookin' awful white right now."

Albert was right. Luke's world spun and his stomach rolled. Before he could sit, Luke's legs gave out. He crumpled next to the horse.

An hour's rest and part of Albert's midday meal of cold

173

chicken and cheese brought Luke back to the living. They headed toward Lawrence. Head still pounding, nevertheless, riding behind Albert was a lot easier and warmer than walking the next twenty miles in bare feet.

It was full dark by the time Luke made it home. All he wanted was a hot bath, supper and his own bed, but what greeted him was chaos. Albert Perkins walked him to the door, explained to Sally, her folks and Luke's, how he'd found Luke, detailing his condition then and now. Then Albert vanished.

Ushered into the living room full of parents, brother, three in-laws and two-year-old son, Luke couldn't get in one word. Pushed to the couch, Luke sat and then like magic, a pan of steaming water appeared at his feet. The muddy socks, now encrusted with something reeking of suspect origin, were the first to come off. He tested the water. A dunk of his right foot, then left. Not too hot. Feet now submerged, he closed his eyes, and sighed. Even better than Ernie's.

"I should've gone with you." James handed a cup of hot coffee to Luke. "We could've fought 'em off. Should've gone."

"No." As tired as Luke was, he rushed his words. "No need. It worked out fine." What would James think if he found out there were guns in those barrels? Luke considered. Could it have been Quantrill who intercepted his load? If so, why didn't he tell him? He'd raided, looted and burned like Quantrill had requested.

"Maybe I'd have lost my boots, too." James patted Luke's knee, interrupting his thoughts. He held up one foot and pointed. "I like these. Finally broke in."

Deciding to put the Quantrill question to the back of his mind, Luke sipped the warm liquid, enjoying the sense of relief and safety it brought. All he wanted was for everyone to leave him the hell alone now. But he couldn't bring himself to order his family out. Instead, he kept his eyes closed and ignored the endless conversations assaulting his living room.

The women fussed over him, cackling and squawking like old biddies who'd just found a wounded, stray chick. The men offered a word or two, but mostly exchanged looks. Only Adam crawled up into Luke's lap and snuggled against his chest, the blanket around Luke's shoulders now encompassing Adam as well.

Within a half hour, Adam was asleep, Hannah lay in the cradle cooing; parents, James, Morningstar and in-laws on their way home. The house grew quiet and dark.

Sally stepped out from the bedroom doorway, her billowing nightgown reminding Luke of drawings he'd seen of ghosts. Pale, long arms, big eyes. Cold. But not Sally. She was always warm. Just not tonight. Tonight he was going to sleep. Sally smiled at him.

"Glad you're back safe. Your nightclothes are laid out."

A nod. If he didn't get off the couch right now, he'd wake up there tomorrow.

CHAPTER THIRTY-THREE

A light knock at the door. Luke's eyes flew open as he rolled toward the sound. Wrapped like a mummy in blankets, Luke flopped off the couch and thudded to the floor.

Another knock.

Sally peered out from the kitchen, mixing bowl in hand. "Who can that be at this hour?"

Luke blinked, struggling to make sense of his world. Sally opened the front door, allowing a blast of cold air and Luke's boss, Elmore Gibson, into the house. Luke wiggled out of the blankets, still caught around his ankles like a fish in a net.

Sally nodded to the visitor. "Please come in. This is a surprise. Would you like coffee?"

"Thanks, I would," Mister Gibson said. "If it's not too much bother."

Sally returned with cups for Luke and his boss, now seated in the rocking chair opposite the couch. Luke pushed blankets aside and fixed his attention on Mister Gibson.

"Since you didn't get back with the rig last night, Luke, thought I'd come over and drive it back myself." Mister Gibson sipped, then shifted in his chair. "You got the goods delivered to Independence?"

How much should he tell his boss and how much should he keep quiet? Exactly who was this man, anyway? More'n likely a Jayhawker. Scum. "Yes, sir. Got it all to Watkins Mercantile, like you asked."

"When you didn't get back yesterday evening, I figured something'd happened." Gibson sipped again, but his green eyes stared at Luke's face. "But this ain't the first time you've been late."

"Ran into some trouble on the way back." Luke massaged the knot on his head. "Got held up, I'm afraid. Took the horses and wagon *and* my clothes." Memories fisted in his chest. "I could've died if Albert Perkins hadn't come along when he did."

"Held up, huh? By who?" A long sigh escaped from Gibson. He looked like he'd just lost his best friend, his turned-down mouth and caterpillar mustache accentuating the downward curve. His shoulders sagged.

"Don't know." Luke chose not to reveal he knew about the guns, unless Gibson asked.

Gibson drained his cup, set it on the coffee table, and then stood, buttoning his coat. "Sometimes Mister Watkins sends supplies back to me." His eyebrows raised. "He give you anything to bring back?"

Lying came easy to Luke. He pursed his lips and shook his head as if deep in thought. "Just the flour barrels like you told me. I tucked the bill of sale in my coat pocket, and *that* was stolen."

Gibson frowned. He opened the door, then turned back and hollered toward the kitchen. "Thanks for the coffee, Missus Colton." Eyes on Luke. "I need you in the office right away."

Before Luke could nod, the door closed and Mister Gibson was gone.

Following breakfast and with body aching in places that hadn't hurt before, Luke headed downtown for a soak at Ernie's before going into work. Whatever Mister Gibson had to say could wait another hour. Luke certainly couldn't think straight at home with Adam climbing all over him and the baby crying.

Warm water and a good cigar called.

Getting out of the tub proved hard. Muscles hurt, a couple bruises were sore, and his face, scraped in several places, was tender. Today, he decided, he'd skip shaving, giving his mustache some company. On second thought, maybe he'd quit shaving altogether. Grow a beard.

Luke nodded at Gibson's secretary, an older widow with two grown daughters. He'd gone to school with the younger one and lusted after the older. She would have nothing to do with a boy three years her junior, a declaration she made clear every time Luke came within spitting range. Luke had courted the one his age but soon learned her sister's influence had rubbed off. Both girls hated him.

But Missus Emmaline Delmartin was polite and rather handsome, in an old way. Luke took little notice of her other than to say good morning and to pick up his pay from her.

Luke rapped on the frame of Gibson's open door and then walked in when his boss looked up from his desk.

"Close the door, Colton."

This was not boding well. That familiar fist grew in Luke's chest as he sat.

Gibson played with the pencil in his hand, Luke following the movement until it made him dizzy. His head still hurt from whatever hit him yesterday.

After a deep breath, Mister Gibson pointed the pencil at Luke. "Mister Watkins would've sent me something. You said he didn't, I know he did." He tossed the pencil onto a note partially written. "What was it?"

Caught. Luke sat up straight praying his poker face was in place. "There was nothing else, Mister Gibson. Nothing. Just empty flour barrels."

"Then tell me why somebody would steal my wagon and horses. They're not worth much." Gibson's black-and-gray mustache covered his top lip, and his mouth appeared as if half was gone. Shorter than Luke by a bit, Gibson outweighed him by a paunchy stomach. Gibson's black hair was striped with gray and his dark-brown eyes were accented with lines running out from them. Luke didn't know how old his boss was, but he guessed early fifties if wrinkles were an indication.

Luke shrugged. "Guess they needed a wagon. Or the barrels. They didn't say why."

Gibson stood, marched to the wall and spoke to the papers tacked on the bulletin board. He tapped at line after line. "You were late for this delivery, Mister Colton." He lifted the paper revealing several more. "And for this one. Says here they never received the goods on this one. Had to send out my other driver."

On his feet now, Luke walked toward his boss, deciding to stay a few feet away in case he decided to finish this with his fists. He peered over Gibson's shoulder. "Keep getting waylaid, Mister Gibson. This is a time of war, you know."

Gibson spun around, fire flashing from his eyes. "What the hell you know about war? You know what I think?"

Despite misgivings, Luke had to know. "What?"

"I think next time you fail to deliver . . . on time . . . you'll be looking for a new job, that's what I think. And I also think you better dig down deep in the back of your muddled memory and decide, once and for all, if you were bringing back something for me yesterday." Gibson stepped closer. "It better be the truth."

CHAPTER THIRTY-FOUR

Luke eyed the clouds boiling in the southern sky. The long trip to Independence yesterday had been uneventful—weather-wise and outlaw-wise. Nothing of any consequence had delayed his travels. Now as he gazed upward, a chill ran down his back. Something didn't feel right. Something about the air. Thick. Nothing moved. He'd passed only a few other freight wagons on this trip home today. One man on horseback galloping the other way, back toward Missouri, had waved a greeting but continued without as much as slowing.

Which was fine with Luke. His one goal today was to get into Lawrence by nightfall. And in one piece, preferably. No walking today. If he spotted two men riding toward him, he'd shoot first, ask later. Nobody was going to hold him up today. He had things to do.

A half turn on the hard seat and he counted the barrels and boxes behind him for the fourth time this morning. However, Mister Watkins from the mercantile in Independence had assured him that the flour and sugar barrels, the boxes of saws, were fine. He and Luke tied them securely, but still . . . would they bounce out? If a barrel top came loose, he'd have a white cloud behind him. What was really in those barrels? Flour, sugar? Luke doubted it since last time it'd been rifles, but he had gone ahead and signed the bill of lading. Skipping breakfast, Luke lit out for Lawrence. His stomach grumbling told him he should've eaten.

Gonna get home with time to spare, he thought. Tired of this trip and tired of this road. Another survey of the sky. Those clouds had a funny green tint. Wind. The wind kicked up as the thoughts connected. Tornado. More than likely he was in its path. No. Not now. Not today.

Up ahead on his right held the promise of a ravine. While it wasn't deep, it was the best he could hope for. He snapped the reins over the horses' backs and took dead aim for it. The wagon bumped, almost knocking him off the seat as he rushed down the embankment. The incline was steeper than anticipated, and the cargo slid from end to end. Nothing he could do now. Getting somewhere safe was priority. He'd worry about the contents later.

The horses seemed to sense impending disaster as well. They pulled together and then stopped easily. Wagon and horses snugged against the chasm's side, Luke jumped off the seat and gripped the reins up near their muzzles. Maybe they wouldn't bolt, leaving him stranded—again.

Wind swirled. Hard to stay on his feet. Luke pulled his hat down tight, turned his back against the wind. Eyes closed tight, he squeezed his body in between his horses, and then mumbled the only prayer he knew—the one Ma had taught him, the same Sally says with Adam.

Fierce, howling winds tugged and pulled. The horses pawed the dirt, shifting their weight from side to side, but somehow stayed upright. Thunder rumbled then pea-sized hail pelted him. Luke turned his face into one of the horses' sides, hoping to shield himself from bruises or broken cheekbones. Small hail chunks grew into balls of hard ice. Sleet slammed him, burning his head and back, his legs.

Yet through it all, his horses stood.

A roar, then the hail let up, as did the wind. Luke chanced a look over the horse's back, and what he saw chilled him even more. A funnel bounced along the ground, away from him, churning up plants and dirt, scattering debris.

Shaking, Luke leaned again against the horse. Damn, that had been close. He'd missed the brunt of the tornado by mere yards. What would've happened if that thing had come directly overhead? He didn't want to think about it. Instead he turned his attention to his animals. A close inspection revealed they'd also come out unscathed.

I must be living right, Luke thought.

Although his legs were rubbery, he walked, leading the animals away from the ravine wall, which towered a mere three feet over their heads, and up onto the road. Patting their necks, he spoke softly to each one. They appeared to be calm enough to continue the trip. He ran a mental inventory over his body. Yep, he was ready as well.

He climbed into the wagon, sat down, picked up the reins, and from out of the corner of his eye, he spotted something small and gray bolt from bush to bush, zigzagging like something was chasing it. A rabbit. Big jackrabbit running for his life, no doubt. Before Luke flicked the reins, both horses reared and took off, galloping as if they'd been poked. Hanging on, Luke slid from side to side, feet braced against the foot rail. He yanked back on the reins until he knew the bits in the horses' mouths would cut them in two.

Still they ran.

A stand of wild cherry bushes loomed ahead, then another ravine. Should he jump off and let the horses run where they wanted? They were going to, anyway. But at least he wouldn't crash with them. Before he decided, the wagon fishtailed, wiggling like worms on hooks.

Yanking, tugging, pleading, cursing did nothing to stop the runaway horses.

All right. I'll jump, he thought. He released the reins and just as he did the wagon overturned, taking him with it. Luke flew off the wagon seat, hit the ground and rolled. Dirt filled his mouth as he tumbled down the embankment and crashed into a boulder.

Luke lay still, draped around the rock. A few blinks, breaths pulled in, then he unwrapped himself. Nothing seemed to be broken. The bottom of the ravine was a ten-foot drop, above was another ten. Certainly easier going down than up, Luke scooted to the bottom, creating a small dirt avalanche under his rear.

Feet now on level dirt, he squinted up at the top. "Dammit to hell! What'd I ever do?"

Although sore and achy from head to toe, he kicked at dirt clods. "No good, lousy horses. No good, stinkin' lousy tornado. No good, stinkin' lousy—"

"I'll be go to hell. Luke Colton, again."

Spinning, Luke frowned up at the top and spotted a man, shotgun aimed at Luke's chest.

There was nowhere to run, nowhere to hide. Nowhere safe. Instead of running, which he wanted to do, he raised his hands.

"You climb on up outta that big ol' ditch, Mister Colton," said the man. He waved the shotgun. "Take it fast, but easy, and you'll live to walk back home."

Luke glared up at the outlaw.

"Just like last time." The bandit let out a laugh, sounding more like a mule braying than a man. He grew serious. "Now come on up and be quick."

Curse words flashed through Luke's head as he scrambled up the dirt side of the ravine. Twice he slid back, but with pure determination, he managed to reach the top, then knelt on the dirt. To his right, the overturned wagon lay on its side, the undercarriage toward him.

The team remained attached, but they managed to stay calm,

waiting for someone to right the wagon.

From the team, his gaze traveled to his left. Scattered like toothpicks lay wood parts. The barrels and boxes, splintered like matchsticks, dotted the landscape. Moans and hints of conversation sailed in the air.

People. Negro people stood around the wagon, mostly hiding behind it, a few clutching the side as if it would protect them. A quick count revealed seven—a couple women, a few children, the rest men. Had they been hiding in those boxes and barrels? Questions bombarded his head. His world turned sideways.

Before he began to make any sense of the situation, someone jammed a pistol into Luke's temple. "Say or do anything, Mister Colton, and you're a dead man."

Something about the man's stench brought back memories. A sneaked peek at the man at his side, and Luke recognized him. Nodding, Luke knew to stay still and quiet, but his mouth wouldn't cooperate.

"Who're these people? They with you?" He squinted against the afternoon sun.

"Told you to shut up." The stinky outlaw pulled the hammer back. Metal scraping against metal in Luke's ear. He closed his eyes, knowing the man would shoot. Boots scruffing through the dirt came up behind him.

"Them darkies," the man behind Luke said. "They're with you, Mister Colton."

"Correction. They were," Stinky Outlaw said. "Now, they're with us. Stolen right out from under your nose." He raised an eyebrow at Shorty. "Quantrill's gonna promote us for sure now."

"Quantrill?" Luke swung his gaze from outlaw to outlaw. None of this made any sense. Had he hit his head and was dreaming? Had to be. "You ride with Quantrill?"

Shorty sneered. "Yeah. He sent us."

"Quantrill?" Why'd his leader do this? Was he double-crossing him?

"You heard me the first time. And you best be scared, Luke Colton. 'Cause nothing stops Quantrill."

Should Luke mention that he rides for him, too? What would that buy him?

Rotten Breath spoke to Shorty. "Get a couple of them coloreds to right that wagon. Then load 'em in." He bent closer to Luke. "You know the routine. Boots and socks off. Now. Haven't got all day."

Still confused, but a glimmer of reality setting in, Luke tugged at his right boot. "Those darkies hid in my wagon?"

The man glared at Luke. "What the hell you think you been haulin'? Potatoes?" He huffed. "Moron. Got sawdust for brains. No wonder Gibson has you haul for him. Too stupid to do anything but drive."

The wagon crashed back onto its wheels, dust flying in all directions. Once it stopped moving, without saying a word, the seven black folks scrambled up into the wagon, their heads hung down. Like they were whipped. Beaten. Like they had no hope.

Luke looked long at the procession. Runaways from the law. They should be returned to their rightful owners. Luke considered. If somebody stole your horse, you'd want it back, wouldn't you? You'd go after the man who stole it, wouldn't you? Stealing people's no different. Property is property.

"What're you gonna do with them?" Luke hesitated pulling off his boot. This was his last pair and he hated the thought of breaking in new ones. Maybe someone would come along and scare off these bandits. He peered into the distance. Nobody either way.

The pistol-wielding outlaw walked over to Luke and the other bandit. "Ready, Luther? I'll drive the wagon while you ride behind. That way you can shoot 'em if they try anything."

"Fine. Be right there."

Luke envisioned a long walk home. Maybe he could reason with them. "Look, just take the cargo, leave me my boots and I won't say a word to Mister Gibson. All right?"

Dark eyes trained on Luke, the outlaw Luther cocked his head. "Didn't know you had coloreds in those barrels, did you?"

Luke wagged his head. "Guns."

"Them blacks fold up nice and tight. They hunker down good for the long ride." Luther raised both eyebrows. "Gave 'em quite the ride you did. Twice. And that ol' tornado come at just the right time, I'm thinking."

Despite Luke's pledge to keep quiet, his mouth disagreed. "How's that?"

Luther's gaze swung from the people settling themselves in the wagon to Luke. "We was gonna just plain shoot you off the wagon, kill you most likely. Even had you in my sights. But that twister swooped down, wind knocked me and my partner off our horses."

Shorty spoke over his shoulder, his attention and gun riveted on the slaves. "By the time you got yourself back up, Mister Colton, gave us enough time to catch up. Easy."

Scratching his whiskery cheek, Luther cocked his head. "Maybe in the future we can do business." He gestured toward Luke's feet. "I wouldn't have to take them boots no more. See, me and my partner know when slaves are moving."

Luke knew he had nothing to lose. "How's that? How d'you know?"

"Feelin' generous today, so I'll tell ya." Luther chuckled. "You know Missus Delmartin. Works for your boss, Gibson?"

Luke nodded.

"That's my sister. She tells me when and what moves." Luther let out an onion-laced laugh. "Yeah, comes in real handy. We intercept the cargo and sell 'em back to their owners. Make a nice, tidy little sum, we do. Cut her in ten percent."

"Missus Delmartin?" Luke looked from Shorty to Luther to the slaves and then back to Luther.

Luther grabbed Luke's shirtfront and pulled him within inches. His words turned icy. "You ever tell anybody, Colton. And I'll have your head in one of those barrels." He let go. "Got it?"

Luke got it. He couldn't nod fast enough.

Luther glanced toward the wagon. "I bet you do. I know where your pa lives."

It all came crashing down around Luke's ears. These were runaway slaves headed for his pa's barn until somebody came to fetch them for the next part of their journey. It made sense. But these slaves would never make it to Pa's barn. They were more'n likely headed back home.

Luke had to ask. "Last time you waylaid me. Were there people in those barrels, too? Along with the guns?"

A long guffaw startled the horses. "You ain't near as smart as you appear, boy." Luther reached down and rocked Luke's shoulder. "Yeah, they was. Made us a small fortune, too. Oh, and Quantrill says to say 'thanks'."

The other bandit hollered from the wagon. "Gotta go, Luther."

Luther waved the gun at Luke's feet. "Now, them boots." He dropped his voice. "Off."

"But—"

"Off, or you'll have a bullet through your leg. Maybe your heart." Luther chuckled. "I ain't a real good shot—but this close, I guarantee I hit what I'm aimin' for."

Luke sat hard and pulled off his boots and his socks. Would they leave him his hat at least?

Luther stuffed the socks into the boots and then tossed them into the back of the wagon, hitting a woman in the arm. She said nothing and arranged them in the wagon.

Would Luke try to save his wagon and horses? Or would he sit in the dirt and let them ride away? He had no hat, no gun, no boots, no nothing to protect himself with. Once again, the robbers held all the cards.

He struggled up to his feet as they rode away, due south. Shading his eyes, he took a step west, toward home, and hoped someone would come along.

CHAPTER THIRTY-FIVE

"Stinkin' robbers." Luke hopped on one foot, brushing pebbles off the bottom of the one he held up. "Stinkin', no good, lousy, thieving outlaws." He set it down. "No good, rotten—ow!"

Luke jerked his foot off the ground and inspected the sole. A thorn stuck out of the bottom, right between his big toe and the one next to it. "Damn, no-good, rotten son of a—" He yanked the barb out as he balanced on one foot. Both feet on the ground, he muttered every oath and curse word he knew, maybe even some he didn't.

"Damn Quantrill." He jerked with another step. "Damn Negroes."

Something rumbled behind him. The sound was familiar, but far off. He turned, peering east, shadows growing long in the late-afternoon summer sun. Squinting, and with a tilt of his head, he could make out a wagon. Coming his way.

Life wasn't so bleak after all. He waited for the wagon and the team to come into full view before waving at it.

By the time the wagon had reached him, Luke had considered what he would say to Mister Gibson. "I quit" came to mind, but he knew that wasn't it. No, he couldn't quit and he couldn't confess that he knew about the runaways. Gibson had friends in high places. Jayhawker friends. They sure as hell wouldn't take kindly to someone who allowed their rescued slaves to be stolen. Sold back into slavery. They'd strike back and maybe even harm his family.

And he especially couldn't say anything about Missus Del-martin. Especially her. He didn't want his head in a barrel, and he couldn't prove anything. And judging by the looks on the robbers' faces, they took their threat seriously.

Even for as long as he'd walked today, pondering the situa-tion, he wasn't sure how to handle the information. Hell, maybe he'd talk to James about it.

The wagon slowed, then stopped. Luke explained his predica-ment and without questions, they nodded to Luke and waited for him to wedge in between boxes in the wagon bed. Sitting. Luke rubbed his feet as they bounced along.

The trip proved uneventful. Both drivers had been pleasant enough, although neither forthcoming with much information. Luke didn't blame them. These days, it was best not to volunteer information, no telling who was on whose side.

Full dark had come upon them by the time Luke spotted the welcoming lights of Lawrence. A farm or two they passed still had the kerosene lantern glowing in the barn. Dropped at home, Luke offered coffee to the men since he had no cash. They both waved him off and continued toward a livery stable.

The next morning, Luke woke to the sound of bacon sizzling and the smell of coffee boiling. He followed his nose into the kitchen. Other than his bruised and battered feet, the rest of his body wasn't too sore. Tired, he was bone tired, but otherwise in good shape.

Sally greeted him with a wide smile and a hug, despite the fork in one hand. "Is Mister Gibson buying you a new pair of boots? We shouldn't have to pay for them."

Luke couldn't help but smile. She was pretty with righteous indignation pinking her cheeks. Too bad both children were up and she was busy cooking. He was tired, but not that tired.

A long kiss would have to do for now. Luke smiled again. As

usual, her blue eyes melted his heart.

"Luke? Did you hear me?"

Frowning, he thought he'd been paying attention, but thinking back, his mind had wandered a bit toward the bedroom. He pulled his focus forward and shrugged.

Sally sighed and forked the bacon over, the slice wriggling on the hot skillet. "I said your brother's coming over pretty soon." She poured Luke a steaming cup of coffee. "And Morningstar and I are going shopping today. Your ma's gonna watch the children. Then . . . we're all meeting over at my folks' house for supper. Won't that be fun?"

Luke's first definition of fun right then did not involve anybody except him and Sally. But his second definition was family suppers. He did enjoy those—mostly. Except when Reverend Burroughs was sermonizing or when his own pa, and now James, ranted about the evils of slavery. Usually, though, the women kept the men in check and the evening was fun.

CHAPTER THIRTY-SIX

James and Luke sat on hay bales in the barn, Luke puffing a cigar and James nursing a flask. Not much had been said that held any depth or meaning, mainly weather-related conversation, cursory brother information, livestock reports, but nothing of substance. Luke felt it coming, though.

Watching the smoke curl from his mouth and up toward the rafters, Luke slid his eyes sideways toward James. Words shot out along with the smoke. "Don't get me wrong. I'm glad you're here." He looked at James. "But, you never did tell me. You staying?"

James threw back a long swig from the flask, then stood and ambled toward the door. He peered out. Luke frowned at his brother's back, waiting for his answer.

Another drink, then James spoke, more to his boots and the inside of the barn than to Luke. "Don't know. Nowhere else to go." He shook his head. "Had to leave Mesilla. Court order. Didn't want to go to Tucson. Been there."

"Tucson's where Morningstar's from, right?" Luke stared at the tip of his cigar. It was better than staring at his brother. He hated the uneasy feeling creeping over him.

"Right. Tucson. But I wanted her to meet Ma and Pa, and of course, you and Sally."

"And?" Luke wasn't sure how he'd react if James said they would stay. Ma would be thrilled and Sally and Morningstar had already become friends. But he wasn't sure he wanted James in his business all the time. Dealing with Pa and Reverend Burroughs was tough enough, but he didn't need an older brother watching his every move. And he would.

James shrugged. "I don't know. Maybe. Don't have any plans right now." He shook his head. "No, that's not true. I plan to visit Grandpa, have a long talk with him. Maybe he'll help me figure out what the hell I'm doing wrong."

"Want me to go with you?" Luke remembered the day Grandpa's heart gave out. James' eighteenth birthday. The day James knelt outside by the woodpile, cradling Grandpa, rocking him. Luke knew he'd never forget his brother's tears.

And three and a half years later, James still wasn't the same brother. Luke had noticed the change, had seen it from the beginning. James hadn't pulled himself together.

Luke looked up at the flask tapping his shoulder. A drink would be welcomed right about now. He finished it off.

James tucked the silver container into a vest pocket. "No, you don't need to go with me to talk to Grandpa. I can do this alone."

Luke understood. He knew there were things James would say at Grandpa's grave that he wouldn't tell anybody else. He'd done it himself.

Looking down at his own feet squeezed into a pair of his pa's boots, Luke pushed up off the hay bale. "I gotta go into town, get something that fits. Wanna go?"

"Only if you'll let me buy you dinner. And maybe a drink."

A smile stretched Luke's cheeks. Damn, it was good having James home.

Chapter Thirty-Seven

Luke wriggled his toes in his new boots. Tight. Too damn tight. But they'd stretch to fit his feet. Right and left foot would form and then they'd fit. And they were better quality than the ones he'd lost. And he could wait. While he regretted losing that last pair—his feet were still sore—they'd been formed wrong. Shoddy workmanship, someone else had complained. They had been cheap, running just over two dollars. But Mister Dorwart, a professional bootmaker, had made these shiny black ones. Expensive, they'd cost Luke eleven dollars, but this pair would last—if he could get them broken in, and not stolen.

Luke and James sauntered down Massachusetts Avenue, tipping their hats to the ladies and eyeing the men as if they might be the enemy. Luke limped then stopped. Maybe the boots weren't going to work after all.

James pointed toward a building two doors up the street. "There's a place. You've eaten there before?"

The Palace Restaurant and Saloon. Yeah, Luke had had more than dinner in there. He nodded. "Let's go see what their special is."

The brothers stepped in. Cooking smells wafted under their noses, twirled around their heads until Luke thought he'd gnaw on a chair if he didn't get real food soon. Ten tables, four or five with people, filled the place. Wallpaper, decorated with white lines, looked cheery.

After ordering and then waiting for their food, James sipped a beer while Luke tilted his chair back, his own beer left untouched on the table. James wiped the suds from his lips then turned to Luke.

"I'm sorry about the other day. I didn't mean to sound like I'm watching every move you make. Spying on you. Hell, Luke. We're family. I'll always back your play. You know that, right?"

Part of Luke's shield melted. He believed his brother. Luke nodded, a thin smile sliding up one side of his face.

A couple of sips of beer, then James turned his gaze on Luke. "Don't mean to pry, but . . . aren't you supposed to be at work today? I mean, I thought Sally said—"

"I gotta go in sometime today. After losing the wagon and the cargo, Mister Gibson sent word early this morning I'm supposed to come in later today. 'Later' meaning after buying boots and eating some grub."

"Maybe he's got another big haul for you." James sipped his beer and spoke over a foam mustache. "Maybe I could go along with you. You know, I can drive, too."

Luke hesitated. While the idea intrigued him, he wasn't sure he wanted James interfering. If he proved more reliable than Luke, chances were Mister Gibson would fire Luke and hire James. What would Sally say? And what if James found out about the slaves? He'd tell Pa and Sally and then there'd be a huge row at home. Pa would confront Luke, blame him for losing the slaves.

Or maybe they'd be glad thinking he was aiding the freed Negroes . . .

"Didn't mean to get personal, Luke," James said. "Just thought I'd ride along. But if you don't want me—"

"Sure, big brother. You can come." Luke shrugged. "Come watch me work."

What the hell had just happened? Why did he agree? What was he thinking? Before Luke could retract anything, two plates heaped with sliced beef, mashed potatoes and fresh turnips appeared before them.

James dug in while Luke played with the potatoes.

Over a mouthful of dinner, James held a fork out at Luke. "Look, you don't want me to go. It's written all over your face along with the sarcasm in your voice."

He might as well come clean. "It's not that I don't want you . . ."

Luke's attention snapped at the sight of two men walking through the doors. Albert Perkins and Smitty Jenkins. Perkins, Luke saw around town on a regular basis, but Smitty had been absent since their foray into Prairie Grove, Arkansas, last winter. They'd ridden back together but that had been six, seven months ago. It was good seeing Smitty again.

Standing, Luke waved his friends over. After shaking hands with both, he introduced them to James.

"You wanna join us for dinner, gentlemen?" James pointed to two empty seats. "I'm sure Luke would enjoy your company. He's probably already tired of mine."

Perkins nodded. "We'll sit for a spell." He turned to Luke. "We're meeting the Iversons. Got some . . . uh . . . business to take care of."

Albert and Smitty pulled out the chairs and sat. Awkward silence shrouded the table. Luke wanted to find out what they were doing and why he hadn't been included, yet couldn't say anything in front of James.

Small talk and pleasantries were bantered back and forth until the Iverson brothers strode in. Gunnar, in the lead, spotted Luke right off. They nodded to each other. Tobias Iverson closed the door, took his hat off and ran a hand through his blond hair, then pulled the hat down tight.

Both men ambled over. Luke stood, shaking hands with his friends, and then introduced James to them. Luke pointed to the remaining empty chairs. "Join us?" But how to get James out of the way? If he asked him to leave, that would be rude. If they all went to another table, that would be rude, too.

Luke wanted to know, needed to know, what was going on.

Gunnar Iverson nodded to Smitty and Albert. "Got some boring business needs discussing, fellas. You wanna meet us over there?" He pointed to his right. "James, don't mean ta ignore you. I'd really like to be sittin' down and talkin' with you. But . . . well, you know how business goes."

"I do." James nodded. "When you're done, join us again."

Albert Perkins stood. "We'll do that. They got good pie here."

Problem solved, thought Luke. Except he was excluded. And it appeared they'd intended to leave him out.

As he and James ate, attempts at small talk proved useless. Luke sawed at his meat like he was cutting down an oak. Fleeting glances over his shoulder, then longer looks did nothing for his appetite. A touch on his arm jerked him back to the table.

"Go on over to your friends," James said. "Join them. I'll pay the check then wander down the street. Meet you later."

He knew he should object, but damn, Luke wanted to know what was going on. "If you don't mind."

James folded his napkin. His plate was clean, Luke's almost untouched.

"Go." James stood and fished coins out of his vest pocket.

Luke pulled up a chair between Gunnar and Tobias Iverson. He watched James close the door behind him and then Luke held one palm face up. "What's going on? Why didn't I know about this?"

Albert and Smitty exchanged glances, Tobias shrugged, but Gunnar lowered his voice. "Don't know how to say this, Luke."

"Then say it plain." A knot fisted in Luke's chest. "What's going on?"

"More guns going out tonight." Gunnar glanced at Luke over

his raised beer mug.

"I can freight out first thing in the morning." Luke studied Albert Perkins whose beady eyes narrowed, if that was possible.

Perkins held up a hand. "The suppliers don't want you moving anything, Luke. They're of the mind that . . . that—"

"That what?" Luke's deep voice lowered to a whisper. "What're they a mind of?"

Smitty pulled his shoulders back. "You've gone guerilla. Work both sides. You can't be trusted."

"What?" Luke pushed his chair back. "What the hell?"

Gunnar shrugged at Luke. "I know. But they're thinking you've gone into business for yourself. They're sayin' that you report those holdups, but you're letting those slaves go free."

"What?" Luke looked from man to man.

"And," Gunnar continued. "They're saying you're selling the rifles and guns you claim got stolen. Then pocketing the money."

"Well, Gawd dammit to hell!" Luke then realized the entire restaurant had stopped to stare at him and his friends. He didn't need that kind of attention. He fumed at the diners as if they'd all been listening in on a personal conversation. "Sorry."

Patrons mumbled, frowned then turned back to their meals. Luke looked from Albert's round face, to Smitty's tight mouth, to Gunnar's blue eyes. Luke's gaze settled on Tobias, the kid who reminded him of Andy. Who told about the weapons in the barrels? He hadn't said a word to the Iversons or Smitty. He eyed Albert Perkins. Of course. He'd happened to have conveniently come along after Luke had been robbed the first time. Perkins had asked all sorts of questions.

Luke turned to face Albert and dropped his voice. "It was you. You were the one lied about me. You're the one, Albert. Nobody else knew what was going on." Luke's words grew louder. "Thought we were friends. Partners. Well . . . you backstabbin' son of a—"

"You can't accuse me of anything, Colton." Albert's hand hovered over his holstered gun.

"What're you two arguing about?" Smitty held up both hands. "Who knew what? Calm down or take it outside."

Luke stood quickly and his chair scooted out behind him. "What do you think, Tobe? You think I've turned? I'm a traitor? You've been damn quiet this whole time. What d'you think?"

Tobias played with the tines of his fork. "Known you a long time, Luke. Don't believe you'd do something like that. But . . ."

"But what?" Luke would either march out of the restaurant or stay and plot another gunrunning mission. It hung on Tobias' answer.

A shrug. Tobias ran his hand across his mouth as if knowing the fate of the universe depended on his answer. His blue eyes trailed across Luke's face then rested somewhere behind him. "I guess I think you're still with us, but I'm not sure."

That was it. Luke knew the rest of them felt the same way. "You're all wrong. I'm no traitor." He snorted. "Looks like our business ventures together, gentlemen, are over." He wagged his head. "And I thought we were all friends. Proves how wrong a man can be."

The four former Cutthroats sat, watching Luke. No one moved or tried to convince him to stay. Or offer an apology.

Luke eyed each man. "The hell with all of you."

Heart thundering, mouth dry, Luke fought the urge to punch the nearest man. Instead, he turned and marched through the restaurant, yanked open the door, and stepped into another life.

Damn them, anyway. Who needs 'em? Hell, he could do better on his own. Hell, *would* do better on his own. His own with Quantrill. He tramped down Massachusetts half searching for James. When he found him, would he share the good news? He knew his poker face needed work, and James knew him well enough to spot trouble.

Either way, he'd plan another lie to tell his older brother.

CHAPTER THIRTY-EIGHT

The last time Luke stood like this was in school, when the teacher had called him up to her desk. There he had stood, hands clenched behind his back. She had accused him of not completing his work, not turning in his homework, not participating in class. He'd watched her mouth flap, words spurting forth like angry bees. Most of what she said he'd heard before. But he hated that tone—the frustration, anger, disappointment—resonating in her voice.

And here he was now, hands behind his back, standing in front of Mister Gibson's desk, listening to him, that same "teacher" tone in his voice. But instead of threatening to tell his ma and pa, Mister Gibson threatened to fire Luke.

"I've given you every chance, more than I should have. Every chance." Sitting behind his desk, Gibson jerked a pencil at Luke's face. "You were supposed to come in yesterday for another assignment. You don't show up. You need a damn good reason."

Luke wasn't about to explain that by the time the Capital Saloon's bartender threw him and James out, it was dark and they were late for supper. Real late. The glares and huffs from the women, the narrowed eyes from Pa, the cold shoulder from Reverend Burroughs were almost worse than this headache. Almost.

Gibson continued. "Nothing to say for yourself." He sniffed. "You take extra days getting back. You don't finish what you've started. Hell, Luke, you've lost three of my wagons and three teams of horses." He held up three fingers. "One supposedly stolen by Indians. Two more by border ruffians. Stolen right out from under your nose. Literally. That alone cost more than two months of your wages. More than you're worth."

That hurt. He'd been doing what he should, maybe not putting his best effort into his job, but he'd come close to losing his life. Three times. Being compared to wagons and horses hurt.

Gibson sat up straighter. "And worst of all, you don't seem to care. If I heard concern in your voice, real, honest regret for losing my merchandise, then maybe I'd be apt to keep you on here." He waved the pencil toward the closed door. "I know your politics lean toward pro-slavery, I know that. I'd like to think your poor judgment in political issues hasn't affected the performance of your duties. But I'd be wrong."

He could take only so much. Luke unclasped his hands and placed them on Mister Gibson's desk. He moved in closer. "Sir? What're you accusing me of? Exactly."

Gibson tossed the pencil to the desk, then pushed his chair back and stood. His voice dropped to a deadly whisper. "I'm accusing you of stealing my goods. My wagonload of merchandise. I think you sold them to the highest bidder."

Steal? Like a common thief? Luke was many things, but a thief he was not. He reeled back. "I don't steal, Mister Gibson. Maybe I'm a little late with the wagon sometimes, but I don't take other people's property and then sell it." He paused and pulled in a lungful of air. "I don't cram somebody into a barrel for days. Hell, I wouldn't do that. Damages the merchandise. I wouldn't even treat dogs like that!"

"Get out." Gibson marched from behind his desk and pointed to the closed door. "Get out. I won't have you judging me. You've collected your last pay from me."

"I know about the guns you've been smuggling," Luke said.

"I know people who'd want to know that."

"You don't know nothing." Gibson's face reddened.

"Quantrill's gonna be mighty interested in your activities, Mister Gibson."

"Don't threaten me. And the hell with him. He's nothing but a killer with a gang of thugs." Gibson poked Luke's chest. "Just let him try something around here. He'll get what's comin'."

Luke's hands fisted.

Gibson's finger drilled into Luke's chest pushing him back a couple steps. Gibson lowered his voice, the deadly growl leaving no doubt. "Get out."

"Fine." Luke's head pounded, his hands fisted again then relaxed. Punching his boss wasn't the answer. Probably even land him in jail. But the impact, his fist on Gibson's jaw, would be mighty satisfying. Instead, he'd have to settle for slamming the door.

Which he did with gusto.

CHAPTER THIRTY-NINE

James needed directions to Grandpa's grave at the Oread Cemetery. Things had changed in the three years since he'd last visited. Houses and orchards grew where only prairie and rolling hills had been. On foot, James headed east, crossing busy Massachusetts Avenue, then out on Fifteenth Street. Rolling prairie, which he loved, shimmered in this morning's warmth. It would get hot today, but he planned to be back at the house by noon, then help Ma with inside chores. Or maybe he'd visit his brother.

If this headache would just let up, he would enjoy the walk more. Fresh air seemed like a good idea at the time, but now after walking for half an hour, he wasn't sure. But he needed to talk to Grandpa.

By the time James spotted the upright markers, he was tired. An hour or so spent at the grave would be welcomed. Not sure where Grandpa was exactly, James meandered through the cemetery, reading markers as he went. One he passed, then returned to.

Thomas W. Barber
b. Ohio
d. 1855

Pa had talked about Barber's killing, which had happened before they moved to Lawrence. It had made headlines around the world. One of the first deaths associated with Mister Lincoln's War. Or also called the Brothers' War, James prayed it wouldn't be *his* brothers' war. Too many brothers and families had been ripped apart already. But, it was the brutality of the pro-slavery supporters that inflamed even the most passive citizens.

A poem written by John Greenleaf Whittier immortalized Barber's death. James had read "Burial of Barber" in *Harper's Weekly.* He shook his head. *Mister Barber, look what you started.*

More ambling through the cemetery until James spotted several fresh graves, if mounded earth and sparse grass was an indication of new. Volunteer Infantry, the 13th Wisconsin. He looked closer at one of the markers. Died 1862. Last year. Typhoid fever had taken this soldier's life. And the one next to it. Then another one. James backed away, as if he could get the fever from just standing there.

Locating Grandpa's grave, far enough away from the recent ones, James knelt then sat with crossed legs. A warm breeze cooled the sweat on his face. He pulled a blade of grass and stuck it in his mouth. The marker tilted just a bit to the left. James pulled until the metal cross stood straight. As if connecting with Grandpa, James ran his hand across the words.

Francis Michael McConnell
At Peace in Heaven
b. Kilkenney, Ireland, February 27, 1806
d. September 15, 1859

Pressure built against the back of his eyes and James squeezed them shut. He rubbed until he felt better, but the world blurred. One tear lingered on his scarred left cheek.

"I'm back, Grandpa. I missed you." He blinked a second tear. "Got a lot to talk about. Don't know where to begin, though. Hope you can hear me." James glanced up into the morning sun and squinted, despite the shade his hat afforded.

205

He spit out the piece of grass. "Since I left here, terrible things have happened to me. But some good things, too. I got married. In a church. You'd like her, Grandpa. She's real pretty and takes good care of me. Sometimes I think I don't deserve her."

He'd thought about that often. Why had Morningstar fallen in love with him? Right there in Tucson at her pa's doctor's office. At that time, especially, he was broken. Physically, mentally and emotionally. Before going to Tucson, and still recovering from Apache abuse, he'd stabbed a man in Mesilla, then was sentenced to time in the Union army. His stint there helped him face his fears, let him grow as a man. Marching across the Sonoran Desert and back to Tucson had helped, but the nightmares kept coming until he knew he'd gone mad. It was Morningstar who helped subdue them, helped put him back together.

But was he put back together? Hardly. James studied the scars around his wrists. Sometimes it felt as if the scars were the only things holding him together.

"Grandpa, tell me what to do." James swatted at a fly on the marker. "Back in Mesilla, all I wanted was to make a home. But that damn army came. I couldn't sit by and watch people starve."

His gaze trailed to sprigs of grass near his knee. "And Trace. Andy. We don't agree on anything. Can't get along at all anymore. Maybe I've let them down." Something wet rolled down his cheek. "We used to have fun together, got along together." He swiped a hand across his mouth. "I miss them, Grandpa." He closed his eyes, tears stinging. "I miss you more."

CHAPTER FORTY

Luke went right to the barn. He didn't stop at the house to tell Sally he was back or to give her the news. No, he didn't want anyone harping about his shortcomings right now. He'd get an earful later. He needed a good cigar and a drink. On second thought, maybe he'd skip the drink. His head still hurt, though not throbbing as it had earlier. A dull ache had set in on his long walk around town, and despite all the air he'd gulped, nothing had quieted it. This headache he'd just have to ride out.

By the time Luke had stormed down a full block, he had wrangled his anger down to a simmer. Maybe getting fired was a blessing. Now he was free to ride with Quantrill all the time and to make a difference in this ugly war. He would prove to Gunnar and Tobias Iverson, to Albert Perkins and to Smitty Jenkins, that he was still on their side, still willing and able to ride with them. Yeah, he'd show them.

Smoke curled around his face and then lazed into the air. Although it was past noon, the wind was beginning to pick up, and even though the barn was well built, it was drafty in places. Luke watched his cigar tip flare as he pulled in more tobacco flavor. He relaxed. Feet burning, he tugged off his new boots and rubbed a big toe.

"Damn boots."

The barn door groaned open. James closed it behind him, located Luke and walked over. "Sally said she saw you come in here." James pointed to a nail keg. "Want company?"

Shrugging, Luke then changed his mind and nodded. "Got any more of that whiskey?"

James held up a hand. "Nuh uh. Don't ever want to see that stuff again." He eased down to the keg. "My head still hurts."

Luke's did, too. But now it had dulled, along with the rest of him. The reality of losing his job was setting in, and he didn't like it. Not one bit. Would James understand? Maybe. Probably. Surely.

"Got fired this morning." Luke spoke to his cigar. "Damn hard to take. And I sure in hell don't deserve it. I did what he wanted. When he wanted."

"Sally know?"

"Nope." Luke blew a cloud of smoke.

"What happened?"

"That son of a bitch accused me of smuggling. Stealing his supplies and selling them for a profit."

"You're not, right?" James flashed a quick smile.

Luke glared. "Hell, no, I ain't." He pointed toward town. "If anybody's smuggling, it's him. Hell, turns out, I've been hauling rifles for him back from Independence."

"Rifles?"

"That's not all." Luke's eyes flashed toward the barn door, then turned on his brother. "He's hauling people. Slaves."

"Slaves?"

"You heard me." Luke pointed his cigar at James. "Did you know that Pa helps them escape? Hell, James, I've even seen 'em! Right in Pa's barn."

James gave a slow nod.

Flashes of heat, like hot pokers, raced up Luke's spine. "Wait. You *knew* Pa was helping slaves? You *knew*?"

"And you're still dead set against helping set them free?" James studied the ground. "Just don't understand you."

"How come you didn't tell me?" Luke jumped off the keg and stormed across the barn. "You *knew* but couldn't be bothered to tell me?"

"Wasn't my secret," James said. "Besides, I figured you already knew."

"Hell, James. Slavery's good for the South. Where would they go without someone owning them? How would the plantation owners survive?"

"Survive? Good for the South?" James balled both hands, his chest rising and falling with each snorted breath. "You haven't seen what slavery does, have you?"

Luke frowned.

James lowered his voice, spitting the words. "It's time you do."

Before Luke could ask what his brother was talking about, James unbuttoned the three fasteners of his shirt. "Two months." He shrugged out of his suspenders, pulled the shirt over his head, and tossed it to Luke.

Unbuttoning his undershirt and pulling out of it, James ran his hand across his bare chest, pointing to various scars.

"Most are whip marks. I got five a day for fourteen days while Trace was gone, trying to get Cochise's brother released and the army to retreat."

Wicked pink lines, some wide, some zigzagged, covered his brother's chest, many circling under his arm, around to his back. A roadmap of Hell.

Unbuttoning and then dropping his trousers and cotton drawers, James turned his back, allowing half a minute for inspection, then turned around. "Got 'em from the top of my head to the bottom of my feet. Take a good look."

Luke did. No man could endure that. No man should survive. How had James survived?

"This scar right here?" James pointed to a ragged pink line

209

on his left side. "I ran a gauntlet, like sailors on the sailing ships. Only mine was Apaches with knives. They said if I got through, I'd be free." His gaze traveled down to the dirt floor. "I'd planned to bring back help for Trace."

"But you . . ."

James squeezed his eyes shut. "Too many. I was stabbed. Cut. Kicked. I was . . ."

Nothing Luke could say or do would help his brother. Nothing but time would heal him.

James continued. "Trace and me were tied against saguaro cactus every time the camp stopped moving or when we weren't working. At night, they tied us to stakes, like animals, so we wouldn't escape. They beat us whenever they felt like it. One time, Trace got hit . . ." He swallowed, opened his eyes and frowned at Luke. "Beat so terrible he was unconscious for a full day. I thought for sure he'd die."

As much as Luke wanted to question right now, he thought better of it and remained quiet.

James wagged his head and brought his brown-eyed gaze up to Luke. "This is damn hard to say, but twice Trace and me agreed to kill each other." He sighed. "Hell"—James looked away—"thinking like that, knowing that dying was better than living . . ."

Luke studied the dirt floor.

James pulled up his drawers and then trousers. He reached for his shirt. The brothers' eyes met. James lowered his voice. "This is what slavery looks like."

CHAPTER FORTY-ONE

Elbows on the table, head resting on his fisted hands, Luke wasn't convinced that all slaves were treated like his brothers were at the hands of the Apache. Surely the white owners had better sense than to whip their property that badly. A needless waste. Those Indians, savages that they were, hadn't realized how important a commodity Trace and James were. If they'd been treated right, his brothers may have worked harder for the tribe and maybe even been allowed to work freely. No, that was stretching it, but James had admitted yesterday in the barn he'd asked Cochise to become a part of the tribe. He'd asked to marry an Apache girl, not the Pima captive, a girl who wasn't Morningstar, and to become a white warrior.

Either James was lying, or he'd been broken, worn down so hard he'd do anything to stay alive. They'd told him no and he would remain a captive until either Trace returned with Cochise's brother, or James died. And, according to James, a day, maybe two more was all he could've endured. Trace barely got back in time.

"You're going to stare a hole in the table, Luke." Sally slid a plate of hotcakes and bacon in front of him. She returned with the coffeepot, started to pour, then stopped. Luke's cup was still full.

Aromas of hotcakes, coffee and bacon mingled, and his stomach rumbled. Despite his hunger, nothing appealed to him this morning. With Sally seated across from him, he forked breakfast into his mouth, eating, not tasting.

Sally reached out and touched his forearm. "You can get another job, Luke."

He focused on Sally's pretty face, her wide eyes clouded with concern.

"You're a good driver, Honey. Mister Gibson had no good reason to let you go. It wasn't very Christian of him and I'm sure my pa'll pray for you this Sunday. But I bet there's plenty of people needing things hauled." Sally pointed her fork toward the door. "I know. You could go work for your pa."

He'd rather eat his new boots.

It wasn't exactly what he'd imagined, but riding next to William Clarke Quantrill caused Luke's chest to swell, his vest buttons to strain, his shoulders to straighten. Quantrill exuded confidence . . . leadership . . . a sense of purpose. All traits Luke knew were within himself, too, if given the chance. It had taken a few words for Luke to join up again with Quantrill. But riding next to him like this . . . proved he was trusted. He was one of *them*.

Proving himself had been relatively easy. Two raids, burning, looting and threatening to kill had sent Luke right up to the front of the pack, where he intended to stay. Satisfying view from here—very satisfying. But the one thing he needed even more than this? Money. He couldn't feed his family on satisfaction, and while Quantrill allowed him to keep some of the loot, Luke wasn't making much.

Things would change tomorrow. Earlier today he'd checked Pa's barn and sure enough, fresh straw was piled in front of the small door. A sure sign someone was behind it. First thing in the morning he'd be able to coax them out of their hiding place and into his wagon. Hell, he'd take them back to their grateful owners and get a reward, plus the bounty on their heads. He couldn't lose.

It angered him he hadn't thought of it before. He was smarter than that. From the first time he'd seen those huddled slaves, why didn't he wait till Pa was gone, then haul them back to Georgia, or wherever the hell they'd come from? As he rode with Quantrill, Luke shook his head. *Dumber'n a fence post.* At least that's what his pa had told him he was a time or two. Right now, he agreed.

He couldn't let on about his plans. That would be suicide if Quantrill and his men found out. Quantrill would want a piece of the action or take it over entirely. He wouldn't let that happen. And James? He sure wouldn't agree to help. That brother had been through a lot, but he didn't understand business. Slavery was good for business. Those men, women, children were needed, unlike James and Trace who were not useful members of the tribe.

Slaves had a purpose.

Behind Luke rode more than a hundred men, all galloping toward a village in eastern Kansas, one he'd never heard of. He didn't care about names. One town or village was about like the other. They all needed to understand that this American war was about each state having its own say over its own destiny. If they allowed slavery, well, that should be up to the states, too. No damn government should have the final say. States had rights.

Endless prairie stretched over the horizon, as if the sky tucked in the edges. As far as he could see, nothing but low hills, grass and occasional trees.

Before full light this morning, Quantrill had gathered everyone and given his usual talk. States' rights, slavery, the Jayhawkers' uncalled-for assaults on other Bushwhackers—the list went on. His words lit the fire in Luke's belly, igniting the need to control his own destiny. To make his own decisions.

During this past week he'd camped with Quantrill along the banks of the Missouri River.

While there was no doubt Quantrill should've been a preacher, other parts of the man disturbed Luke. According to Quantrill, everything done by Jayhawkers was cause to kill. And he blamed his family's demise on the North as well. Luke couldn't blame him there. From what Quantrill had said, his pa had been beaten to death, his ma hacked with an ax, his brothers and sisters dragged off and molested and then killed. Who wouldn't want revenge?

But still, something nagged at Luke. Something didn't fit. He pushed aside conjecture and focused on today's mission. Burn down the Pratt farm. Rumors flew that Pratt and his wife helped slaves move north, as well as the story that Mister Pratt had led a raid against one of Quantrill's groups last month. Lieutenant William Gregg, the man Luke had met in Cane Hill, Arkansas, captained the group. Gregg, Luke had been told, received wounds in that recent raid and might never walk again.

Endless prairie stretched all around Luke. Gentle hills rose to his left reminding him of Lawrence. Going home. After today's raid, he was going home where he'd fall into Sally's open arms, and after loving her, he'd sleep for a week. He'd been gone five days now, but it felt more like years. Sleeping on the hard ground, always wondering if a band of Jayhawkers or ugly Union troops would slit their throats, kept Luke from resting. His nerves were frayed, but everybody else was just like him. Edgy. Exhausted. Wanting to get this over until the call came again. After a day or two at home, Luke knew he'd be ready. They all would.

Especially Quantrill.

Cole Younger and Clarke Blackhorn rode up beside Luke. Cole held up a hand. "Hold on a minute, Luke."

Tugging back on the reins and waiting for the rest of the men to pass, Luke stopped and regarded his companions. Although he liked Cole, Luke always kept a distance between them. Too many times Cole had killed for no good reason. Luke wasn't afraid of Coleman Younger, but he didn't trust him. Clarke Blackhorn was worse. That man, although much shorter than Luke, was upholding the Quantrill family penchant for malevolent violence. Blackhorn killed everybody who came within spitting distance. Luke kept him at arm's length, too. Cousin or no cousin of Quantrill's, Clarke couldn't be trusted.

"What's going on?" Luke popped the cork from his canteen. The water slid down his dry throat like a hot knife. Between the wind and the dust, Luke was always thirsty.

Cole and Clarke sat on either side of Luke. Clarke pulled off his hat and ran a forearm across his face, his greasy hair brushing his shoulders. "Damn heat. Next we'll have rain."

Luke nodded. Had they stopped to talk about the weather? Hardly. He waited.

Clarke snugged his hat over his mop of coffee-colored hair. "Quantrill wants us three to do a little extra for him."

Eyeing Clarke, Luke frowned. "What kinda extra?"

"The kind that gets us noticed when Quantrill passes out rewards."

Cole plugged his canteen and wrapped the strap around his saddle horn. A drop of water hung at the corner of his mouth.

"He wants us to head over to Independence and take down that storekeeper."

"Who?"

"The one you've been hauling freight back to Lawrence for. Old Man Watkins." Cole pointed east. "We'll cut off right here, should get there by tonight."

"Then," Clarke said, "we'll drink us a time at the Red Bird Saloon. I hear the women there have the biggest . . ." He cupped his hands over his chest and grinned.

While that part of the plan appealed to Luke, killing the storekeeper did not. Although Watkins must've known about the slaves in the barrels, he sure as hell didn't deserve to die. If Watkins would promise not to help more slaves and run guns, would that be enough? Would he have to die?

It had been one thing to raid a house or stage stop of known Yankee sympathizers, but it didn't feel right walking into somebody's store—in the middle of town—and point blank shooting him. Especially Watkins, a nice enough man.

Cole leaned forward and spoke across Luke to Clarke. "Gonna bring his head back, ain't we? Just like ol' Archie Clement's done a time or two."

"I like your thinking, Cole," Clarke said. His black eyes caught the sun's reflection and sparkled. "We can be exactly like him. And I ain't never brought back a head before. Hands and feet, but never a head." His thin lips rose at both ends. "This'll be a first."

Luke glanced from man to man. He'd heard stories of Clement's raids. "Cut his head off? You're talking not just killing, but decapitating?"

"That's the beauty of it, Luke," Clarke said. "We bring back a treasure. Quantrill's gonna downright wet hisself, he'll be so happy. Hell"—he nodded to Luke and Cole—"he's liable to give us a promotion."

Luke rode with them despite wanting to turn back and go home. But how would it look to Quantrill, who'd let Luke ride up front, if he "got soft" and refused to kill Watkins? Quantrill would never trust him again. More than likely, he'd throw him out of his Raiders. Maybe even kill him. He'd seen that happen once. A fella named Benjamin Parker had made a few raids on his own and Quantrill wasn't pleased. The *Kansas City Daily Western Journal of Commerce* reported Parker's death as a result of militia fire, but rumor ran through the ranks that Quantrill himself had pulled the trigger.

With Parker dead, Quantrill quashed any and all other desires for his leadership position. Everyone was happy to leave William Clarke Quantrill in charge.

The closer they rode, the more Luke questioned this assignment. It didn't feel right. True, Watkins was the enemy and this was war, but beheading? The idea turned his stomach. Luke knew he'd have to intervene somehow. Cole and Clarke would have to settle for just killing, and leaving Watkins' head on his shoulders.

Lights dotted the distant expanse of prairie. Ahead, the town spread out for a mile or two and winked a welcome. One corner of Luke's mouth slid up. Within moments he'd be out of the saddle, boots on the ground, beer in hand. A bed would be welcomed tonight; the past week on the unyielding ground was less than restful, rocks and stickers marring his sleep. No, he'd looked forward to that part of Independence, Missouri, all day. It was tomorrow that worried him.

Bright rays warmed Luke's face as something kicked his foot. "Up and at 'em, Colton. Sun's already up." Cole Younger slipped a suspender over his left shoulder and kicked Luke again. "Got us some Yankees what need killin'."

The room blurred then came into focus. A couple more blinks and Luke recognized the washstand in one corner, Cole standing by his bed tucking in his shirt in the other corner, and Clarke sitting on the side of his bed picking at something between his front teeth. He sucked like he was eating a cob of corn.

Despite all the alcohol last night, Luke hadn't slept well. He'd tossed and turned on the lumpy mattress. Visions of dancing heads parading through his mind all night robbed him of sleep. Yawning, he tasted supper, beer, whiskey and cigars. The flavors rolled around in his mouth, colliding with each other and creating an offense that assaulted his nose. No amount of running his tongue over his teeth would clear the essence of last night. Shrugging it off, he tugged on his shirt, smoothed down his hair, planted his hat on it, and nodded.

"I know a place for breakfast," Luke said. "Food's good and lots of it."

Cole opened the door. "Now you're thinking like me."

Over hotcakes, bacon, sausage, eggs and potatoes, the three men planned how to waylay Ben Watkins. Most likely, it wouldn't be as simple as Clarke suggested. Just walk into the store, order him to the back room, then *wham*. Off goes his head. Cole opted for something more exciting. They'd walk him down the street, shoot him in broad daylight, cut off his head and then hightail it out of town before Watkins' body hit the street.

Luke stayed quiet. Cold-blooded killing like that wasn't what he believed in. Shooting somebody in self-defense, but not outright murder. And while Watkins was a Yankee, a Jayhawker no less, he deserved to die. But no, cold-blooded murder was not something he'd be a part of.

A plan formed. Maybe he would pretend to rob the store, then when Mister Watkins pulled out his gun, Luke could shoot him. Self-defense. That would work. Hell, that way he'd still be able to ride with Quantrill and keep his place in the front of the pack.

Over breakfast, Luke presented his plan. It would be easy. Easier than Clarke's.

"Still don't see what the fuss's about, Luke." Clarke speared a third slab of sausage. "Like my cousin says, 'the only good Yankee's a dead one.' "

His plate clean except for egg remnants, Luke sipped his coffee and spoke over the cup. "I can sure understand Quantrill wanting revenge. I mean after the way his folks, brothers and sisters were killed—"

"What?" Clarke stopped chewing and frowned. "What're you talking about?"

Luke shrugged. "He said his family'd been butchered by Jayhawkers. Hell, Clarke, you of all people should know that."

Chewing again, Clarke sawed at his ham. "I do know what he says. But they ain't dead." He chuckled. "Ol' Willie likes to tell people his folks were all chopped up. Makes people feel sorry for him. But truth is, they're all fine. Hell, I visited with them last month." His gaze scanned Luke and Cole. "Willie. He's a corker, ain't he?"

Luke stiffened. After all this time, riding with William Clarke Quantrill, admiring him, and yes, feeling sorry for him. How could a leader lie—bold-faced—to his men? He was no man seeking revenge. Quantrill was nothing but a cold-blooded killer who took advantage of the war to quench his lust for blood. What else had Luke been told that was a lie? Luke swallowed hard. Maybe it was time to get out of Quantrill's clutches. Luke would fight for the Southern cause, but he wouldn't be associated with coldhearted killings. Luke retained a shred of pride and if he continued riding for Quantrill, that shred would disintegrate.

Besides, the man was a lunatic. Luke thought back to other gruesome killings he'd figured were tragedies of war. The man trapped inside a burning barn, the way-station manager run through over and over with his own saber . . . the list grew.

Decision made. As soon as he could, Luke would leave crazy Quantrill and his bloodthirsty raids. He'd go back to Lawrence and sell slaves.

He turned to Cole.

"What about you? How'd you get tangled up with Quantrill?"

Dark eyes trailed across the table then up to Luke's face. "Kinda personal question, don't you think?" He pulled in air then took a sip of coffee. "But since you're good to ride with, I'll tell you. Couple years ago, my pa went Union. But those bastards killed him anyways. So me, my older brothers and three of my sisters have gone Reb. We owe Pa."

Now *that* he understood. Revenge for a needless killing Luke agreed with. This other deal with Clarke knotted his stomach.

CHAPTER FORTY-TWO

By the time the three made their way down to Watkins Mercantile, Luke couldn't breathe. He knew his boots touched ground, the boardwalk creaking and groaning with his weight, but nothing seemed real. Was this a dream? Was he really about to help kill Mister Watkins and then behead him and take it back to Quantrill? The liar Quantrill.

Cole reached for the mercantile's door handle. Luke put a hand over Cole's and spoke in a low tone. "Let's put our bandannas over our faces so nobody'll recognize us."

"Who cares if they do?" Cole elbowed Luke out of the way. "Anybody in there's gonna be dead in a minute."

Clarke stepped close cocking his gun, his coffee breath blowing in Luke's face. A sneer raised one side of his small mouth. "And dead men don't talk."

Without another word, Cole jerked on the handle and marched in, Clarke and Luke on his heels. He wagged his pistol at Ben Watkins.

"Give us all your money. And be quick about it."

Watkins' hands flew up. "Ain't got but a dollar, maybe two." He cocked his head toward the money box. "Take what you want. Just don't shoot me."

"Shut up." Clarke whipped out his .44 Colt. "Get back in that storeroom." He cocked it. "Now."

Easing toward the back of the store, Watkins continued to plead.

Like lightning it hit Luke. A plan! He'd knock out Watkins and tell Cole and Clarke he was dead.

Clarke pushed Watkins toward the back room while Cole emptied the money box. Just as Watkins had said, a couple of dollars, Union script at that, lay on the bottom.

Plan in place, Luke walked with Clarke toward the back. The front door opened, the tinkling bell announcing customers, and in stepped two men.

Watkins hollered, "Help!" He ducked down on one knee.

Luke and Clarke spun toward the men while Cole shot. Bullets pinged into shelves.

Smoke saturated the air. Luke coughed and shot. Needing to reload, Luke took cover behind the counter and crouched next to Cole, who was also reloading. Clarke knelt behind a flour barrel and fired.

"You no-good riffraff!" Watkins grabbed a broom leaning against the wall and swung. It plowed into Clarke, sending him reeling back against Luke.

With a grunt, Clarke regained his feet, brought his Navy Colt waist high and fired. Watkins lurched left, and missing its mark, the bullet slammed into a jar. Crockery exploded. Watkins aimed the broom at Luke. "You. I know you."

Bullets zinged into goods. Smoke choked the air making it hard for Luke to see Watkins. Or Cole and Clarke for that matter. Luke kept his head down and ran at the store owner.

Reloaded, Cole stood, aimed and shot. His gun clicked, but only a miserable thin flame erupted from the barrel. He cursed. Another click. Nothing.

Luke head butted Watkins in the stomach. *Whump.* Both men rolled to the floor. A moment of somersaulting, then Luke managed to land on top. "Hate to do this, old man. Gonna knock you out for your own good."

Watkins held up a hand desperate to fend off the attack.

Luke brought the butt of his six-shooter down hard on Watkins' head. The man groaned and then lay still. Had he actually killed him? He'd struck him harder than intended. No time to check for a pulse.

A bullet splintered the shelves behind Luke. He ducked. But before he could straighten up and fire, one of the customers shot again. Clarke doubled over, sagging to his knees.

"I'm hit, Cole. I'm hit." Clarke gripped his stomach and crumpled to the floor. On his side, he wriggled toward Luke and Cole. Blood oozed between his fingers and he left a red trail as he inched forward. He shook.

Escape. They had to escape if they wanted to stay alive. Luke grabbed at Clarke, snagging his shirt. Cole clutched Clarke's vest and they hefted him toward the back room.

The two customers followed, shooting and reloading. "Damn Bushwhackers! You'll die for this!"

Luke fired, missing one of the men by inches. Instead of shooting again, Luke released Clarke and ran headfirst into the other customer, sending both into a shelf. Bolts of calico tumbled off the shelf and landed against the men.

Cole hollered from the back room. "Clarke's good as dead. Let's go."

"Back door." Luke scrambled to his feet and headed for the storeroom. A glance at Clarke. Blood coated his shirt and pooled on the floor. Eyes wide open, his last gasp had been one of agony.

More gunfire. Bullets tore into the wooden doorjamb. Luke zigzagged between crates, barrels and boxes. He yanked open the back door and bolted into daylight. Cole's labored breathing drew heavy on Luke's neck. With any luck, they'd make it to their horses and then get the hell out of Independence, Missouri.

If they could get down the alley and around the corner, they'd make it.

Luke ran with every ounce of energy he could muster. Boots pounded behind him. He hoped they were Cole's. Shouts and gunfire rang out a bit farther back. Luke rounded a corner and discovered he was on the main street, Watkins Mercantile a few buildings up.

Their horses were tied across the street and up the block closer to the store. Why hadn't they thought to tie them farther down this way? Yep, thinking like a fence post, Luke thought. Cole and Luke shrunk back against the end of the building and hid in the morning shadows.

"What d'you think we oughta do?" Luke holstered his pistol and discovered his hands shaking. Shouts filled the street.

Ducking into the street then back to the shadows, Cole reloaded his revolver. "Whatever it is, gotta be quick. They're coming at us from both sides."

Boots thudded down the alley; shouts from the street grew louder.

Luke peeked into the street. Saddled horses, two as luck would have it, were tethered less than thirty feet away.

"There they are!" someone shouted from the alley.

Luke dashed for the closest horse. Saddle horn in hand, he swung up and gigged the stallion as hard as he could. Bullets slammed into the street, little dust clouds pinging all around the horse's hooves. Leaning over, the saddle horn jabbing into his chest, Luke yelled and dug his boot heels into the horse's side. He ran.

He galloped out of town, down the end of main street and out of the business district. Pounding hooves behind him, he glanced over his shoulder. Cole, head down, hunched over his horse.

Luke's horse ran. Strong, fast, born to run. And he was grateful he'd picked him. Cole's horse struggled to keep pace. Knowing he should slow down allowing his partner to catch up, Luke thought long and hard before he pulled on the reins. Galloping now would do.

A longer look behind him revealed no posse, no angry hordes of riders on their tails. But they would be. It was only a matter of time.

CHAPTER FORTY-THREE

"Wish it'd been me that'd been shot."

Cole frowned at Luke. "Why?"

" 'Cause Mister Watkins recognized me."

"Hell, Luke, you killed him." Cole enunciated each word. "Dead men don't talk."

The end of the cigar Luke had found in the saddlebag flared as he pulled in tobacco-laced air. "Don't know for sure he died. Maybe I killed him, maybe I didn't. But I bet before I get home, everybody in Lawrence'll know it was me that did it."

"He's dead." Cole snapped a small branch and fed part of it into the campfire. Sparks shot out as the leaves disintegrated. "Hell, Luke. You buffaloed him real good. Caved in his skull pretty slick from where I was."

"At the very least, I'm a horse thief. You know what they do to them, don't you?" The noose tightened around Luke's neck. He coughed and spit. "Hell, I can't never go home."

A long slow nod. Cole looked west, now a dark expanse of prairie. "Looks like you'll be riding with Quantrill from now on."

Not what Luke wanted to hear, but what he'd been telling himself all afternoon, after they'd slowed to a walk. After they'd figured the posse wasn't on their trail. After the rain had washed away all signs of their passing. Although soaked to the bone, Luke knew the rain was a sign. Not a religious man, this last gunfight had changed him, though. The fact he'd survived made him think that somebody "up there" was telling him to change his ways.

Stars winked red and silver. A million of them. Luke thought back to times when he and his brothers would lie outside in the summer, enjoying the hint of cool air, and name all the stars.

Ma had pointed out the constellations, the ones she knew. Big and Little Dippers, Andromeda and Triangulum. She'd also point out planets, Saturn and Mars. Luke and his brothers talked of being birds and flying there, then looking down on Earth and waving to Ma and Pa.

Cole stretched out next to the fire, his head resting on the saddle. "We'll catch up with Quantrill tomorrow, get some coffee there."

Luke eyed Coleman Younger. Was this where Luke wanted to be? Sitting in the middle of nowhere, clothes soggy, stomach gnawing on itself. Stolen horses. And one of Liar Quantrill's henchmen next to him.

Luke fell asleep thinking about his poor decisions. Look where they got him. Running. Looking over his shoulder. Jumping at every sound. Would he hold beautiful Sally again or see his son and daughter grow up? No. He wouldn't bring ugly to their world. He could blame Quantrill, James and Pa for pushing him like they did, but he knew the only one to blame was himself.

Stomachs grumbling, they rode due west, backs to the rising sun. Cole said Quantrill had mentioned raiding a farm outside of Franklin next, so west Luke and Cole headed. While they rode at a slow gallop, Luke mulled over his choice of friends. At one point, he'd been terrified of Quantrill, then later enamored with his fervor, his belief in his cause. And now? Now Luke saw Quantrill for what he really was. He was no hero.

On the other hand, Luke was safer in the middle of the Raiders than he was out alone on this prairie or in Lawrence. He'd have a better chance of survival if he rode in the middle of the pack and stayed low. When this war was over, if it ever was, he could go home and start over again. Or could he?

What about Sally? She expected him home by now. He'd told her he was searching for work out of town. Only be gone a couple of days he'd said. At least she had James and Pa close by. James. Luke considered his brother. He'd spent the past three years wishing his brother would move back to Lawrence, and now when it looked like that might happen, he rides off for God knows how long. What was he thinking?

In the distance, smoke rose in three columns. Now he could smell it, wind pushing the stench of burning wood and flesh. Had to be Quantrill.

Luke and Cole arrived after the looting. Jesse James rode to meet them.

"It's a beauty, ain't she?" Jesse pointed to the collapsing barn, its groans and sighs piercing the late-afternoon air. "Went up like that." He snapped.

"Get any goods, Jesse? Like jewelry? Or women?" Cole shifted his weight in his saddle and licked his lips.

Luke thought more about food than women right now. "Got any grub? We ain't had a bite since yesterday morning."

Jesse frowned, his eyes trailing from Cole to Luke. "Where y'all been?"

"Takin' care of business," Cole said. "You got anything or not?"

"Some jerky in my warbag." Jesse untied the canvas bag hanging over his saddle horn, dug in and then handed each man a strip. He took one for himself.

Luke ate to no effect. There was not enough to ever fill him. He needed more. Much more. Water would be good. The river had been a ways back and this meat made him damn thirsty. He pointed at the canteen also hung on the saddle horn.

Thirst quenched and some of the stomach rumbling gone, Luke surveyed the area. Nothing like Pratt's farm, this one was big, furrowed fields in all directions, corn about a foot high, big stone house with a wide veranda running the length of the south side. Counting at least four outbuildings, all but one burning, Luke realized this must have been home to a rich person.

The name didn't matter. One Free Stater was about like the rest. Those Jayhawkers needed to be taken down, shown their thinking was wrong, that states had a right to make their own decisions, not laws shoved down their throats like Senator Jim Lane was trying to do. The more Luke thought about it, the more determined he became. He would do whatever was necessary to see the Confederates win, or, by damn, he'd die trying.

Luke followed Cole as they wound their way past dying animals, distraught women and one black man, rake in hand, turning in circles, gesturing to the women then back to the smoldering barn. Wood creaked and groaned as the last flames finished off the house.

He sat, mesmerized by the glowing embers, the acrid smoky wafts of burning flesh, the crash of falling timber that used to be someone's home. Luke sat, wondering what he would do if this was his.

Most of the Raiders, including Cole and Quantrill, had ridden off by the time Luke pulled his gaze from the scene. Still focused on the horror, it reminded him of the battle in Prairie Grove, Arkansas, where the Borden house had burned and his friend was killed. Many men killed.

Why did people have to die? Visions of Clarke, clutching his stomach, grimacing like that, his final breath in Luke's face . . . why? Because this was war.

Luke drew in a lungful of smoke, coughed, then gigged his horse north, toward home.

He caught up with Cole and Quantrill within half an hour. Although it was now dark, their trail had been easy to follow. Hoofprints of that many mounts weren't hard to miss. Besides, he knew where they were going. An area just south of Lawrence with plenty of Black Jack oak trees for cover, brush for the horses to eat and a small stream with fresh water.

Tired. Luke was not just tired but exhausted. And from the looks and grunts of the men, they were, too. After seeing to his stolen horse, Luke found a patch of ground that looked good for a night's sleep. He settled his saddle to use as a pillow, the horse blanket to lie on, and then he sat on it. Feet burning, he grabbed his boot and yanked.

"Got a second, Colton?"

Luke's gaze trailed up Quantrill's sooted trousers, vest, shirt and then face. Nodding, Luke released the boot, and pushed up to his feet, which still complained about being squeezed too tight.

Quantrill stepped away from Luke, who followed the boss as if an invisible string tethered him. Quantrill's voice, instead of its nasal monotone, took on a deeper quality, almost a baritone.

"You live in Lawrence, don't you?"

Luke nodded.

"I understand your pa has a farm on the outskirts of town. Don't he?"

Again a nod. Where was he going with this and what did Pa have to do with anything?

Quantrill faced Luke and stared at him. "What side this war your daddy on?"

Luke swallowed hard. He had to lie. "Only side there is." He pushed aside memories of the last time he'd spoken with Pa. Arguing over slavery and state's rights. Luke remembered calling him "pigheaded" and then slamming the door. He'd wanted to call him other names, but Ma had walked in.

"Good." Quantrill looked around at the men bedding down for the night. "Tomorrow we'll give your daddy a visit."

Blades of ice stabbed Luke. What'd he want with Pa? And what if runaway slaves were hiding out? What would Quantrill do to Pa? To him? He didn't want Quantrill and his Raiders anywhere close to Pa and his farm. But sitting out at the edge of town like it was made it a likely place for Quantrill and his boys to hole up.

Why hadn't Luke thought of that before? His need to defy Pa and go his own way would now probably cost everyone their lives. Even James, who would fight alongside Pa.

"You don't look so good, Colton." Quantrill slapped him on the shoulder. "Must be tired." He tossed a final comment over his shoulder as he walked away. "Can't wait for tomorrow."

CHAPTER FORTY-FOUR

The closer they rode to Lawrence, the tighter Luke's throat squeezed. A myriad of questions flew through his mind, spinning his world as he loped next to Jesse James. Behind him, over a hundred hooves beat out a rhythm similar to his heart's beat. Afraid of the answers to his questions, Luke listed all the possible solutions to this mountainous problem. He caught Jesse's eye and then reined closer to him.

"Got any idea why we're headed to Lawrence?" Luke hoped Jesse knew and would tell him the truth. "There's other towns better'n that one."

Hat snugged down around his ears, Jesse looked more like a ghost rider than a man riding across the prairie. Jesse's dark eyes seemed to disappear in his head, and with that three-day beard covering his cheeks, he appeared more like a drawing than a real person. Luke frowned. Maybe he was more tired than he'd thought. The spectral scene didn't disappear when he rubbed his eyes. Jesse stared back.

"Lawrence has everything we want. Those damn Jayhawkers'll die right in their own beds. And your pa's barn's gonna make us a real good hideout. We'll be right there when we raid. Nobody'll suspect a thing. Till it's time."

"Then what?" Luke already knew the answer.

"Bang! Bang!" Jesse used his free hand to point and shoot. "That ol' bastard Jim Lane's gonna die." Another shot. "And soon."

By the time Luke spotted the MacDervishers' barn on the outskirts of town, he'd decided to quit Quantrill and his rowdies. Enough killing, bloodshed and heartache. Enough. There had to be a better way to make people see the answer wasn't fighting. The answer was . . . well, he didn't really have an answer but he knew it wasn't killing, especially when it was more than likely going to be Pa. He'd do anything to keep that from happening.

The Raiders pulled to a stop, a few pointing toward the town's outbuildings.

Luke reined up next to Quantrill who had waited for him. Luke squinted into the midday sun, his hat doing a poor job shading his eyes.

"I'm thinking my pa's barn ain't the best place for your headquarters, Mister Quantrill. It's small and close to town. And he's always in it." Luke pointed over his shoulder. "There's a couple others that would be better."

A long cold stare from Quantrill turned Luke's stomach.

"Like who?" Quantrill jerked a finger over his shoulder. "Old man MacDervisher? He's no good. Got too many Jayhawkers coming and going." He stepped in close. "When the time comes in a couple weeks, his barn's gonna be the first to burn. And I hope to Hell all his friends are inside when it does."

Burn? Here in Lawrence? Luke sat hard against his saddle. Would Pa's barn be the second, even though Quantrill would use it? Probably. Quantrill had earned his reputation as a ruthless killer.

Mustering up enough courage to ask, Luke blurted out the question before he could reel it in and think it through. "You plan to burn down Lawrence? Why?"

Quantrill spun in his saddle, his eyes narrowing. "Hell and damnation, Colton. Do I gotta spell out everything for you? Draw you a picture?" He waited, eyes locked on Luke's.

Apparently. Luke nodded.

"This war," Quantrill said, "won't be over till we live in the Confederate States of America. This war"—he pointed toward downtown Lawrence—"rests on the back, nay, the *hearts* of the men and women of the Confederacy. The men and women who desire to live life their way, not at the beck and call of some government dictator. No sir, our citizens deserve and *expect* to be treated as the intelligent, law-abiding, hardworking people they are."

This man could sure speechify. Luke knew that Quantrill was somewhat of an orator, but never before had he heard such fervor. Lured by the sermon, several of Quantrill's Raiders had ridden closer. Luke counted ten, with more coming. Cole and Jesse sat side by side on their horses, Archie Clements reined up as well. Like bees searching for nectar, the Raiders craved attention from Quantrill.

A strong breeze tugged at Luke's hat. This part of Kansas provided no good place to get out of the wind. No high hills or even low mountains served as windbreaks. From out of nowhere, Luke realized he hated Kansas. It held nothing but hot wind, death and bad memories. Ma and Pa were the exceptions. And Sally. He vowed that if he survived this war, he'd move west, maybe toward Mesilla and his two brothers.

Quantrill droned on. "We'll turn this country into what it should be. What it needs to be. Nay, what it *must* be in order to survive." His shoulders squared and he sat up tall in his saddle. He met the gaze of every man surrounding him. "You . . . are the answer. You are the ones who can make a difference." A long nod. "We'll start tonight. And finish tomorrow."

CHAPTER FORTY-FIVE

With Pa's barn now in full view, Luke scrambled for a plan. How could he keep Pa from revealing his true allegiance? There was no doubt that if Pa mouthed off, told Quantrill what he really thought, Quantrill would cut him down at the first opportunity.

Late afternoon, Quantrill, Jesse and Luke rode into the farmyard, the other thirty or forty Raiders waiting less than a mile back, hidden on the far side of the hill. Pa's house beckoned like a soft bed to a tired man, but Luke couldn't rest right now. Maybe never.

A buckskin horse stood tied to a wild cherry bush on the side of the house, its golden red dun coat shining in the afternoon light. At easily sixteen hands, he stood higher at the withers than most horses. What a beauty! Had Pa bought a new horse? He'd talked of increasing his stock and maybe going into the horse breeding business. At first glance, this stud might be the ticket Pa needed to really make some money.

"Wait here." Luke reined up and swung his leg over his saddle. "I'll see where he's at." Maybe Quantrill would wait and maybe he wouldn't.

Quantrill nodded. "Go fetch your pa and we'll talk."

Five long steps and Luke knocked then pushed open the wooden door, squeaking as it swung. How many times had he promised to oil it?

Biscuits. Stew. Coffee. The aromas attacked his nose and he

followed them into the kitchen. Ma stood over the stove, wooden spoon in hand, the other hand wiping matted hair away from her temple. A smile blossomed as she looked up.

"Luke!" She spread her arms expecting a hug. He swept her up into a bear hug, not caring about the stew dripping down the back of his vest. With this war coming home, there was no telling how much longer he'd be able to do this. He squeezed.

Ma wiggled. "Set me down, son." Her feet dangled inches off the floor.

He released her. "Sorry. Guess I don't know how strong I am." He glanced around the kitchen, then through the door into the parlor. "Where's Pa?" His thumb jerked over his shoulder. "And is that his new horse?"

Luke snagged an extra carrot from the counter and munched.

She stood back, hands fisted on her hips. "Luke Jeremiah Colton. Don't you recognize your brother's horse?" Pinked cheeks turned red. "He bought him right before you took off last week."

Recollection fluttered through Luke's mind. James had talked about buying a horse, about where he would stable him. A vague memory blurred of looking at stock with James, but that was the end of it. Carrot parts still in his mouth, he reached for a biscuit.

Ma swatted his hand. "James needs that horse. Good thing he bought it."

The smell of stew tantalized Luke's appetite. Would Ma allow him to have a bowl before everybody else? Not hardly. He didn't even get a biscuit. He turned his attention from his stomach back to James. "Why's that?"

Ma's Irish green eyes lit up. "My Lord, you haven't heard. Your brother has a job."

"Doing what?"

She stirred the stew. "Driving for Mister Gibson. We didn't

think you'd mind. He took your old job."

The back of Luke's neck needed rubbing. Bad. He gripped it and squeezed, but nothing helped. Mind? Of course he minded James got his job. More that he'd been fired from it. And not for good reason.

"He needed a job," Ma said. "It's starting to look like James and Morningstar are staying in Lawrence. They're wanting to rent a house." Ma smiled. "You'd like that, wouldn't you? I know your pa and I hope they stay."

Stay. Go. It was too much to take in all at once. He nodded and forced a smile. Ma cocked her head and pointed her spoon at Luke's chest.

"Where've you been?"

Luke had to get back to Quantrill before that man came inside the house. He inched toward the door. "Over at—"

"Sally's worried half to death. You been by to see her?"

"I'm going—"

"Did you find work?"

Luke shook his head. "Not—"

"How about driving for your pa?"

"I—"

"You know who's hiring?"

"No."

"The undertaker. He pays—"

"I'll check the barn." Holding up one hand to stop the question barrage, Luke backed away.

Scooting out the door, he waved at Quantrill and Jesse, then pointed at the barn. "Wait. I'll be right back."

Trotting toward the barn, he wondered what he'd tell Pa. Nothing but lies came to mind. Just as he tugged on the barn door, someone inside pushed on it. It swung open. Luke and James came nose to nose.

James, ax in hand, raised it over his head, then let out a long stream of oaths. "You 'bout got your fool head caved in, little brother."

"I thought you were Pa."

"You need spectacles. I'm taller." James set the ax down, resting one hand on the handle. "Where've you been? Sally's worried—"

"I know. And I'm sorry about that." Luke pointed inside the barn, hoping to keep James looking the other way. Maybe he wouldn't spot Quantrill.

"Where's Pa?" Luke moved around James who now faced toward the barn. Luke considered the two Raiders waiting in the yard, more than likely fidgeting to get off their horses and then cut a deal with Pa.

James set the ax against the inside of the barn wall, mopped his forehead with a sleeved arm. "Pa's hauling hides over to Franklin. Should be back in a couple of days. Thought I'd help with chores." He spit and ran the same sleeve across his mouth. "Damn it's hot. Why'd you want Pa?"

"Business."

"What kinda business?"

"Damn you're nosy." Luke stepped back. "*My* business."

A shadow crossed Luke's face. James whipped around. Quantrill stood less than three feet away. Jesse James waited a step behind his shoulder.

"Your pa home, Luke?" Quantrill pushed by James and stood in the barn's darkness. He eyed James. "You're likely not this boy's pa." His gaze traveled boots to hat. "More like a brother, I'd say. You two look alike, by damn."

Knowing he had to say something, Luke fought for air. "This here's my older brother James." His eyes met his brother's and he gave his head a slight wag. "And this is William Quantrill and Jesse James. Friends of mine."

Silence thundered in the barn until James nodded and stuck

out a hand. "Heard about you. Glad to make your acquaintance."

Luke turned to Quantrill. "Pa's gone on a business trip. Won't be back for a week or two." He dared a second glance at James whose eyes had narrowed. Luke knew that look since he'd caused it many times. But so far, James wasn't giving away his true feelings, it looked like he would play his part.

James reached around and picked up the ax, its long handle solid in his hand. He stood in the doorway, watching.

Quantrill peered around the darkened barn, then nodded to Jesse who backed out into daylight. "Too bad," Quantrill said. "Been looking forward to meeting him." He gripped Luke's shoulder and squeezed tight enough to make Luke wince. "Soon's he gets back, let me know. All right?"

"Of course." Was Luke's voice higher than usual?

"Gonna take a look around and make sure it'll suit me." Quantrill didn't wait for approval. Five minutes later and a few mumbled words, both Quantrill and Jesse ambled to their horses, mounted, then waved over their shoulders.

Once the men rode out of sight, James yanked on the back of Luke's vest until both men stood inside the barn. James shook a pointed finger at Quantrill's disappearing back. "What the hell was that?"

Luke shrugged. Words refused to form.

James gripped the vest tighter, his knuckles turning white. "You know who that was?" He pointed the ax handle toward the dust trail. "Quantrill. The meanest son of a bitch around. Hell, Luke, his name's been splashed all over the papers. He's killed more men than all the Confederates put together."

"Let go of me." Luke clutched his brother's hand and jerked it off his vest. James was right. He had no business riding with people like that. Maybe he should accept the fact he messed up. No. They made him do it. If his family and James just saw states' rights and slavery like he did, understand like he did, then he wouldn't have been forced to ride with Quantrill.

"And Jesse James." James spread his arms wide. "Don't know much about him, but hell, I've heard of his older brother. A killer and no-good cutthroat. Jesse's cut from the same cloth, I'm sure." He glanced away and then back at Luke. "Is that where you've been? Riding with them?"

"They're not so bad." Luke smoothed his vest. "They—"

"They *kill* people, innocent people." James stormed across the barn and yanked his gun belt off a peg near a stall. He spun toward Luke. Angry words shot out like bullets. "They goddamn kill people. Hell, once they know where we stand, because of you—first chance they get they'll kill me—*after* they kill you. Then Morningstar."

"But—"

"Then Sally. You want that?" James yanked on the end of his gun belt, cinching it tight around his waist. "After Sally, if they don't kill your kids, they'll come after Pa, then Ma." He crossed the barn in seconds, his words ringing. "Is that what you want? You want Ma to die by the likes of them?"

Luke shook his head.

James, now inches from Luke, lowered his voice. " 'Cause that's exactly what you're gonna get." He pushed Luke aside and stepped into the hot afternoon sun and stormed toward the house.

It couldn't end here. Not now. Certainly not like this. Luke grabbed his brother's arm, but James pulled out of the grip. Luke ran to catch up, then stood in front of him. James sidestepped, but Luke countered the move with his own. He pushed against his brother's chest. "Wait." Damn, this would be hard, but it had to be said. "Let me explain."

"Huh." James stepped to his left.

Luke stepped with him. "I'm done with Quantrill." He rushed

the words. "All right, I'll admit I've been riding with him for months. Me and my friends, along with Jesse and Frank . . . and Cole Younger."

"Cole Younger? Good God, Luke!" James yanked his hat off his head and ran dirty fingers through his hair. "Don't you ever read the paper? Don't you know what these men are doing? Who they're killing? Who they're stepping on to get what they want? Who—"

"I know." Luke hung his head. A beetle marched over his boot toe and slid off into dirt. "I've rode with them long enough to know. Even done some of it myself." He looked up. "But I've never killed. Just in that battle down in Prairie Grove and that was because the armies got us trapped in crossfire. Otherwise, James, you gotta believe me." His brother's eyes locked on his. "I haven't killed anybody that wasn't trying to kill me." *Except maybe Ben Watkins back in Independence.*

Luke held his breath. Silence except for James' breathing. Somewhere in the distance crows cawed, a horse whinnied. Farther away, the clang of a bell, church maybe, spun across the prairie.

That's it, Luke thought. James hates me and has every right to. Still, he stood inches from his twenty-two-year-old brother. A brother who looked like him, acted like him, was more like him than either wanted to admit. James, of all the brothers, would understand Luke's rebelliousness. Something in his soul compelled him to do what he thought was right, to act sometimes without thinking.

James let out a long sigh. "Just like you, I was taught to always back your brother's play. Reckon I just did that."

Luke nodded.

"But I don't have to sit around waiting to be slaughtered by worthless Rebels. I won't stand for somebody burning down what I've worked for or to kill who I love." James' stare traveled

241

over Luke's face then down to the ground. "They're calling this the Brothers' War. I reckon it is. So, if you want to ride with Quantrill, I won't stop you." He looked deep into Luke's eyes. "But you won't be my brother anymore. The Luke Colton I know died in the war."

CHAPTER FORTY-SIX

Luke dismounted and stood outside his own house. If he went in, Sally would expect answers to hundreds of questions. Was he ready to give her the truth? How could he not? She deserved the truth—finally. On the other hand, if he went in, he'd have to say good-bye because James was right. Quantrill and his Raiders would come after Sally once they found out he was quitting. Luke couldn't face that. And even if Quantrill allowed him to live, there was still the matter of killing Mister Watkins and stealing a horse. For the last few days, he'd lived looking over his shoulder and he knew that eventually somebody would find him. The noose would be in his future within moments.

And should his children have a murdering horse thief for a pa? They also deserved better than that. Maybe James and Morningstar would take in Sally and the kids after he was hanged.

The door flew open and before he could move, Adam tackled Luke's legs. Both went down, Luke managing not to fall on his son.

"Pa. Pa." Adam's wide smile reflected the traditional Colton family smile. It was genuine and contagious.

Right then Luke knew the answer. What the hell had he been thinking? He would make it up to his wife and kids, be the man he needed to be. But was it too late? He prayed it wasn't, but in his heart he knew it was.

Sally knelt next to them. "I'd about given you up for dead.

I'm so happy you're home!"

Looking up, Luke gazed into the prettiest blue eyes he'd ever seen. They blinked back at him.

"Supper's about ready. You hungry?"

In order to truly change his life, mend his fences, the first thing Luke knew he had to do was somehow return his stolen horse. When questioned, he'd told his family he'd borrowed it from a friend who had extras at the time, as his own had come up lame. Sally bought the story, Pa needed a bit more convincing, but James just shrugged grunting one-word answers whenever Luke spoke to him.

Five days dragged by while Luke knocked on every door looking for the evasive job. The town had dried up, everyone afraid of everyone else. No one bought or traded goods. Few people ate in the restaurants. It seemed as if everyone felt a change in the air. What it was, Luke couldn't say, but no one would hire him.

With every man who looked sideways at him, especially the sheriff and deputies, Luke cringed. The days took their toll, waiting for that click of cold handcuffs around his wrists, the words *murderer* and *horse thief* whispered in his ears. He walked the town like a condemned man waiting for the gallows.

Sitting at the supper table the fifth night, Sally cut up Adam's meat and spoke to Luke. "Know what I heard in town today?" Her eyes narrowed then widened. "A fellow rode in from Independence and said that a store owner there got attacked and robbed last week."

Luke's fork hung midair. "Which store?"

"Let's see." She sawed at the last piece of beef, then looked at the ceiling. "Larkin? Lassen?" Her eyes fixed on his. "You been to Independence lots of times. Know which one I mean?"

He did. Gambling that he was wrong, he said, "Watkins? You

mean Watkins Mercantile?"

"That's it. They said one man was killed. Four or five masked gunmen stormed into town and beat Mister Watkins, stole all his money, then strolled out the door." Sally bounced the baby on her knee. "I feel so sorry for his wife. Can you imagine what she's going through now?"

No, he'd never thought about it like that, and Luke fought the urge to correct her "facts." He kept his voice interested but calm. "So, Mister Watkins died? I knew him. Nice man."

Sally shook her head. "No, they say he's recovering. One of the robbers got killed, though. Shot seven times I heard. All bloody and gruesome. Some man named Clarke Blackhorn." She paused. "I've heard that name before. Have you?"

Choking down his piece of meat, Luke sipped his water before answering. "Seems to me I have. Bad hombre. Glad the likes of him are gone."

But now things had changed. Not only was Ben Watkins still alive, but alive enough he could identify Luke. Any day now there would be a posse riding up to his door, ordering him out, a long rope in their hands. One look at little Adam working hard to control his fork and get his meat into his mouth, and the fledgling smile of his baby daughter jabbed Luke in the stomach. How could he have made such disastrous choices?

"Something else I heard," Sally said over her mouthful of supper. "The robbers who got away?"

"Uh-huh?" Luke's attention stayed riveted to her words.

"Two of them stole horses—valuable horses." She smiled. "One was the sheriff's horse. Can you imagine? How stupid you gotta be to steal a sheriff's horse?"

Stupid enough. He did not want to know the answer to the next question, but something compelled him to ask anyway.

"They know who those robbers were?"

Sally nodded, putting down her fork. "Fella said Mister

Watkins mumbled a name. Sounded like 'Luke,' like yours."

"L-Luke?" There was that damn stuttering again.

She picked up her fork and speared a piece of meat. "Common enough name." Her eyes trailed over Luke's face. "I'm so glad you weren't there. I worry every time you go out looking for work. With all those ruffians out there, please be careful."

His mind spun. It wasn't on being careful right now. It wasn't on supper. It was focused on taking the sheriff's horse back without getting caught. Ten times harder since Watkins could identify him. A plan. He needed a plan. Then it hit him. Maybe he could kill two or three birds with one rock. He'd take Pa's slaves, along with the stolen horse, borrow one of Pa's horses and march the slaves back to their owners. He'd collect a reward, maybe enough to buy a horse, then leave the stolen horse tied near where he'd found him. Then he could ride home with a clear conscience.

Of course Pa would be furious and worried to find the slaves gone, but with Luke's properly placed warnings about an imminent attack by Quantrill, maybe Pa would think that crazy guerilla leader had something to do with it.

Yep. For once, he had planned ahead. This time, he knew what he was doing. He would take them to one of those Mississippi or Arkansas border towns and turn them over to someone who would pay him for bringing them back so they could be returned to their owners.

CHAPTER FORTY-SEVEN

The sun hugged the horizon, its golden rays warming the bedroom. Luke slipped out of bed, dressed, then strolled to the barn. Today he would start on his path to redemption.

After giving the sheriff's horse oats and plenty of water, he packed the saddlebags with supplies. He led the stallion to the house, gave Sally a tight hug and long kiss, telling her he was going to Independence to check on Mister Watkins and to look for work. Shouldn't be gone more than a couple of days.

Before she could ask too many questions, he rode off into the sunrise. Telling the truth strained his shirt buttons.

Reining up at his folks' house, Luke knocked then stepped inside, knowing Ma would already be up and cooking. Bacon and coffee smells wafted across his nose. His stomach rumbled.

"Ma? It's me. Luke." He followed his nose into the kitchen. Ma stood at the stove, a fork in her hand. "Where's Pa?"

"How about a hug or peck on the cheek for your ma before questions?"

A rule he had broken many times. He gave her both, then set her back on her feet.

Ma beamed. "You boys've grown up big and strong. Makes me proud."

"Thanks." Luke vowed to give her cause to be proud. "Pa?"

She forked the bacon, turning it over in the cast-iron pan. "Your pa's a bit poorly this morning. Something's not sitting good on his stomach. I've made him pumpkin seed tea. Always gets rid of the ache."

It sure did. Luke thought back to a couple of doses he'd received. He'd spent half the day in the privy, but it got rid of the ache.

"Hope he feels better soon." Luke pointed over his shoulder. "Just came by to tell you I'm heading over to Independence. Hear there's work. Nothing else anywhere around here. I'll be gone a day or two." He looked up the stairs. "Where's James?"

"Star wanted to mail a letter before the stage leaves. They walked into town, but should be back shortly." Ma stopped, planted one hand on a hip, the other waved the fork at Luke's face. "You just be careful. I hear there's border ruffians around."

"I'll be fine." He planted a kiss on her forehead. "Think Pa would mind if I borrowed one of his horses? I'm takin' back the one I borrowed."

She paused, glanced toward the closed front door, then sighed. "I suppose so. He can use his older one until you get back." Ma frowned. "You need to be looking for a horse of your own since yours is permanently lame. Gonna put her down, are ye?"

Luke nodded. One lie was as good as another.

Ma waggled a finger at him. "Can't go always borrowin', can ye?" Her Irish accent thickened the words.

Luke chuckled. Every time Ma got angry or concerned, out popped the accent.

"Tell Pa thanks and I'll bring him back good as new." Luke hugged her again. "See you in a couple of days. Ask James to stop by the house, check on Sally. And tell him I'll buy him a beer."

"You have to go now? Today? Maybe ask around town—"

"I have, Ma. Bye." Before she could give him more advice, Luke eased the front door closed, afraid of bothering Pa. The less he knew, the better.

Luke strode across the yard to the barn, the voice in his head telling him to hurry. Would the slaves still be there? He stopped when he opened the barn door. What would he do if the holding site was empty? That was easy. Ride to Independence and return the horse is what he'd do.

First things first, though. He saddled Pa's horse, which had been stabled in the largest stall. Luke admired the sleek coat of James' buckskin. Muscles rippled across the back. A fine piece of horseflesh. He led Pa's horse outside and tied it with his stolen one.

Back into the barn. He slid the door to the holding site aside, and peered in. Three sets of eyes blinked back.

Luke squatted and then eased in for a better look. A man, a woman and a small child stared at him, their eyes blinking at the unaccustomed light. Luke whispered, "You're safe with me. We're moving. Come on." He scrambled out of the opening, hoping, praying Pa wouldn't be standing behind him when he stood and turned around.

Nobody. Luke's chest relaxed. Just the way he'd planned. He stood close enough to the man to pin his age at around twenty-five. A short beard covered his face and his dark eyes emitted sadness, yet resiliency. The man stood at Luke's height, but with the bulging muscles in his arms and neck, he resembled a bull. Luke's eyes watered. This man hadn't bathed in days, if not weeks. Maybe not even years.

"I'm Mister Colton." He regarded the woman. Shorter than him, her body appeared muscled. Looking to be in her late teens, her ebony skin glistened with sweat, her eyes flashed defiance, maybe hatred. She clutched the child to her side.

She nodded and glanced toward the door.

"Let's go." Luke held his breath as he opened the door. Again, no Pa.

Luke pointed to his stolen horse for the man to ride with the child, and Luke would take Pa's horse and the woman. They'd ride double until he could sell these slaves back to their owners. The plan was working well.

Five miles outside of town, Luke reined up near the Kansas River. Using wild cherry thickets for cover, he allowed the horses to drink their fill. The two slaves kept their eyes on Luke, scrutinizing his every move, even as they squatted at the river. Uncomfortable, still he knew he was doing the right thing.

"What's your name?" Luke asked the man.

"Ezekiel, sir."

Luke turned to the woman who clutched the child behind her. "And yours?" He held up a hand. "I'm not gonna hurt you or the boy. Just wondering what I should call you and where you're from."

She took a deep breath. "Polly, sir." She paused long enough for her eyes to trail over Luke's face. "This here's Henry. He's 'most four."

What Luke hadn't noticed until then was how much lighter Henry's skin was than the other two. "Is he both of yours, ma'am?"

Polly shot a look at Ezekiel. "No, sir. He's just mine, sir."

"I see." Luke knew there was a story needed telling, but not now. "Where're you from?"

"Georgia, sir," Ezekiel said. "And Polly's from Arkansas." He stood close to Luke. "We ain't goin' back there, is we, sir?"

"No. Just curious." Luke stepped away, the nearness and stench close to unbearable. He held the horses' reins. "Time to go."

CHAPTER FORTY-EIGHT

A melancholy dusk covered the earth before Luke stumbled upon a cave. They built a small fire in the back, and then rummaged through the saddlebags until they found enough to make a meal.

The jerky he'd packed, along with dried fruit from Ma's cherry and apricot trees, would make a filling supper. Not as good as Ma's Sunday fried chicken, but enough.

Luke attempted small talk, but neither slave spoke more than giving short answers. Even little Henry was quiet. They eyed each other like pumas and bears deciding who would live and who would die.

With supper finished, Luke brought in the two saddles and saddle blankets. Pleased with himself for thinking ahead, he'd also brought a rain slicker and a bedroll. The four of them would sleep dry and well tonight.

At first light, Luke and Ezekiel fed and saddled the horses. Polly cooked the rabbit Luke had shot at sunrise. It crackled over the open fire, the aroma making Luke's mouth water. After eating, they repacked the saddlebags. Polly's hands, callused and rough, were gentle with the boy as she helped him on the horse. His green eyes and light-brown hair reminded Luke of his own son. At least his son's future was brighter than this child's. As a slave, Henry couldn't decide his future, couldn't marry who he loved, couldn't live life his way. But then again, as he grew, he'd be useful. The South needed him. Luke found comfort there.

Keeping off the main road, Luke headed east planning to cross over into Missouri by nightfall. So far, they'd traveled well, making at least fifty miles yesterday. As he rode, his plan took shape. He'd take them as far as Arkansas, find someone willing to buy them, head up to Independence, finish his business there, then trot on home. It was working out well.

Full dark found them still riding, but in Missouri, Luke was sure. He'd traveled this route many times and was confident his little party could head south first thing in the morning. Then two, three days and they'd be in Arkansas. Although prairie surrounded him, a hill off to his left offered a bit of shelter.

Unsaddling his horse, Ezekiel stopped, turning to Luke. "I been this way 'fore, sir. We been headin' east now two days. You takin' us back?"

The man's broad shoulders straightened. Luke shook his head. "We *are* heading east, you're right. But over in Independence, they got conductors that'll take you to safety. It's better there than in Lawrence."

Did he buy it? Luke doubted this slave was stupid. Maybe he couldn't read or do numbers, but he had exhibited a load of common sense in the two days Luke had known him. Maybe because he was in his mid-twenties. Luke's oldest brother Trace was also full of common sense.

Luke would have to keep an extra-sharp eye on this one tonight. Ezekiel finished unsaddling his horse.

Sometime before sunup it had rained. Luke woke to the smell of fresh air, a light cooling breeze. Damp. His clothes and hat were damp. His bedroll damp. Rubbing his eyes open, he blinked at Polly, sitting on a saddle blanket, the slicker around both her and the boy.

"Good mornin', Mister Colton," she said, a timid smile on her face. Her eyes shone. "Smell good this mornin', don't it, Mister Colton."

"Does for a fact."

Polly looked at her son. "Know what it smell like, sir?"

Luke sat twisting his back, hunching his shoulders. "No. What?"

"Like freedom." Polly stroked her son's head. "Clean, fresh freedom." Her smile blossomed.

That sack of grain sat on Luke's chest again. He pushed aside guilty thoughts. Had to be done. His gaze took in the wet campfire, the wood gathered for the morning meal soaked. All sense of bliss crumbled.

How could he sleep through rain? Must've been tired. The glistening prairie grass slid under his knees while he stretched up to his feet. Wet. Everything was wet. Damn rain. Why couldn't it wait a day or two?

He stretched out his arms, twisted his torso. Squinting into the morning sunrise, he spotted Pa's horse, still hobbled and busy munching on grass. Just one horse. Where was the other one? His stolen sheriff's horse.

Missing. And Ezekiel. Both gone. Luke glared at Polly. "You know he left?" His words shot out.

"Yes, sir." Her eyes darted toward the north.

"You know he was planning to?" Luke moved in close to the runaway.

"No, sir."

"Where'd he go to?" Luke asked himself more than her.

"Don't know, sir."

"Dammit to hell!" He kicked at a clump of grass, glared again at Polly, fisted and then unfisted his hands.

Luke stomped in every direction looking for a sign, any sign, of which way Ezekiel had ridden. Unfortunately, the deluge

253

covered his tracks. No hoofprints, no parted grass, no dirt clods pushed to one side. No, nothing. That damn runaway slave was flat gone.

His circular path spiraled farther and farther out until he realized camp sat at least a hundred yards back. Would she be gone now, too? If she was still there, should he tie her up? However, with the child, chances were she wouldn't run. It would be tough going if she did. But then again, she'd run this far from Arkansas. Nothing to do about Ezekiel, but he could certainly be more careful with Polly.

Anger erupted. He muttered, mumbling oaths and curses, anything that popped into his mind. Most of his things, including the stolen horse, gone. Should never have taken his eyes off that Negro. He didn't trust him, never had.

He stormed back to camp. The minute Polly spotted him, she stood, wrapping Henry in the slicker.

Everything was ruined and Luke needed to fix it. His future had depended on Ezekiel, and now with his running off, that ungrateful fugitive had shattered Luke's chances of making some money. Damn him! Luke grabbed Polly's shoulders, tight. She winced.

"Where'd he go? Tell me." He shook her. "Where?"

"Don't know, sir." Her wide eyes, once full of jubilation, now radiated fright.

"Yes, you do!" His hands tightened on each shoulder, the blouse material bunching in the grip. "Tell me!" Luke's gaze trailed to Henry. "You know. You tell me!"

With Polly still in his grip, Luke leaned toward the child. Polly yanked out of Luke's hands and with it, her blouse ripped right down the middle. The blouse hung in tatters around her waist, her dingy shredded camisole covering only bits and pieces of her ebony skin.

Both froze. Her thin straps did little to cover her shoulders, pink lines branching out across the top of her chest. Luke wanted to avert his eyes, but couldn't pull his gaze away. She turned her back to him. Bumpy lines, scars covered what he could see. One zigzagged across her shoulder and down under the camisole.

The bottom fell out of Luke's stomach. Words refused to form.

Polly's words were soft. "Master always took the whip to me when he was angry." She turned to face Luke. "You gonna beat me, too?"

"Beat? Whip?" Luke winced at what must've been painful. "No, I ain't. Guess it's not your fault Ezekiel ran off." His eyes traced one of the wicked scars. "Why'd your master whip you? What happened?"

The light in her eyes turned dim. "When I told him I . . . was with child, *his* child, he said I lied and that . . . well, it weren't his." A tear slid down her cheek. "After Henry was born, Master borrowed me out to any man who had an extra dollar. Said I owed him for lyin'."

Luke swallowed hard, all anger drained.

"Then," said Polly. "I heard they was gonna sell me permanent to some man, and Henry was gonna be sold to a different plantation." A second tear sat on her eye. "I couldn't let that happen. I gotta be with my boy. So I ran. Ran until a fella picked me up and took us to a safe house. We hid up in his attic for a day or two."

"Where was that?" Luke asked.

"Don't know, for sure, but they called the conductor Elwood Smith. But that fella only visited me once. Most of 'em . . ." Her eyes roamed the sky then stopped on Henry. "I'd lie with every man in the world just to keep my son."

She wouldn't "lie with" him, Luke vowed. He turned his back, now embarrassed to have seen her partially naked. "Fix

255

yourself, Polly. I ain't gonna hurt you."

"You wanna—"

"No." He knew exactly what she offered, and under different circumstances he may well have taken her up on it. But not now. Emotions in his chest collided—pity, contempt, outrage. No way in hell he'd sell her back. She'd been to hell and now that she was out, he'd be sure she continued her journey to freedom. She and Henry. Maybe what Sally and Ma said was right. Maybe Pa, even James, with their anti-slavery rant, was right.

For the first time, Luke understood slavery. It wasn't pretty. It was ugly. Damn ugly.

CHAPTER FORTY-NINE

Too far to ride back to Lawrence with a runaway slave and a four-year-old, Luke decided to continue on to Independence and take Polly and Henry to Mister Watkins. His general store would be a hiding place for a while, especially since Watkins knew about escaped slaves. Or at least he should have since it was his barrels that hid slaves earlier this year. Although Lincoln's so-called Emancipation Proclamation had been issued months before, it affected only certain states. Luke wasn't sure which ones it applied to, and judging by the slaves still hiding, many people didn't know, either. Slaves weren't free, that's all Luke knew.

Skirting the road, Luke walked his horse while Polly and Henry rode. No way would Pa's horse carry three. Not easily at least. He certainly didn't want to harm his only means of transportation, especially on this road. He'd been stranded three times already, and he wasn't about to add a fourth.

Late-afternoon sun warmed Luke's back as the first buildings of Independence danced on the horizon. While he'd walked, he'd gone over endless conversations in his head with Mister Watkins.

Luke chose pleading ignorance and innocence as the best route. Watkins had taken quite a blow to the head, and there was a chance he didn't remember who clobbered him. Luke knew he'd pretty near perfected a decent poker face, but daggers of doubt edged into his confidence when it came to bold-faced lying. Too often he'd practiced on his wife. Maybe that would come in handy.

A stand of oaks outside of town would have to do as a hiding place for Polly and the boy. If Henry didn't fuss or run around, chances were they wouldn't be detected. Undergrowth near the river covered the bottom half of the trees. It was in there they would hide.

With the second rabbit Luke had shot and some jerky in the saddlebag, he felt sure he'd left enough food before heading into town. If all went well, he'd come back for Polly before full dark, and while they hid in the store, or wherever fugitives stayed, he would spend the night, dry and comfortable, in a hotel bed. After breakfast, he'd visit with Watkins then start home for Lawrence, and the beginnings of a new life.

That was the plan.

The door to Watkins Mercantile creaked open, that little bell jingling, as Luke stepped in. He cringed. It was that bell and those customers that had ruined everything. Certainly Clarke Blackhorn wasn't supposed to get killed. It had been a while since Luke had stepped foot in this store. Hopefully, it would be his last.

He rethought that. "Last" was so . . . permanent.

A careful study of the store revealed three customers browsing—one woman selecting a bolt of calico and two men discussing the various qualities of the pickax each one held. They stopped, staring at Luke. He nodded to the men, tipped his hat to the woman who flashed a man-eating smile, then all three returned to their efforts.

Stepping out from the back room, a man, older than Luke but not by much, nodded to him. "Howdy. Help ya?"

All the air out of Luke's lungs, he struggled to breathe as he edged toward the man. "I'm looking for Mister Ben Watkins." Luke swung his gaze left to right. "He in?"

The man stopped, eyebrows knitting. "Depends. What d'you need him for?"

Luke lowered his voice as he walked up close. "I've got some merchandise he might be interested in. Thought we could do some business."

"Ben's my uncle. You can do business with me." The man motioned Luke aside while the woman brought the fabric up to the counter.

As the man cut the calico, wrapped it, discussed buttons and thread with her, Luke roamed the store. He tried peeking in the back, but the door was closed halfway, giving him a partial view of more crates.

The woman thanked the man, raised one perfectly shaped eyebrow at Luke as she turned, then sashayed out the door, her bustle in full swing. The bell tinkled. Nice, Luke thought. Nice.

"What kind of merchandise you talkin' about?"

The man's voice in Luke's ear brought him back to reality.

"It's rather of a personal nature, if you don't mind." Luke deepened his voice. "I'd rather speak with your uncle. He in the back?"

Hesitation spread over the man's pockmarked face, his sandy brown hair oiled down hard. The part in the middle wasn't straight. "I'll see if he wants to talk to you. What'd you say your name was?"

Luke hadn't said, didn't want to. But unless he could come up with something else, fast, he'd have to stick with what he knew. He blurted out, "Luke Colton from Lawrence. Worked for Gibson's Mercantile. Hauled freight for your uncle."

Damn! Why was he always volunteering information that wasn't asked? Another kick in his britches would be called for about now. The man frowned deeper, then mumbled something, turned on his heels trudging to the back room.

"I recognize your name," one of the customers said. The ax

in his hand glinted in the evening sun as he marched toward Luke. "Saw it on a wanted poster this morning."

"That's right," said the other one, sidling up to Luke. "Says you robbed this here very store. Hell"—he glanced at his friend—"even stole a horse, the sheriff's horse."

"What?" Luke prayed he was ready for the charade. One man grabbed his upper arm while the other one pulled Luke's gun out of its holster. The barrel jammed into his ribs. Luke jerked his arms skyward. "What're you talking about?"

"You know what we're talking about. The robbery last month. You tried to kill Ben Watkins." Metal scraping against metal as the pistol's hammer pulled back thundered in Luke's ears. The man spoke to the other customer. " 'Tis a head scratcher, Bill. This man here marches in bold as you please, like we ain't got the brains to figure it out."

"Now wait a minute, fellas," Luke said. "You got it all wrong. I ain't held up anybody. I've been back in Lawrence with my wife. Ask her. Ask my brother. Been haulin' freight with him. They'll tell you. It wasn't me." Luke hadn't planned on telling strangers this rehearsed story, but it came easily, nevertheless.

The ax man pointed to the door. "We'll see how your story checks out with the sheriff."

Luke froze. "Hold on." He regarded both men. "You said it yourself. If I did what you say, why in the world would I march in here? Huh?" Luke held up both hands. "Be kinda like suicide, wouldn't it?"

The man pushed Luke forward. "Get moving."

Again, that damn bell tinkled as the man pulled on the door handle.

"Wait a minute." Ben Watkins' voice called from the back room doorway. "Where you going with him?"

"Says he's Luke Colton," Bill said. "He's the fella tried to kill you."

The gun-toting man nodded. "Gonna let the sheriff sort it out."

Luke turned at Ben's voice, shaky, weak and tinny. Still, maybe he'd just bought Luke a few extra minutes. Luke produced a wide smile. "Mister Watkins. Heard you got hurt. Sure sorry to hear about it. You remember me?"

Watkins, his nephew at his side, wobbled into the store and propped himself against the counter.

He frowned, cocked his bandaged head at Luke, then straightened up. Bill's grip on Luke's right arm tightened.

While Watkins caught his breath, Luke jumped in. "These fellas here think I had something to do with your robbery." He fidgeted against the stranglehold making his arm tingle. "You mind telling them it wasn't me? You know I wouldn't do anything like that. You know me."

Time froze while Watkins thought. The two customers shifted their feet and weight. Ben's nephew looked from man to man. Luke prayed. While it wasn't so much a real prayer like he'd heard Sally and her pa say, still it was a message sent Heavenward. Something about changing his ways if he got out of this mess alive.

Watkins' clear eyes met Luke's. "Sorry, son. Can't say for sure it wasn't you."

"But you can't say for sure it *was* me." Luke's heart sat heavy in his chest.

Watkins motioned for him to move in closer. "Yeah, you're the one."

"What?" Luke's voice rose higher. The gun barrel aimed at his head.

"Yeah, you're the one hauls freight for Gibson, don't ya? I *do* know you. You're Luke Colton." Watkins shook a pointed finger in Luke's face. "Came by here, let's see . . . month or so ago."

"Two months, yes sir," Luke said.

"Then how'd the sheriff get his name?" the ax man asked.

"My uncle told them, that's how." The nephew gripped Watkins' elbow. "Best sit down now, Uncle. All this excitement's not good for you."

Watkins wobbled as he turned. "I know, I know. Quit fussin' over me. Just like a layin' hen over her eggs." Two steps then he spoke over his shoulder. "Let 'im go, boys. I must've said his name 'cause I sure as hell couldn't remember my own." A chuckle followed him into the darkened room.

The grip on Luke's arm relaxed and so did the tightness in his chest. Heart still thundering, he managed to speak over it. "No harm done, men." He pointed toward the back room. "Now if you'll give me my gun back, I gotta talk to Mister Watkins." He stepped away.

"Not so fast."

Bill nodded to his friend. "Let's take him down to the sheriff. I'd feel better knowing for sure this fella's innocent."

"But I am." Luke knew he'd get struck by lightning for lying, but there wasn't a cloud in the sky. "No need to waste the sheriff's time. Mister Watkins told you he was mistaken."

"Mister Watkins has been confused, but he said your name yesterday." Bill jammed the gun barrel into Luke's ribs. "Now the sheriff knows who did it, he's gettin' up a posse right now." He turned to his friend. "We just saved him the trouble."

"Sure as shootin' did."

Luke planted his feet. "I'm telling you. You got the wrong man."

"But we want the sheriff to say so." Bill nudged Luke. "Let's go."

Luke walked down the street through a gauntlet of gawkers. Women reached for their children while the men reached for their guns. The farther he walked, the longer he had to concoct a better story.

The sheriff bought none of it. Instead of a friendly pat on the shoulder, he locked the cell door, smirking. Luke glared out between the bars. "At least get a hold of my older brother. We drive freight together. He can tell you we were hauling for Mister Gibson."

Those iron bars grew warm in Luke's hands. This was not part of the plan. The sheriff's wide shoulders rose and fell with laughter. "Sure you was. And I was in Paris eating crumpets with the Queen." He turned around and stood close to Luke. "You Kansas prairie fairies are all alike. You think you can waltz into *my* town, beat *my* businessmen, and then steal *my* horses." He spit as he spoke, but Luke didn't dare try wiping his face right now. "The judge'll be here soon enough. He'll deal with you then."

"Sheriff," Luke said. "I can assure you I don't have your stolen horse." Then Luke decided to try out his Colton family charm. He pushed a smile onto his face. "With that robbery, I'm sure it's an honest mistake. I can see how Mister Watkins got me mixed up—"

"Ain't no 'mixed up' about it, Mister Colton. Mister Watkins just yesterday remembered your name." The sheriff's eyes narrowed. "Now, why d'you suppose he said your name?"

CHAPTER FIFTY

Five endless days passed while Luke sat in jail. Half the town stopped by the jail, wanting to see who'd stolen the sheriff's horse and beat the poor shopkeeper.

With Mister Watkins still an invalid, Luke's only choice was to ask to see Watkins' nephew and tell him about Polly and Henry, where they were. The nephew promised to take care of the matter and get them to safety. Luke hoped Polly would have sense enough to stay put until someone came to help them.

At least that was going right. On the other hand, the sheriff took pleasure in parading past the cell, reminding Luke the judge's arrival was imminent. Soon, very soon, his trial would start, then be over like *that*. He'd snap his fingers, then gloat. Luke would swing. Maybe by this time tomorrow, the sheriff said, Luke's boots and horse would both be up for grabs.

No amount of pleading or logic would dissuade the sheriff. And the jail, along with its iron bars, was secure. When he wasn't worrying about Polly or Sally, Luke worried about himself. He couldn't swing for this. If stupid Cole Younger hadn't wanted to make a show of killing Watkins, they'd never have been caught. Damn Cole. Damn Clarke.

On second thought, damn *himself*.

Luke sat on the hard bunk and stared at the closed door. With only a tiny window in his cell and one in the empty cell next to his, it was dark. At night, he couldn't see his hand in front of his face. Sitting here, now fully aware of his future, something moist pressed against his eyes.

At twenty, he was gonna swing. His world would end.

Then it hit him. *Just like James.* His brother had been accused of killing a sheriff a couple years back, and he ended up with a rope around his neck. James rarely mentioned it, except when he was drunk one time, then the whole story erupted. Thankfully, James said, people stepped forward and got the judge to free him at the last moment. But that terror still lay just under James' surface.

"I'm telling you, it *is* Mister Gibson's signature, Sheriff." Loud, frustrated words penetrated the wooden cell door. Luke stood. The voice sounded like James.

Mumbles, curses. Then silence. Boots stomping Luke's way.

The inside jail door flew open, light barreled in. Luke recoiled like a vampire. He squinted at the sheriff. Behind him stood James.

The sheriff jerked his thumb over his shoulder. "This here fella says he's your brother." After a long, scrutinizing look, he stood back. "Sure enough is. Don't that beat all. You two look enough alike to be twins."

James moved up next to the sheriff. "Brought a letter from Mister Gibson confirming we were hauling freight over to Franklin same time they say you robbed Watkins' mercantile. Stole a horse." He held it up. "But the sheriff doesn't believe it's Gibson's writing."

Glimmers of hope flooded Luke's chest. He nodded at the scribbled curlicues. "It's his. But maybe take it over to Mister Watkins—he might recognize it."

Luke held his breath while James and the sheriff spoke with Watkins.

Within half an hour and like music to his ears, the cell door clicked open and Luke stepped into freedom, apologies from the sheriff sailing out the door. Luke couldn't get away fast enough. James and he rode without speaking until Independence turned into a memory.

James and Luke reined up at the river and allowed their horses to drink. The brothers stood, looking at the horses, the prairie, the sky, anything but each other.

Luke took a long breath. "Thanks for coming for me. I don't know how you convinced Mister Gib—"

"I didn't." James shot a withering glare at Luke. "When I got word from Albert Perkins what was going on, *I* wrote it."

"Albert told you?"

James nodded. "I lied for you, Luke. Flat out lied for you. You're damn lucky Perkins had business in Independence." He yanked off his hat, ran a shaking hand through his hair. "Hell, Luke, I even distracted Watkins from comparing Gibson's signatures on the bills of lading."

"Don't know how you did, but—"

"This is the last straw, Luke," James ranted. "Last straw. I'm done with your bad judgment, your lies and half-truths. I'm done with you doing what's best for Luke Colton. I'm done with . . ." He lowered his voice and faced Luke. "You. I'm done with you."

"Done with me?" Luke clenched his fist wanting to swing. "What about what Andy did to help you last year? At sixteen, he moves to Mesilla to keep you from getting killed or killing yourself. You were a mess. Said so yourself. He quits his job, leaves home. Hell, James, he joined the Union army for you, even got shot—all to help a brother." Every muscle in Luke's body tightened. "And now you're saying you're not willing to do for me, what our little brother did for you? What makes *you* so damn special?"

James' face remained emotionless, although his brown eyes shifted.

Luke's words turned soft. "I needed your help. Bad. You were the only person who could save my life. I'm sorry you had to get involved. I know how you feel about lying, but you did it for me. I'll always be grateful."

James cocked one eyebrow.

Luke scanned the horizon and then returned his gaze to James. "Hell, go ahead and be done with me. I probably deserve it. But know this . . . I'd do anything for you, in a heartbeat. I always back my brothers' play."

CHAPTER FIFTY-ONE

August 14, 1863

The August heat stifled all of Luke's energy. Even the act of sitting on the porch fanning himself turned wearisome. Last night was the third night in a row all four of them had slept outside on the porch. A wet blanket strung along one end, fanned by gentle breezes, cooled the air enough to allow them to catch a couple hours of sleep. The baby fussed and fidgeted most of the day, Adam whined and complained more than usual, and Sally . . . Luke couldn't live with her. When she was especially cranky, like now, he found chores in the barn that needed his attention. The cigar and flask hidden under the hanging harnesses near the stalls eased some of the ringing in his ears.

While Luke sat in the barn this morning, the barrel under his rear turning hard, he thought about the past month. Once his brother sprung him from jail, he stayed home more, worked harder fixing the roof and odd jobs around the house, visited his parents without incessant prompting, and even helped James and Morningstar move into the Eldridge Hotel. While James was guarded in his conversations with Luke, he now spoke in complete sentences and more often—politely.

It surprised everyone, especially him, when he wrote a letter to his brothers in Mesilla. Luke told Trace and Andy what he and James were doing, inviting them to visit. His brothers. He missed them. When they were kids he thought they'd always be together. But when Trace turned nineteen, he went off on his own following the Santa Fe Trail down into Santa Fe, and finally ending up in Mesilla. His leaving hurt, but Luke had his other two brothers—one older, one younger. But then a year after Trace left, James left. And life would never be the same.

"Luke? You in there? Luke?" The barn door screeched open. Smitty Jenkins, flanked by the Iverson boys, stormed in. Jenkins slid the door shut. The three men glanced around as if expecting the Union army to be waiting.

"What's going on?" Luke dabbed out his cigar and corked the flask. "What're you doing here?" It wasn't like his former "Cutthroats" to barge in. Judging by the looks on their faces, the news wasn't good. In fact, it looked grim.

Smitty, his lanky body imposing, peered down at Luke. "You haven't heard?"

Luke shook his head.

Tobias and Gunnar glanced out the windows then moved in closer to Luke and Smitty. Luke's gaze flitted from man to man. "What's going on?"

Gunnar gave a deep sigh, one that comes with bringing terrible news. "It's Quantrill. Cole Younger."

Smitty kicked at dirt. "There's been an accident, Luke." He pointed east. "Over in Kansas City, that women's prison over there."

Luke had heard that three of Cole Younger's sisters, along with two cousins, were jailed there. All because they were related to Cole. That and the fact they were aiding the Confederates' cause.

"It burned down." Tobias shook his head. "The women, the women killed. Ceiling and walls collapsed, they couldn't get out."

"My God." Luke sagged against a post. "How many?"

"They're saying around eighty," Smitty said. "A couple were cousins of Quantrill and some were friends of the James boys."

He swiped his mouth with a sleeve. "Younger's out of control, and Quantrill's steaming mad. He's blaming Jim Lane and his cronies for it."

Gunnar lowered his voice. "Quantrill's out for blood. Lots of it."

"Hell, Luke," Smitty said. "He's aimin' straight for Lawrence. We're riding out right now to join him. Figured you'd want to come along."

"What we gotta do," Luke said as he headed for the door, "is warn everybody. Get the women and children to safety."

Smitty grabbed hold of Luke's arm. "You ridin' with Quantrill? Or against him?"

Feeling like he'd been hit in the face with ice water, Luke frowned up at his friend. "He's fighting a losing battle." Luke took in Gunnar and Tobias' wide eyes. "He can't win. And he shouldn't be coming here to fight. Leave civilians out of it."

"Civilians?" Smitty stepped back, his hands clenched. "Who the hell've you been killing? I don't remember uniforms on most of them people. They were civilians."

"Dammit, Smitty. Ain't you been reading the papers? It's over. The war's about over. The South's gonna lose. States' rights is gonna lose." Luke found himself uttering his pa's words. "Most the slaves been freed. What we gotta do now is figure out how to put us back together."

"You're a bigger damn fool than I thought." Gunnar shoved Luke backward. "Right now when you're needed most, you run and hide. Turn traitor."

Tobias hitched up his britches, repositioning his gun belt. "Thought you still saw things our way." He turned his back and stepped into the daylight. Gunnar shook his head followed by a deep sigh. He disappeared into the brightness of day.

If Quantrill was hopping mad, then it wouldn't be long before he'd strike. Luke caught up with Smitty at the barn door. "How long ago did this happen?"

Smitty Jenkins turned around facing Luke. "Yesterday. They're still identifying bodies."

He stepped toward his horse, then stopped. "Came by to tell you Quantrill's headed for your pa's house right now."

CHAPTER FIFTY-TWO

Luke wrapped Sally in a hug close to his chest. "Awful news."

By the time he finished the story, he knew what had to be done. Move Ma and Pa somewhere safe, find James and Morningstar, tell them. Sally and the kids would go to her folks' house. Nobody would harm a minister, a man of the cloth. The Burroughs were safe. He had a flash of the minister's body lying on the steps of the church in Cane Hill, but no, Beckett had been caught in crossfire. That had been an accident, hadn't it?

Once that was done, he'd sound the town's alarm. Fortunately, with just under three thousand people living in about one square mile, it wouldn't take too long to warn everyone.

"You really think Quantrill will hit here?" Sally pulled out of Luke's grip. "Don't you think he'll go after Senator Lane and leave the rest of us alone?" Her panicked words broke Luke's heart. Damn him for bringing this on her. He knew once Quantrill or Cole found out he'd quit the cause, Luke would rise right up there next to Lane on Quantrill's "need to be killed" list. No doubt.

"I know he will." Luke grabbed up the baby. Her blue eyes so innocent.

"You do?" Sally stopped packing and turned to Luke. "How?"

Would he say? Tell her the truth? Her wide eyes demanded answers. Luke's chest rose with the pull in air. He fought for the right words. "I've been riding with him. But not anymore. I'm done."

Eyes narrowing, Sally's lips pursed. "You've been lying to me? All this time? Luke—"

"I'm sorry. So sorry." Luke tried to hug her but she moved back, out of reach. "I did what I thought I should do."

"Lie to me? What about your folks? And James? You lie to them, too?"

Luke nodded. "Not James. He knows."

"Fine." Sally stuffed the rest of her clothes into a canvas bag. "Great. Brothers stick together even in something like this. He should've . . . I should've . . . you should've—"

"No time to argue right now. Gotta get you all safe." Luke picked up the bag over Sally's glares. "We'll work this out."

Sally snatched the baby out of Luke's arms, turned her back on him and stormed outside. He followed. She waited for Luke to lift Adam into the back of the buggy, then handed the baby to him while she climbed into the buggy. Taking the baby from Luke, she snugged Hannah into a basket by her feet. Sally glared at Luke and spoke through clenched teeth.

"This isn't over." She clucked the reins over the horse's back and clattered out of the yard.

Luke galloped to his parents', hoping, praying his friends were wrong. Would Pa and Ma agree to leave or at least stay with the Burroughs until Quantrill had killed Lane? He doubted it, but Luke would insist. Pa wasn't as strong as he once was, and while Ma was expert at killing chickens and still mighty feisty for her age, Luke could pick her up and sling her over his shoulder like a sack of potatoes. She wouldn't like leaving, but at least she'd be safe.

Luke knocked at the front door, then marched in. "Ma? Pa? It's Luke. Where're you at?" No smells of lingering breakfast, no Ma calling out from the upstairs bedrooms, no Pa sitting on the settee. Luke dashed upstairs confirming no parent in any of the bedrooms, then flew downstairs and out the front door. A glance at the barn told him what he'd missed earlier. The door was open and two darkened figures moved inside. Did they have new runaway slaves?

As he ran he thought about what he'd told Ma and Pa about the three missing slaves. They'd bought the story that while Pa was sick, one of the other conductors came by and helped the Negroes on their way to freedom. It had happened before, Pa said. Made sense. Usually he helped when the slaves were moving, but not always.

Out of breath, Luke rushed into the barn, its darkness momentarily blinding him. He squinted at Pa. "We gotta go. You and Ma. Head over to the Burroughs'. You should be safe there."

Ma propped the rake against a post and ran her hands down her apron. Arms full of harness and ropes, Pa muttered something and then turned to face Luke. "What the hell you goin' on about, son? What'd you say?"

Tugging on Ma's arm, Luke used his head to point outside. "Quantrill and his Raiders are heading this way. It's gonna get ugly. They're gunning for Lane, but will take down anybody and everybody that's in their way!" He pulled his ma toward the open air. "Grab what you gotta have, then let's go. No time to waste."

Pa finished hanging the harness and ropes on the wall. "Now just hold on a minute there. What's all this about?"

Luke recounted what he'd learned, leaving out the fact that until just recently he had been one of the Raiders. A trusted Raider at that, someone who rode alongside Quantrill. No, his folks didn't need to know right now. Undoubtedly Sally would tell them soon enough.

"And I figured nobody would hurt a minister." Leastways, he thought, not on purpose. "That's why you'll be safe with Sally's folks." Luke figured his heart would explode right out of his chest if they didn't get moving. "Please, come. Please."

Pa and Ma shot a long look at each other, then Pa nodded. "All right. We'll go. But just for a couple of hours. We won't impose on the Burroughs for very long."

Hoofbeats in the yard. Several horses loped through the front gate. Luke knew the identity even without looking. But he did look. Icy hot jabs of fear raced down his back.

William Quantrill. Frank James. Cole Younger and two others.

Luke pushed Ma and Pa back into the barn. They had to hide. Pa wouldn't tolerate having Quantrill on his property and sure as shooting he'd mouth off. That Partisan Ranger Bushwhacker would kill Pa dead, maybe Ma, too. Luke couldn't let that happen. He'd brought all this to them and now he had to protect them.

"Gotta hide." Luke's panic tightened every muscle.

Pa thrust out his chest. "I ain't afraid of—"

"You need to be. That's Quantrill and his top men. They'll kill you." Luke's gaze flitted from the open barn door where he spotted Quantrill stepping down from his mount, back to his folks. The slave hiding hole. Big enough.

"In there." Luke brushed aside the straw, yanked open the small door and pushed Ma's rear as she crawled inside. Pa twisted and turned to get in. Luke mounded the straw in place just as Quantrill strode inside.

"Colton." Quantrill swaggered farther into the barn, followed by Frank and Cole.

"Howdy," Luke said. Did he sound nervous, scared, terrified? He put down the rake and reached over to shake hands with Quantrill. "Just doin' chores."

How dumb was that? Quantrill was not stupid and could figure out pretty easy what was really going on.

"Your pa around?"

Luke shook his head. "Nah. Travels a lot."

"Fine." Quantrill spoke over his shoulder. "We'll set up headquarters here. Frank, you go in the house and rustle up some dinner. Cole, you ride back to the others and let 'em know where we are."

"Yes, sir."

Quantrill strutted across the barn, away from the concealed room. "Nice barn. Your pa's done well for himself. Yeah, it'll do fine." He stopped and turned to Luke. "Till you burn it down." Chuckles followed him outside.

When Quantrill was several yards away from the barn, Luke scrambled for the door hiding his parents, pushing straw aside. "Pa? Ma? Gotta get you outta here." He sat back on his haunches. "I'll distract Quantrill. You two get out and run for the ravine."

Ma nodded, her stoic face set hard. Pa pushed his way out, then helped Ma. Luke gave her a quick hug, then hurried outside.

While Luke talked to Quantrill, he watched his folks scurry outside, plaster themselves against the wood barn, and then disappear into the scrub oak shrouded ravine. Though not religious, he found that he was sending a lot of prayers Heavenward these last few days.

It took all of Luke's concentration and words to convince Quantrill that he needed to go into town. He promised to scout the perimeter and report back on army movement. Quantrill had agreed only after Luke promised results.

But what he *had* to do was get James and Morningstar to safety.

Wide Massachusetts Avenue bustled with more activity than usual. Luke jogged down the main commercial street dodging men and women scurrying back and forth, many toting baggage and armloads of packages. Two or three men made a show of loading their rifles and guns. At the north end of Massachusetts and a block around the corner stood the Eldridge.

Luke pushed open the doors and trotted past the desk clerk who called out, "Hear the news?"

Sliding to a halt, Luke backed up. "What news?"

Leaning over the counter, the man said, "Women's prison burned down. Quantrill's coming here to take revenge."

Nodding, Luke started off but the clerk's voice stopped him. "Got nothing to worry about, though."

Luke turned around. "How's that?"

Rolling his eyes as if Luke was a total moron, the clerk sighed and pointed east. "The army's got soldiers posted every five feet along the border. Ain't no way them ruffians gettin' through and comin' here. No, sir. We're safe."

There was some comfort there as well as information Luke would not share with Quantrill. It was clear Quantrill would strike from the south, where Pa's barn was, and from the east. With soldiers patrolling the perimeter, that might stop most of the threat. Luke allowed an easier breath. However, would they also come from the north? Probably not. That was Indian country and no white man lived there. No reason for Quantrill to go that way, although there were plenty of woodlands along the river. Good hiding place.

Luke would keep an ear to Quantrill's plans. He could alert the town before the Raiders struck.

Luke bolted up the steps to the third floor and pounded on James' door. It jerked opened.

James frowned. "Yeah? We were—"

"Quantrill's on his way. He's at Pa's barn right now. There's gonna be a lot of blood shed and I don't want it to be yours." Luke pushed his way in and nodded to Morningstar now clutching James' arm. "I'm gonna take you to Sally's folks. You'll be safe there."

"Slow down." James stood back, allowing Luke inside the room. The four-poster bed took up much of the space, its quilt giving off a homey feel. Luke pulled off his hat and took a deep breath. "You heard about the prison fire?"

"Made me cry," Morningstar said. "We heard it at breakfast this morning. Can you imagine those poor women?"

Luke shook his head. "Three of those were Cole Younger's sisters. And two cousins." His eyes met James' hard stare. He knew what his older brother was thinking. If this didn't slice and dice his relationship with James, then nothing would.

Morningstar's mouth turned down. "How horrible."

"Quantrill had a cousin in there, too. He's out for revenge and he's gonna start with Senator Lane." And maybe me, Luke thought.

"What's he doing at Pa's barn?" James' ran a hand across his mouth. "They all right?"

"For now." Luke pointed toward the door. "They're hiding in the ravine. Can you get them and take them to the Burroughs'?"

"Yeah." Three long strides took James across the length of the room, oaths and mutterings trailing after him. He stopped at the window overlooking the Kansas River. More muttering, then James turned to Morningstar. "Get a change of clothes. I'll take you to the Reverend's. Luke's right, you'll be safe there."

She nodded. "What about you?"

A long look at her, then James shifted his gaze to Luke. "After I get our folks, I'm staying with Luke. I always back my brother's play."

CHAPTER FIFTY-THREE

Luke and James passed the next two nights in Luke's old bedroom. They stayed close to Quantrill, who'd taken Pa and Ma's bigger room. Cole Younger occupied James' former bedroom while Frank slept downstairs and many of the men out in the barn. It had been reported four hundred men were gathering for this raid, and to Luke, it looked like two or three hundred were camping out of sight in the woods behind the barn, reminding him of the fighting at Prairie Grove. Even Luke's former Cutthroat friends were here. The Iverson boys were surprisingly missing. Maybe they were on their way.

With Frank sleeping inside, watching him was easy for Luke. Almost like he'd planned it.

What he hadn't planned on was how long Quantrill took to make decisions. Was he waiting for something? There were rumors Senator Lane was hiding out and Quantrill had sent scouts to find him. When they did, then Lord have Mercy, as Reverend Burroughs would say. It would be a bloodbath.

The entire town had shuttered and locked doors and windows while soldiers marched up and down the streets, ready to shoot anybody looking suspicious. Luke and James, telling Quantrill they were scouting and knew all the local hideouts, visited the Burroughs one night. They didn't stay long. There wasn't much to say, especially since none of the women would speak to Luke. And Pa's comments were directed at James.

He deserved their silence, he knew. After this was all over and

Quantrill was either killed or arrested, Luke would tell no more lies nor make such stupid mistakes again. He'd get a job and settle down. Or die trying.

CHAPTER FIFTY-FOUR

August 20, 1863

Luke held a coffee cup to his lips and spoke over the rim. Quantrill lounged in Pa's favorite chair. Early-morning sun warmed the room.

"Mister Quantrill, they find Senator Lane yet?" Luke cast his eyes sideways at James, standing in the kitchen doorway drinking coffee.

Quantrill shook his head. "Bastard's gone into hiding." He pointed a thick finger toward town. "But I'll find him. And when I do, I'll tear his worthless hide into a million pieces. His own ma won't recognize him."

There was no doubt Quantrill would do just that. Luke had witnessed it many times. A quick glance at his brother who'd lost some color in his cheeks. Damn Quantrill for bringing this on Luke's family. Then he rethought. No. Damn *me*.

A plan. Maybe they could murder Quantrill. Quantrill hadn't fully accepted James into the Raiders. He kept his words guarded when he was in the house. Luke rethought. Killing Quantrill would be close to impossible with all his lieutenants in the house. Still, he'd watch for a chance.

James set down his cup and pointed to the barn. "I'll tend to the horses." He shot a nod at Quantrill. "May need them soon."

"I'll help." Luke downed his last gulp of coffee, set the cup on the table and started for the door.

As he turned the knob, the door flew open, Cole Younger

pushing inside. Behind him trailed several Raiders.

"Found Lane." Cole thumbed over his shoulder. "Found that Jayhawking scum."

"Where's he at now?" Quantrill eased to his feet, a smirk sliding up his bearded face.

"Headed back into town taking the Fort Scott road. He don't know we're on his tracks." Cole chuckled. "Got Lieutenant Gregg following him. He'll be to town in an hour."

Quantrill's head did a slow up and down. He handed his coffee cup to Luke. "Come on, men. It's time." As he swept through the door, he tossed instructions over his shoulder. "Luke, gather the men in the barn. James, you come with me. Cole, good work."

Packed shoulder to shoulder in the barn, the men mumbled, grunted and checked their weapons. The excitement set Luke's nerves on fire, and from the looks of it, everybody else's as well. In an odd sort of way, Luke liked gatherings like this, getting ready for a masculine show of force. Too bad people would die.

Not if he could help it. Luke mentally listed then discarded ways to alert the town. "Men," Quantrill began. "The time has come. The day of reckoning is upon us. We'll show the good people of Lawrence what we're all about. It's time for Washington to know we mean business. It's time for those leech-sucking Jayhawkers to go to hell. And we'll help 'em."

Shouts and hoorays rumbled off the wooden walls.

"You all know what to do." Quantrill swept his gaze across the barn. "Let's do it!"

Pushing, elbowing, men poured out into the warm summer morning. Luke and James trailed near the rear, twenty men still behind them.

Before reaching the barn door, Quantrill grabbed Luke's arm. James stopped next to his brother. Cole Younger and Smitty Jenkins stopped behind them, blocking any retreat.

"You." Quantrill frowned. "Luke Colton." His dark eyes bore into Luke's soul.

"Sir?" Luke could only guess at Quantrill's thoughts. The outlaw's face, other than his narrowed eyes, wore no expression.

The Raider leaned in close to Luke. "Thought I could trust you. Thought you were one of us."

"What?" Luke's mouth turned bone dry.

"You're a lying, backstabbing son of a bitch traitor. I *know* what you've been doin'. Warning the town, helping slaves escape. You're a Jayhawker spy, Luke Colton, and I hate spies. *Detest* 'em." He turned to James. "And you're no better. You'll die with your brother. But not until we quarter him and feed him to your hogs."

Cole wrenched Luke's arms behind his back and tied his hands. Smitty grabbed James.

"What's going on?" Luke, no longer brave, no longer full of bravado, swallowed fear. His heart pounded in his ears. He would die and James with him.

Smitty Jenkins finished tying James' hands. Eyes wide and wild, James jerked and pulled, trying to free himself. He kicked, screamed words Luke didn't understand. Was his brother crazy? Seeing Indians?

The more James fought, the more men grabbed at him. He fought harder, but Luke knew not to thrash around. Until lately, he'd been the one doing the tying.

Quantrill moved in nose to nose with Luke. "It's over." He stepped back and then balled a fist, plowing it into Luke's left cheek. Luke spun crashing into the ground.

James fought harder against the arms pinning him. He glared at Quantrill. "Killer. Murderer. Hope you rot in hell!"

Quantrill balled a fist and plowed it into James' stomach. He smiled at the *umph* and impact. James doubled over.

"You know what to do, Cole." Quantrill nodded to his second

in command. "Light the match yourself."

"Yes, sir."

Someone yanked Luke to his feet and marched him over to the small door hidden in the stall. The straw, mounded so carefully, now lay scattered, spread out in front.

Quantrill followed. "Thought I didn't know that your pa helps escaped slaves? Found this the first night we were here. Pretty clever." He nodded. "We'll be payin' your pa a little visit real soon. *Thank* him for taking our property."

Strong hands shoved Luke inside the narrow confines. Before he could back in farther, James stumbled face first into Luke. The brothers squirmed, trying to sit upright.

"Make yourselves comfortable," Quantrill said. "Hell's comin' boys. Hell's comin'." He stood back, then kicked the door shut.

James rammed his shoulder into it, but a rake handle shoved up against the door kept it securely closed.

It was not totally dark, so Luke could make out his brother in front of him, but it was too dark to see well. Footsteps, laughter faded. Horses whinnied and then galloped off.

Luke pulled in air. Not just straw-laced air. Smoke.

"The barn!" James wiggled, plowing elbows into Luke's knees.

"Gotta get outta here." Fighting down panic, Luke struggled to figure out how to save his brother, himself and the entire town.

James kicked at the two-by-two door. Luke squinted at the wood planks of the barn's outside walls. Smoke curled under his nose. He coughed and choked. Would the wood break if he and James kicked hard enough?

Heat licked his face. "Kick the walls. With me." Luke scooted around, his feet now aimed at the outside wall. He kicked. With only a couple of inches of room to maneuver, he couldn't get much power behind his legs. James slid next to him.

One kick. Two. Three. Four.

A board splintered. Luke's eyes teared as he coughed. James lowered his head and gave the boards another stomp. Both men coughed.

Hot. Damn hot on Luke's back.

"Again." Sweat ran into Luke's eyes.

One kick. Two. *Crack.* The board splintered. Luke put his shoulder into it and shoved. His head stuck into fresh air. He pushed the rest of his body through and knelt while James wiggled into freedom.

James ran. His long strides took him across the pasture and down into the ravine. Luke followed, with his tied arms behind him, he struggled to stay upright.

Scrambling up the far side of the ravine, James stumbled, sliding down into a scrub oak. The limbs scratched his face, grabbed at his clothes.

"No more. No whips!" James thrashed against the clutches of the bush. His eyes squeezed tight, he muttered, then shouted something sounding like Indian talk.

Luke knelt by his trembling brother. "What's going on? You're all right. Nobody's got a whip." He wished he could use his hands to get James out from the bush and make him realize where he was.

"James? It's me. Luke."

Sobs and muttering slowed.

"James, you're in Kansas. You're safe." Luke considered. *Safe from the Apaches, at least.*

Opening his eyes, James scanned the ravine. His gaze rested on his brother. "Luke?"

Luke nodded.

"Sorry." James' shoulders heaved. "Being tied up . . . a slave . . ." He let out a long stream of air. "Never goes away."

"Understood." Luke didn't, but what he'd just seen shoved a

knot into his throat. Nobody could shake as hard as James was doing right now. They had to get untied and into town.

"If you can get out of that bush there, big brother, maybe we can untie each other." Luke wiggled his fingers. He had just enough feeling left.

Five minutes and they were free. Blood trickled down James' cheek from the scratches.

He wiped it off. Smoke filled the sky, wind carrying it east. The brothers stood at the edge of the pasture as the barn and house lit up, flames shooting out from everywhere, flicking from one end to the other.

Mind made up, Luke rubbed his wrists. "James, you get to the Burroughs'. Keep everybody safe. I'll go into town and see what I can do."

"I'll go with you." James spit out a mouthful of dirt. "I can help."

"No. I gotta do this. Take care of Quantrill. Alone."

CHAPTER FIFTY-FIVE

Smoke billowed toward him as he ran. Was the entire town in flames? The dirt road, littered with people running and screaming, felt like it stretched hundreds of miles. Luke couldn't get to town fast enough. He dodged desperate people, wild horses, buggies with nightclothed children on board—running out of town as he ran in.

As Luke rounded the corner on Fifteenth Street, he stumbled over a body. He plowed into the dirt road, pebbles gouging his palms. Luke rolled over, then sat up, rubbing his smoke-burned eyes. This early in the morning, shadows were dark and Luke struggled to identify the man he'd fallen over.

A closer look. Reverend Snyder. Luke froze. A reverend? They were supposed to be safe from bloodshed. And judging by the dried blood, this man of the cloth appeared to have been dead for a while. Maybe the first to have been killed by Quantrill's Raiders? And what did that mean for Reverend Burroughs? And Sally?

Luke ducked as he stood. Bullets whizzed past, planting themselves into the prairie dirt near his feet. Screams, shouts, more gunfire. Although still several blocks from downtown, flames shot up from the buildings and nearby houses. Men swarmed past, running the other way. Women, their children clutched in hand, rushed toward safety.

Sulfuric gunpowder stink clogged his nose as Luke zigzagged over more fallen men. Closer into town, bodies lay like jumbled

287

twigs, some strewn across the sidewalks, a few out in the middle of the street. Massachusetts Avenue was alive with the dead, dying and raiding.

Gotta find Quantrill. Luke recited the mantra as he loped, hiding in shadows as often as possible.

Raiders on horseback rode into stores while Raiders on foot staggered out of the stores, hauling whatever loot their arms would carry.

A gun. Luke needed a gun. He bolted down an alley and kicked in the door to Otis Mercantile. Inside, men grabbed armloads of weapons, ammunition, boots, shovels and candy.

Spotting a revolver on the floor, Luke sprang for it, hiding it under his shirt. Men appeared too busy to pay much attention to him. A box of bullets lay on the floor against the counter. Luke scooped them up and ran for the back door.

"Luke! You're supposed to be dead!"

Luke glanced over his shoulder. Cole Younger aimed a revolver at Luke's chest. Luke ducked and ran, zigzagging around crates and boxes in the back room. Bullets whizzed past, splintering the wall next to his head. Luke launched himself through the door, slamming it.

He ran.

On the street, other Raiders whooped and hollered, sharing bottles of whiskey while hurling threats of mayhem to citizens unlucky enough to get in the way.

And still Luke ran. Glances over his shoulder showed no Cole on his heels. But that would be just a matter of time he was sure.

The Eldridge Hotel, a flagship of the town, sat at the north end of the street, and Luke could have spotted it from where he stood—four blocks away. Catching his breath in shallow doses, he thought he made out flames shooting through the inky smoke. Was the hotel on fire?

He ran.

Maybe he could help pull people out. Thank God James and Morningstar were safe. Maybe Quantrill would be nearby. Then he could shoot the bastard and the Raiders would leave.

The noise, the stench, the air—none of it felt real. Ignoring his own safety, Luke pushed through the street, using horses as shields.

Within a block of the hotel, Luke peered left, then right. While he loaded his stolen gun, the Dix home, engulfed in flames, roared. The Johnson house, which once held a large family, was a pile of smoking rubble. Luke could only guess where the six children had hidden. He wanted . . . no, *had* to believe they'd made it out.

Could he take quick refuge in the Methodist Church? Surely Quantrill wouldn't burn a place of worship. But this one, the one Reverend Burroughs toiled in, was close to the Eldridge Hotel. Luke turned the corner only to be brought up short by the flames, the Hell-like furnace roiling from the church.

"Underestimated you, Colton."

Luke spun around. William Clarke Quantrill stared at him.

Quantrill raised his .38 Army Colt waist high. "Put down your peashooter." He waggled his gun at Luke's. "Thought by now you'd be burned up. Guess I was wrong."

"C-church," Luke stuttered. "You burned a church." What about Frank's new stained-glass window? He'd spotted it recently set in the front wall.

"I said *gun down*. Now." Quantrill sneered, his eyes narrowing.

As much as he hated to, Luke set his gun down, but within reach if he were to fall. He'd keep Quantrill talking long enough to figure something out.

Quantrill nodded. "Good boy. The church. Those do-gooders think God's gonna protect them. Think God has all the answers." He aimed for the stained glass and shot. Colored glass exploded, pieces falling on Luke's hat.

"But—"

"God ain't got nothin' to say. But *I* do." Quantrill cocked the hammer. The metallic sound grated against Luke's already-frazzled nerves. "You know what I say?"

Luke shook his head.

Quantrill raised his voice. "I say make your peace 'cause you got 'bout two seconds."

"You son of a bitch." Luke's gaze flicked from Quantrill's gun to his eyes. "You've done enough killing to burn in Hell for eternity! My folks . . . these people've done nothing to you." Luke swept his arm around the burning piles of buildings. "They don't deserve this. Leave them alone."

"Don't deserve?" Quantrill stepped back. "Who the hell d'you think you are? You sniveling, backstabbing traitor. I took you into my army, treated you well. Then you turn on me, and now *you're* telling *me* what to do?"

Luke's words wouldn't stop. "Leave Kansas alone. People here ain't doing nothing to you!"

The stench of burning wood and bodies swirled around Luke until he knew he'd throw up. He wanted to kill Quantrill, but his gun lay at his feet, close, but not close enough. "Call your men off! They'll listen to you. The war's over. Call them off!"

Quantrill waggled his gun. "Crawl back under that rock you came from, you bastard." He brought it up, aiming at Luke's chest.

Luke sidestepped and grabbed. Instead of metal, he got arm. He held on and swung at Quantrill's face. *Whack!* While his fist throbbed, the impact felt good.

The Bushwhacker stepped back, then came at Luke like an enraged bull. He flew into Luke, taking both men to the ground. Wind knocked out of him, Luke struggled for air.

Fists to his face brought him back. Luke lashed out, rolling on top of Quantrill. Anger, hatred, fear pushed Luke. Something hard pressed into his side. He grabbed at the revolver.

Quantrill's eyes flashed.

Luke pulled at the gun and pointed it skyward.

Bang!

Luke's ears rang. In that moment, he loosened his grip on the gun and felt Quantrill grab it. Acrid gunpowder mixed with smoke stung his eyes. Quantrill pushed Luke, who somersaulted, stopping a few yards away.

Bang!

Pain seared his side. Luke's world faded, growing fuzzy as he rolled onto his back. He clutched his right side, his fingers coated with sticky crimson. Freezing cold. Boiling hot. His body shuddered. Luke flopped over and forced himself to his knees.

His gun. Where was his gun? Through the smoke and white flashes, Luke spotted his stolen gun to his right, within grabbing distance. He stretched and reached, swinging the weapon up. He pulled the trigger.

Click.

He pulled again.

Click.

Quantrill hovered over Luke, that smarmy smirk spreading across the Raider's face. "Nothin' worse than a two-bit pistol. 'Less it's a two-bit traitor."

Luke sprung like a mountain lion and head butted Quantrill, the force knocking the gun out of his grip.

Luke grabbed it and, without aiming, shot.

Quantrill gripped his upper arm. "Damn you!" He kicked out, his boot connecting with Luke's face. The gun sailed out of his hand. Luke tasted blood.

Get up or die. Rolling onto his stomach, he pushed up. Another boot to his ribs sent him flying, crashing into the church's rubble.

Luke gripped his side and lay on his back. He prayed for just a little more strength.

Quantrill towered above him, gun in hand. His eyes on fire. He tugged at his torn sleeve, soaked in blood. "Damn you." He drew a bead on Luke. "I should kill you for this right now. But that gut shot's gonna give you three, four days to die." He cocked his head. "Maybe I'll stay around to watch."

Luke's curses and damnation sprayed the outlaw leader. Gut shot like Luke was, the pain folded him.

Quantrill knelt next to Luke. "Want me to shoot you again? Save you the agony of dying slow?" A long chuckle rolled through the Raider. "No, no, you need time to think about dying. To feel life ooze out of you, drop by drop."

From this position on the ground, Luke could see a pair of boots stand next to Quantrill. Boots he recognized. A slow trail upwards confirmed his suspicions. Cole Younger.

"Let me kill 'im." Cole pointed his revolver at Luke. "I owe 'im. Here's for my sisters in that prison."

Quantrill stood and glanced at Cole. Without a word, Quantrill kicked Luke in the ribs again. The impact sent him careening into a wall. The Bushwhacker dropped his voice.

"Changed my mind about letting you die slow. Gonna let Cole here kill you. This's for my cousin, Clarke. He didn't deserve to die." He nodded at Cole, who made a show of cocking his gun.

Metal scraped against metal.

Cole's eyes narrowed, flames reflecting in them. He licked his lips.

Luke closed his eyes, knowing this would be his last moment alive. But he couldn't let that happen. Using every ounce of energy he could muster, Luke cringed, moving to his left.

Bang!

Flames tore across Luke's eyes and then danced. All went black.

CHAPTER FIFTY-SIX

"Luke? You dead? Luke?"

A familiar voice swirled around his head. Luke pried one eye open. It snapped shut at the bright light blinding him. A hand slid under his head, lifting it. Something metal pressed against his lower lip. Liquid poured into his mouth.

Both eyes open, Luke gulped water and stared up into his brother's face. "Where . . . ?" Water trickled down his chin. His fuzzy surroundings coming into focus, he realized the ground under him wasn't dirt. It was soft.

"Lie still now," James said. "Morningstar's coming with bandages."

"Did I kill 'im?"

"Who?"

The man's name wouldn't come. But he'd never forget that face, those eyes staring at him. Or the other fella's face, grief etching hard lines as he aimed the pistol. Right at Luke's head.

James' voice broke his thoughts. "You're damn lucky. Bullet just grazed your head. Took some of your scalp with it, but your hair'll grow back." James smiled. "Have a helluva scar, though. *Two* scars."

The muddled words didn't make sense. A couple deep breaths, then more of his world pulled itself together. Luke blinked into what must have been a hotel lobby, if couches, rug, chandelier and counter were any indication. Men and women jammed the room, all talking or crying at once.

Luke gripped his throbbing head. "James?"

"I'm here."

Nothing made sense. "Where's here?"

"City Hotel." James shrugged. "Quantrill decided not to burn this place. Moved everybody from the Eldridge over to here."

Too many questions reeling in his head, Luke chose one. "Is it over?"

James nodded, but pain dulled his eyes. "Yeah."

Remnants of this morning pulled itself together. "Ma. Pa. They— ?"

"Everybody's in one piece. When Quantrill pulled out of town, I rushed in trying to find you." James patted Luke's shoulder. "Looks like I did."

Knowing the full story would come out later, Luke chose another question. "How'd I get here?"

"Over there." James pointed to a man standing on the far side of the room. "That man?"

Luke surveyed the blurry crowd, some huddled in the corners, some sitting on the floor, weeping. Others prowled.

Luke followed his brother's pointed finger and then nodded.

A slight grin crawled up one side of James' face. "After Quantrill left, that fella was walking through the streets and came across you lying face up, like you were dead. He said despite the blood, he recognized you. Knows you from drinkin' down at Dulinsky's Tavern. Said he thought you were still alive. He and another fella hauled you in here."

"What?" Luke tried to focus on the man. No recognition.

"I thanked him, but he said to tell you that you owe him a beer." James' shoulders jiggled with the chuckle. "One a day for the rest of your life."

It hurt to smile, but Luke managed.

CHAPTER FIFTY-SEVEN

Enjoying the light breeze, Luke sat on his in-laws' front porch, the rocking chair under his rear needing another pillow. Should he get up and get one, or wait until Sally was within earshot? No, right now smells of cooking supper wafted through the front door whetting his appetite for what smelled like chicken stew. Sally was the reason for those smells. So as to not interrupt her cooking, he could ease up to his feet himself and get his own pillow. After all, it'd been six days since he'd been shot, and he was mending well. On second thought, a pillow to rest his arm on would help.

He thought again about getting up. If he did, no doubt Adam would come bouncing along, grab his leg and both would topple over. The wound on his side would pop open, and then he'd be back to having more stitches and louder clucking from the mother hens gathered under this one roof. Living with one on a normal basis was hard enough, but now with Morningstar, Ma, Missus Burroughs and Sally . . . that was three women too many.

At least they were all speaking to him again. He couldn't decide which was preferable.

Tomorrow would be better. As they'd headed out this morning, James and Pa had said their work on Luke's house would be finished today. They could move back in tomorrow. While the barn had been torched and was nothing but a pile of black wood, the house was singed, but the flames had gone out before doing much damage. The worst part was the looting of all their belongings. Sally's pretty dresses, her dishes, even the children's toys—ripped and strewn—left in a trail of mayhem. Most of their furniture sat in the yard, smashed and burned. Little of their past remained intact.

As Luke sat, his side burning, he thought about the past six days and the upside-down town of Lawrence. Everyone was devastated from the attack. Few buildings remained unscathed. Pa had reported only four buildings were left standing on Massachusetts Avenue. But that wasn't the worst part. He'd said all in all, over one hundred and seventy-seven men and boys— innocent men and boys—had succumbed to Quantrill's raid, many shot as they were dragged from their homes or as they ran away.

One piece of the puzzle still bothered him. Why had Quantrill allowed the guests at the Eldridge Hotel to scurry over to the City Hotel, unmolested?

Reverend Burroughs stayed busy presiding over funerals. With the Reverend's sermons, and Missus Burroughs consoling the hundred weeping widows and mothers, both would be busy for days yet to come.

Morningstar, with her medical background, tended to the sick and injured, when she wasn't fussing over Luke. There was comfort in her touch. His surgery at the City Hotel, while painful, could've been worse. Morningstar pulled the bullet out before Luke had drunk half the bottle. The damage from the whiskey was almost worse than damage from the bullet. His head pounded for a full day.

Pa's buckboard pulled into the yard, James riding in right behind. He waved at Luke. Pa helped the Burroughs and Morningstar from the wagon, climbed back up, whistled at the horses and headed toward the barn. The women hurried onto the porch and fussed over Luke. He assured them he was fine, and no, he didn't need more coffee, didn't need to lie down, didn't need more pain powder. Still fretting, they clucked into the house.

After tending to his horse, James stepped onto the porch, sat next to Luke and rocked.

"You feelin' better?" James swiped a sleeve across his forehead.

Luke nodded. "Every day." Sharp jabs shot through his side. Not healed quite yet.

"You know what I heard in town?" James straightened his shoulders, working out kinks.

"What?"

"Remember when your pal Quantrill herded everybody from the Eldridge to the City Hotel?"

Luke bristled at "pal," but reined in his irritation. He raised both eyebrows. "What?"

A wag of his head, then James shrugged. "It makes sense why he saved the City Hotel. It seems the owner's a friend, and old Quantrill stayed there a time or two. The Eldridge is owned by a Jayhawker, so he torched it."

"And none of the guests got hurt?"

"Not one." James pulled an envelope from his pocket. "Got this today. Came on the first stage since the burning." He waved it in Luke's face.

Peering at the scrawled handwriting, he recognized it. "Letter from Trace." He reached for it. "What's it say?"

James snatched it out of grabbing range. "It says it's mine, is what." He unfolded both pages and smoothed them on his pant leg. "If you're nice to me, I'll let you read it."

"If you're nice to *me,* I just may do that." Luke was dying to know what his brother had written. Were he and Andy coming for a visit? Andy getting married? Another baby for Trace? They couldn't have heard about the devastation of Lawrence yet. Curiosity piqued, Luke held out a hand and hoped his hangdog expression worked on his older brother. He grimaced extra hard and groaned.

Letter held out to one side, James stood and stretched even farther. Even if Luke could get out of the rocker, it would hurt too much. James stepped toward the door, and then handed it to Luke. James patted the top of Luke's head. "I know you don't read too good, baby brother, so I'll decipher it for you. Start with the first word and I'll be back before you can figure out the second one."

James' chuckles didn't fade until he stepped into the house. Luke had no problem reading Trace's handwriting. He scanned both pages and then settled down at the beginning. The farther he read, the worse he felt.

According to Trace, the army was pulling out of Mesilla and some of the day-to-day law duties were being returned to him and Andy. Martial law had been rescinded and Trace, with Andy's help as deputy, had already arrested one drunk and broken up a couple of fights. The third paragraph spun a knot in Luke's chest. All was forgiven and Trace said he understood what James had been doing when he tried to start a revolution. Because of James' involvement, he had been instrumental in the army pulling out.

Trace asked if James and Morningstar would consider coming back. A man named Bergstrom was willing to give James his old job back.

The letter fell to Luke's lap. Would they go? Could he let James leave again? Especially now when they were becoming brothers once more. What would Ma say? And Pa? They would be devastated. No more family dinners, the children bouncing on Uncle James' knee. No more Morningstar and Ma together baking blueberry pie—his favorite. James and Pa wouldn't go hunting this fall like they'd discussed.

Lost in thought, Luke ignored the screech of wood across

wood—someone dragging the other rocking chair to face him. Eyes down, he wasn't ready to talk. How could he say hello and good-bye so soon? Luke peered at the porch's plank floor, wishing he could dive into a knothole near the toe of his boot. James' breathing. Its impatient huff waiting to discuss Trace's news.

"Looks like two months in jail was worth it." James picked up the letter and folded it. "Mesilla's gonna get back to normal pretty soon."

Luke took in his brother's wide eyes, one corner of James' mouth turning up. Luke mumbled, "You goin' back?" That hollow fist planted in his stomach—just like three years ago when James stepped into the stagecoach. Luke, Andy, Pa and Ma had stood on the boardwalk waving good-bye, wondering if they'd ever see him again.

James nodded. "I think so. I'll ask Star after supper, but since all this happened"—he waved the letter toward town—"we've been talking about it."

A cold knot stuck in Luke's throat.

James produced a grin. "Come with us. You, Sally and the kids. You'd like New Mexico. No Jayhawkers, no Bushwhackers. Hell, you can even get a real job." His famous family smile spread across his face. "Just think. All four brothers . . . together."

Images of Luke's folks pushed into his mind. His shoulders slumped. "I can't leave Ma and Pa. I'm the only son left." On the other hand, moving to Mesilla would be a new start. Luke toyed with the idea. Moving far away, out of arms' reach, might be the right idea. If Mister Watkins recovered sufficiently and remembered for sure who clobbered him, well, it would be the hangman's noose for Luke. No doubt.

And maybe the sheriff would find out that the letter was a forgery and arrest both of them. So, it was a good idea for James to leave. Soon.

And what about Sally? Would she be willing to go? Probably not, and certainly not with him, especially with their problems so raw. He'd have to do a lot of fence-mending with her before proposing they move to Mesilla. Starting all over, this time with Sally and the kids. He'd make it work.

James sighed long and low as he stared out into the prairie, the setting sun turning the waving grass light pink. "I know Ma and Pa will be alone, but we got our own lives to live. Stop frettin'. It'll take a couple of months for Pa and me to rebuild their house. I wasn't going until then. And you're almost well enough to help, so it'll rebuild faster." He looked at Luke. "At least think about coming. All right?"

Before Luke could nod, Pa stepped out from the house and onto the porch. "Supper's ready. Your ma says come and get it or she'll throw it out. Now that'd be a plumb shame to waste Sally's good cooking."

Pa's smile faded with his chuckle as he glanced from James to the letter in his hand. "You both look like someone died." He frowned at the letter. "Bad news?"

The brothers answered at the same time.

James shook his head. "No."

"Yes." Luke nodded.

ABOUT THE AUTHOR

New Mexico native **Melody Groves** has a deep love for anything cowboy and Old West. Melody was raised in southern New Mexico, but spent a few "growing up" years on Guam and in the Philippines. Besides being a freelance writer, she plays rhythm guitar in a band. When not strumming, she keeps busy as an Old West reenactor, shooting either sheriffs or bad guys on Sundays in Albuquerque's Old Town.

Winner of five first-place writing awards, Melody is a member of Western Writers of America and SouthWest Writers. She writes magazine articles, screenplays, novels and nonfiction books and contributed to a collegiate history encyclopedia.

Melody is a contributing editor for *Round Up* magazine for Western Writers of America. She lives in Albuquerque, New Mexico, with photographer husband, Myke. www.melody groves.com.